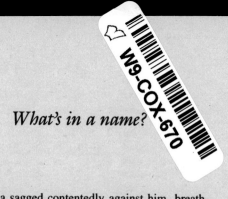

What's in a name?

Georgianna sagged contentedly against him, breathing in the warm, spicy scent of him. How she loved him, she told herself.

The same thought seemed to have occurred to him. He raised her face to his and kissed her with a thoroughness that left her breathless. Heedless of impropriety, of her father, of the dog tugging at her hem, he kissed her as though he wanted to drown in her.

And Georgianna kissed him back just as thoroughly.

When he stopped kissing her to gaze lovingly into her eyes, she was able to think again. A brilliant crimson stained her cheeks as Georgianna came to a terrible realization.

She did not know who she had just kissed!

Miss Pennington's Choice

MEGAN DANIEL

CHARTER BOOKS, NEW YORK

MISS PENNINGTON'S CHOICE

A Charter Book/published by arrangement with
the author

PRINTING HISTORY
Charter edition/November 1988

ISBN: 1-55773-119-5

Charter Books are published by The Berkley Publishing Group,
200 Madison Avenue, New York, New York 10016.
The name "Charter" and the "C" logo are trademarks
belonging to Charter Communications, Inc.

PRINTED IN THE UNITED STATES OF AMERICA

10 9 8 7 6 5 4 3 2 1

ONE MIGHT THINK it logical to assume, when attending a lavish London ball in the heady victory year of 1814, that the swirling silks and revolving regimentals bedecking the smiling members of the *haut ton* masked nothing but high spirits and happy dispositions. For, after all, how could one be less than thrilled when in the presence of the Russian czar, the Prussian emperor, and any number of princes, counts, dukes, earls, ambassadors, and plenipotentiaries and wearing a gown that cost as much as a country parson might earn in a twelvemonth?

But alas, not even the course of the most privileged existence can always run smooth. There were those in the glittering group who were unhappy and those who were fearful, those who were envious and those who were uncertain. There were even a few who were as bored as fashion demanded they appear.

In the case of Miss Georgianna Pennington, however, lovely and lively and twenty-one, the bright smile was wholly sincere and the joy unfeigned and infectious. And it remained so for at least the first half of the evening.

It wasn't until after midnight that an unfortunately overheard conversation caused her smile to falter alarmingly.

Then, for the remainder of the evening, though she pasted the smile back onto her piquant face, it held a brittle edge, as though fashioned by Mr. Wedgwood and as vulnerable to breakage as one of his finest pieces of translucent china.

Miss Pennington's evening had started on a high note. She never thought of herself as a great beauty, being too small and too dark and too slender to warrant that appellation. But she knew she looked well this evening in a simply cut though elegant gown of teal blue silk taffeta that whooshed with a tantalizing whisper of sound with every turn she made. Her slippers were of silver that matched the gauzy shawl draped around her snowy shoulders, and a silver lace ribbon was threaded through her dusky hair. That hair, so heavy and wavy that, if she but knew it, nearly every man who saw it immediately wanted to run his fingers through it, was pulled up into a topknot from which a few elegant curls had been allowed to escape to cascade around her face.

Though she was certainly no schoolroom miss, this was Miss Pennington's first London ball—she had spent most of the past four years living abroad with her diplomat father— and she was gratified to learn she was not to be condemned to prop up the walls all evening. Though not at all in the current mode of tall, blond goddesses, there was that in her manner, an easiness and a liveliness, that could not but attract. Crowds of young men vied for the honor of dancing with her or bringing her glasses of lemonade and chilled champagne. Her dance card was filled even before the orchestra began tuning their instruments for the first set of the evening.

Any young woman must be gratified by such a success, and Georgianna Pennington, for all her independent turn of mind and her lack of romantical notions of the world, was no exception. She found the attention highly gratifying.

Of course, the young lady's case was not hindered when the madly handsome, madly popular Alexander, Czar of all the Russias, approached her as soon as she entered the brilliantly lit ballroom. Striding across the glistening parquet floor on his long legs and bowing over her hand with a courtliness almost forgotten in England, he asked to be put down for a waltz. Not to be outdone, the dashing Prince Metternich then inscribed his name onto her card with a Germanic flourish. These were old friends of Miss Pennington for they had all met some months earlier in Frankfurt and more recently in

Paris when Alexander entered that city at the head of the victorious Allied Army.

Georgianna, traveling with her father and the other diplomats in the army's wake, had naturally found herself at many of the same balls and parties as these new folk heroes, and everyone in the London ballroom this summer night envied her the knowledge. She, in her lack of conceit, was merely glad to have found herself not totally without acquaintances in a room full of strangers.

The cachet of the patronage of the Heroes of Europe soon made everyone at the ball take notice of Miss Pennington. They saw the sparkle in her eyes under a high brow, the curve of her high cheekbones that seemed made for smiling, and her delicate, slightly pointed chin. Many wished to know her better; a few less well favored females simply wished she would go away.

On her arrival at the ball, several gentlemen pressed for the privilege of leading her into the first set, but this Georgianna saved, as was her wont, for her father. She had been used to begin every ball she attended by dancing with him, not from any misplaced sense of duty but because he was truly her favorite partner.

For four years each had been the sole family of the other. At the death of Mrs. Pennington, each had consoled the other's wrenching grief. They had traveled the world together ever since. They were more than father and daughter; they were friends who genuinely enjoyed each other's company.

"Well, puss," he teased her as they waited to go down the movements of the opening dance, "I see you've already begun to set London on its ear just as you did Berlin and Madrid and St. Petersburg."

"Oh, please, not on its ear, Papa," she said with a mock frown. "Rather on its mettle, I should hope." They laughed together a moment. "I must admit," she went on with a sparkling smile, "that it would be gratifying in the extreme to end up as the belle of the ball, though I know how ignoble that must sound. Do you think me horribly puffed up in my own conceit, Papa?"

"I find you wholly enchanting, Georgie, as well you know."

"Well, I do know it," she acknowledged with another laugh, "but then you are strongly prejudiced in my favor, totally blind to my myriad faults, and a consummate diplomat into the bargain."

"True enough, but the other gentlemen in the room are neither all diplomats nor prejudicial in their judgments, I am certain, and any one of them will verify the truth of my claim."

"Well, I am not at all certain I agree with you, for I am not classically beautiful, you know. I expect it is just that everyone is so disposed to be gay now that the world is finally at peace again. Is it not wonderful, Papa? How glad I am that this *wretched* war is over at last." Her bright smile faded. "So many young men gone. So many of our particular friends never to be met with again."

"Yes," said Sir Richard, his smile evaporating as well. "And you, my love, have been forced to see so much more of its ugliness than any young lady should have had to face. I feel it strongly that I have been so unfair as to expose you to such horrors."

"Other women have faced far more, Papa. They have lost husbands, brothers, sons."

"Well, the war *is* over now," he said briskly, "and this is no conversation for a young lady to be having while dancing at her first London ball. Especially when she is looking as enchanting as you are tonight, puss, and when every gentleman in the room is falling over his feet for a chance to dance with her."

"Well, I do hope it shan't go that far, for I so hate having to pick them up again," she said and laughed delightedly once more as they went down the center of the set. Stepping lightly and smiling hugely at each other, they made a handsome sight as they glowed in the light of a hundred candles from a chandelier overhead. Then the movements of the dance took them apart. As Georgianna turned back to smile at him, she felt proud.

At forty-five, Sir Richard Pennington was still a strikingly handsome gentleman and showed to advantage his perfect black evening dress and snowy linen. The streaks of gray threading his thick dark hair only added to the sense of dignity and power he conveyed. And the brown eyes, very like his daughter's, brimmed this night with good humor.

So lighthearted did Georgianna feel that her smile beamed equally on everyone in the set as she glided past each dancer with a swirl of her whispering skirts. Unfortunately, so win-

ning was that smile that one very young gentleman trod on the
toes of his hapless partner. He had not been attending that lady
at all and was instead wholly occupied in craning his neck
over his shoulder for another look at the beguiling Miss Pennington.

When she came together with her father once more he said,
"You see? What did I tell you? The chaos has already begun.
It looks to be a diverting evening, and I expect to enjoy myself
hugely watching all the beaux falling at your feet, Georgie."

"Well, I do hope we shan't have to summon a doctor or call
for burnt feathers and vinaigrette to revive any who might
languish for want of a dance with me." Her eyes twinkled
with a merriment that removed all trace of arrogance from her
words. "And there is something very off-putting, don't you
think, about a gentleman who goes into a decline before one's
very eyes merely because one doesn't require yet another glass
of lemonade?" Miss Pennington was not in the least romantical.

"Oh, cruel beauty," he said with a chuckle as he led her
around in the promenade. "Perhaps I'd best stay well clear in
case they come to fisticuffs over you."

"Stuff! I shan't let them, for I've no intention of playing
favorites, though I *might* suffer one of them to compare my
eyes to chocolate bonbons as that sweet Mr. Schalikoff did
last year in Moscow." She couldn't help letting a giggle
escape at the memory of the young Russian soldier on his
knees making a perfect cake of himself.

"Young puppy!" said Sir Richard. "If ever I'd said anything half so preposterous to your mother she would have
married Bingley instead of me. Threatened to once, you know,
when I told her merely that her eyes were blue pools and I was
like to drown in them."

"Papa!" said Georgianna on a lilting laugh. "Surely you
never said anything so absurd! I wonder Mama agreed to have
you at all after such a laugh as that must have given her."

"Well, I admit I never tried it again. Very unpoetic woman,
your mother. It was my brother's idea, at any rate. Convinced
me that gently bred ladies liked pretty, poetical compliments."

"How little Uncle Jamie knew of Mama."

"True," he said and spun her around. Then, smiling fondly
down at her, he added, "You are so very like her."

"I hope so, Papa," she said softly as the set came to an
end.

The party swirled about them as the dancers swirled about the floor in the newly fashionable waltz, a roiling sea of silks and satins in every color of the rainbow. Georgianna met several people she liked very well and many more that she found absurd, for she was at heart a very practical, sensible young lady. With the help of her aunt, Lady Jane Piedmont, who was officially introducing her to the *ton,* she was soon feeling quite at home. Having served as her father's hostess for several years, entertaining ambassadors and military officers and even royalty on more than one occasion, Georgianna had a degree of poise and confidence rare in one so young.

"I see I was in the right of it," said Sir Richard to his daughter some two hours into the festivities. He was beaming with good cheer, a smile writ large on his rugged, tanned face. "I expect to have a half dozen gentlemen, at least, calling on me by morning begging to be allowed to pay their addresses to you."

"Oh, I do hope not," she said with a chuckle, "for I would so hate to put you to the trouble of dashing all their hopes."

"What? Has there not been a single fellow lucky enough to impress you?"

"Oh, I found several to be graceful partners, and one or two were quite conversable. But I cannot picture myself spending any great amount of time with any of them without growing bored to flinders. Most gentlemen are so . . . well, so silly, Papa."

"What about Briarley? I noticed you stood up with him twice."

"Yes," she said with a frown belied by the twinkle in her eye, "and the second time I did, the Honorable Mr. Briarley had the effrontery to tell me that my eyes are more beautiful than those of his favorite hound in Leicestershire." She groaned. *"Much* worse than Mr. Schalikoff's bonbons."

"Much!" agreed her father with a laugh. "Well, Corning then. You seemed in high gig when he took you in to supper."

"Did I? But then I was very hungry, you know."

"Minx! Well, perhaps when we reach Vienna you will find your prince, the lucky dog."

She closed her fan and looked squarely at him. "You sound as though you are looking forward to handing me over to a husband. Are you so eager to be rid of me, Papa?" She said it lightly, but there was an edge in her voice, a tiny note of hurt.

"No, no," said Sir Richard quickly, "not at all, not at all.

It's just that I . . . that I should like to see you happy, Georgie."

"I am happy, Papa."

"Good," he said and stared at her a moment with an unusually serious look on his face. "Good."

Then a gentleman with a very small waist and a very large Adam's apple bowed over her hand, intoning, "My dance, I believe, Miss Peffington."

"Pennington," corrected Sir Richard, and father and daughter shared a soft chuckle as she took her partner's bony arm and joined the set forming at the center of the room.

An hour later, Georgianna said to her chaperone, "Isn't it a lovely party, Aunt Jane?" She had just finished a heady waltz with a Captain of Dragoons, and her face was flushed with pleasure and exercise. Her brown eyes sparkled like shiny marbles. "It is quite as nice as any we attended in St. Petersburg."

"So I should think," replied her dowager relation. The Lady Jane Piedmont would certainly not concede that a mere Russian could do anything, even to arranging a ball, better than an Englishman.

"I expect we will have many such parties when we get to Vienna. It is going to be very gay."

"I should imagine so," her aunt agreed. "They say all the world and his wife will be there."

"I do hope Papa will not be so busy with diplomacy and such that he will have no time to dance."

"Have no fear, child. I have never known your father to miss the best parties. And though I cannot entirely approve of this new dance that is all the crack—such physical intimacy, you know, and particularly in public, is not at all the thing—I notice that he is enjoying it quite as much as you are."

"Oh, Papa is an excellent waltzer. In fact, it was he who taught me."

"Humph," came a sound from Lady Jane for she could not think it at all proper that her niece had been raised in such a . . . singular fashion. There had been far too much license, in her opinion, and far too much time spent in the exclusive company of gentlemen. But she would say no more on that head since she knew well enough that neither Georgianna nor her father would pay her the slightest heed. They had been happily disregarding her advice for years. "I also notice that Mrs. Patterson performs the waltz beautifully," she went on.

"Your father has taken the floor with her *three* times this evening."

"Three times?" said Georgianna with a glance across the room. Her eye alighted on her father where he stood conversing animatedly with a strikingly lovely woman of about five-and-thirty. She was elegantly gowned in deep rose silk and her hair, of a blond shade midway between honey and burnished bronze, was graced with a pair of silver-tipped rose-colored plumes that swayed delicately as she laughed. "Three times?" she repeated. "Are you quite certain?"

There was something in her voice that gave her aunt pause. Lady Jane looked hard at her niece, and both her face and voice softened. "Quite certain, Georgie," she said, then added more briskly, "and nothing could please me more. Though I know it may distress you, my love, it is time and past that your father began looking about him for another wife. To my mind, there could hardly be a more perfect candidate than Suzanne Patterson."

Georgianna's eyes, very large in her face, had not left the vision of her father chatting so comfortably with the beautiful widow. "He loved your mother very much, Georgie," added Lady Jane with a note of true sympathy and understanding in her voice, "but four years is more than long enough to mourn. Richard is still a young and vigorous man. He deserves a life of his own. He deserves not to be alone."

"But he is not alone . . ." she began, only to be interrupted by a gentleman in a peacock-blue coat and overstarched linen.

"It's the quadrille, Miss Pennington," he said with a deep bow and a sleek smile, "and you faithfully promised it to me. I venture to say we shall make quite a sight in our blues. Every eye shall be upon us." He seemed rather more taken by that realization than Georgianna was; she felt a strong urge to tell him to go away. But she was a well brought up if unconventional young lady, so when he said, "Shall we take our places?" she merely offered her hand.

"Of course, Mr. Winkel," she said and smiled, but the smile did not quite reach her eyes and her expression had lost much of its usual charm.

It was perhaps fortunate that the complex movements of the dance allowed little opportunity for conversation, for Georgianna was uncharacteristically silent for the duration of it. Though she flawlessly glided through the *entrechats*, the *glissade*, and the *pas d'été*, her thoughts were otherwhere.

She hardly noticed the attention that Mr. Winkel had promised they would attract and which had, as he predicted, come their way. Her glance kept straying not to the self-satisfied face of her partner but across the ballroom to where her father still stood deep in conversation with Mrs. Patterson, whom Georgianna knew to be a widow of several years standing.

A three-noted, lilting, and very musical laugh wafted across the floor from the lady in question just as Georgianna and her partner danced by. Quick on the heels of the feminine laughter came a familiar and beloved masculine chuckle that followed Georgianna across the room. She determinedly turned her attention back to her partner and the devilishly difficult steps of the mazy dance. By the time the orchestra wound out its finale and she allowed herself to look back at where her father and the lovely Mrs. Patterson had been standing, it was to discover that they had both disappeared.

Young Mr. Winkel must have wondered what he could possibly have said or done to bring such a frown to Miss Pennington's dainty brow. He made a deep bow over her hand, reluctantly accepted her assurance that she hadn't the slightest desire for an iced cake or a glass of orgeat, and finally drifted off to search his conscience and to resolve to find some manner of redeeming himself in her eyes.

Suddenly feeling a strong need for fresh air and fresh thoughts, Georgianna escaped the ballroom—and her next partner, whom she could see crossing the room in her direction—by slipping out through a pair of French doors and onto a terrace overlooking the gardens. There she stood in the shadows, breathing deeply of the soft summer air.

It had been a long time, more than four years, in fact, since she had seen on her father's face the particular smile he had just bestowed on Suzanne Patterson. The only woman she had seen him honor with it before had been her mother.

In an age and a class where marriages were made to advance family fortunes and prestige and where love was considered to be of no consequence in such decisions, Sir Richard and Annabelle Pennington had been gloriously, deliriously in love. He refused to travel without her, so she accompanied him to every diplomatic post he held, taking their daughter with her. They had been blessed with only the one child, but Georgianna had been enough. They had been a very happy family.

At seventeen, Georgianna herself had fallen in love, or so

she thought, with a young lieutenant attached to her father's diplomatic mission in Madrid. Her parents, though wishing Georgie were not quite so young, had given their consent to an engagement. They wanted their only child to marry for love as they had done. A date for the wedding of Miss Georgianna Pennington and Lieutenant Giles Farnham was set.

But then the world fell apart. On one horrendous, unforgettable nightmare of a night in Madrid, while her husband was in the field conferring with Lord Wellington and her daughter was visiting with a Spanish friend, Annabelle Pennington was caught in the fire that destroyed their hired house. Though horridly injured, she had lived long enough to bid her husband and daughter, hastily summoned to her side, a loving farewell, and then she died.

Georgianna and her father returned to England. For a while, Georgianna feared he would die too, or at the least lose his sanity. He sat for hours, days, weeks, alone in his study, barely eating, consuming enormous quantities of brandy, seeing no one but his daughter. He refused even to look at the urgent letters sent to him from the foreign office.

Putting aside her own searing grief as best she could, Georgianna cared for him. It was now out of the question that she should go through with her planned wedding. She would not leave her father. She believed that for now Sir Richard needed her far more than Lieutenant Farnham did.

After six months of more or less wallowing in his grief, six months in which his daughter sympathized and reassured, coaxed and cajoled, and finally bullied and commanded him to come back to life, Sir Richard finally seem to awake somewhat. He reluctantly returned to his work. The foreign office sent him to Regensburg rather than back to Spain. There was no question but that Georgie would go with him. She became his housekeeper, his hostess, his confidante.

For all this time her loyal Giles waited patiently. He wrote long letters from Spain assuring Georgie of his love and his understanding. But when her father was sent to Germany, he begged Georgie not to go. This, however, she refused to agree to. Her father needed her.

By the eighth month apart from her, Lieutenant Farnham was begging Georgie to set a new date for their wedding. She tried to bring herself to do so, she really did, but the time never seemed quite right. After ten months, he was threatening to come to Regensburg and carry her off by force. It was then that Georgianna wrote very kindly but firmly to formally end their engagement.

She felt some pain at losing him, but it was less than she would have supposed. She could only assume that she had loved the young man less than she had thought. The idea of living without him was merely painful whereas the thought of leaving her father was totally insupportable. When, not long afterward, she heard that Lieutenant Farnham had married a Spanish lady, she found herself rather more amused than hurt.

In all the years since, she had met no man who had even tempted her to consider leaving her father. She had met no man who could come close to him in all those qualities she thought indispensable in a man.

All these memories now flitted through her mind as she stood in the summer night smelling the roses climbing a trellis just below the terrace. Music drifted around her as she stood in the shadows; the marble was cool through the thin soles of her slippers; and she ached. That look, that particular, private smile with which Sir Richard had blessed Suzanne Patterson, had made Georgianna miss her mother with an intensity she hadn't felt in years.

Another couple floated out through the French doors. Georgie, needing to be alone yet a while, moved farther along the terrace, into even deeper shadows. She leaned on the stone banister, gazing out over the garden where tiny lights twinkled in the branches of the trees and couples strolled arm in arm along the gravel pathways.

And then she froze. A voice below her sounded clearly in the night air. "I cannot do it to her, Suzanne," she heard her father say. "You must understand." Despite herself, Georgianna could not help but look down. They were seated on a bench almost directly beneath her. Her father was holding Suzanne Patterson's gloved hands in both of his and gazing at her with a look of tenderness and love mixed with pain. "I am all Georgie has," he went on. "She has been so used to looking after me, to running my house, to playing hostess at my parties. Can you not see how impossible it would be to ask her to take second place to you? I could not . . ."

"Shhh," said Suzanne, and Georgie saw her reach up and gently lay the fingertips of one hand on Sir Richard's lips. "Of course I understand, Richard. I wouldn't dream of trying to take Georgianna's place. One day soon she will be married, and you will be free to do as you please. I have waited a long time to find you, Richard. For now it is enough to know that you love me. That you want me. I can wait a while longer for the rest."

And then they said no more, at least not with words, and Georgie found she could not bear to witness what they were saying with their actions.

All the sparkle went out of the evening and out of her eyes.

Some time later, in the carriage on the way back to their house in Curzon Street, Sir Richard once again asked Georgie, oh so casually, if she had met any gentleman who particularly took her fancy. She waited a long time before answering. "Should you really like to see me married, Papa?" she asked in a small voice, thankful that the darkness of the carriage made it impossible for him to see her face.

He reached across the carriage and took her gloved hand in his. "Georgie, it will be the saddest day of my life when I lose you, but I know I shall have to and probably quite soon. I've been uncommonly lucky to have kept you to myself this long. What a selfish dog I should be to try to hold on to you forever. You deserve a husband and a family and a life of your own."

"A life of my own . . ." she repeated softly, turning her face to peer out into the darkness. Her aunt's words came back to her. He deserves a life of his own, she had said. He deserves not to be alone.

The carriage drew to a halt before their town house, and they spoke no more until they were safely inside. "Shall we ride in the morning?" said Sir Richard as they climbed the stairs.

On any other occasion, Georgianna would have leaped at the chance to ride in the park with her father, particularly at an hour early enough to allow them a good run. But now she hesitated. She found herself wondering if perhaps Mrs. Patterson would also be in the park as she had been on two other mornings in the past week. "Thank you, Papa, but I think not. I had planned to begin sorting and packing in the morning. So much to be done, you know, before we leave."

"I see," he replied as they stopped before her bedroom door. Try though she might to suppress the question hovering in her mind, Georgianna found herself asking, "Does Mrs. Patterson go to Vienna, Papa?"

"I believe she did mention that she was planning to join the festivities. Should you mind if she accompanied us, Georgie?"

"Accompany us?" Now she really wished she had not

asked. "Why . . . why no, Papa. Not if you wish it, but I . . ."

"Good!" he said heartily. "Good. Well then, off to your bed, and remember when you begin your packing that you are to buy yourself at least a dozen dashing new gowns in Paris."

"Good night, Papa," she said listlessly despite the proffered treat of the gowns. She kissed his cheek and closed the door.

Rose, Georgianna's maid, was waiting patiently and full of eager questions about the ball and all the swells who were there. "For I knew you'd be a hit, Miss Georgie, I just knew it, so pretty as you looked, and you'd dance with all the Royals, and I expect the regent himself fell in love with you."

"The prince was not in attendance," said Georgie half-heartedly.

The maid unhooked her mistress's gown and eased the drift of blue silk over Georgie's ebony curls. "Well, I'll wager every other gentleman there fell head over ears for you. Which one did you like best?"

"Oh, not you too," Georgie snapped in a manner wholly unlike herself. "Is the whole world determined to marry me off in the next fortnight?"

Rose, hurt by her mistress's tone, did not reply but silently hung the gown away and handed Georgie a flowered dressing gown.

"Oh, forgive me, Rose," said Georgianna at once. "It is just that I have the headache a little. I'll do my own hair. Here, give me the brush and go on to bed."

"Yes, miss," said Rose, doing as she was bid. Then with a curtsey she was gone.

Georgianna sat before her mirror, her accustomed place and pose whenever she had something serious to discuss with herself. Her itinerant life had left her with few intimate friends, and she had developed the habit of talking things over with her own reflection when a knotty problem seemed unwilling to untangle itself. Though she and her father were unusually close, there were certain subjects one could not, if one were a proper young lady, discuss with any gentleman, even a much loved father.

She pulled the silver-backed brush through her dark, heavy hair in long, even strokes, studied her reflection, and thought for a long time. Anyone who knew her well would have been able to follow an entire inner dialogue as it announced itself on her face. And the exact moment she reached a decision of sorts was perfectly clear to the mirror, her only spectator.

"Well, Georgie," she said finally to her image. "Though it is the most lowering thought imaginable, you had best admit it. Suzanne Patterson wants to marry Papa, and he wants to marry her, and you do not like it one bit." Now that the words were out, she was emboldened to go further. "But why should he not? Aunt Jane is quite right. Papa is still a young man. He has every right to find his own happiness, and you have no right to try and stop him. Such selfishness on your part is insupportable."

Her brush strokes became somewhat less gentle as she warmed to her topic. "And it is perfectly clear that he will not marry Suzanne, or anyone else, as long as you are still unwed. He said so himself in so many words. Therefore, you must take immediate steps to find yourself a husband. It is the least you can do for him."

There, she had said it. And she knew as soon as the words were out of her mouth that that was just what she was going to do. Georgianna had never been one to sit on a problem when there was some action that could be taken.

Her lively charm and generous spirit disguised a will of iron. Her determination, which her father preferred to call her stubbornness, had stood her in good stead through the years. It had caused her to learn to speak a half dozen languages with perfect accents, to overcome an early fear of water to become a veritable mermaid of a swimmer, and to look after her father at his lowest ebb with the tenaciousness of a hen with a single chick. When Georgianna Pennington decided to do a thing it was as good as done.

And so she must at once set about the task of finding herself a suitable husband, thus freeing her father to wed Mrs. Patterson. Which meant, of course, that she must set about the task of falling in love, for she didn't *think* she could bring herself to marry without it, not even to please her father. The hairbrush moved harder and faster now as she considered the likeliest plan of action.

"Vienna," she proclaimed finally. "I shall fall in love in Vienna. There will be dozens of gentlemen there. Hundreds. Surely I can easily fall in love with at least one of them." The thought, so pleasant a subject to most young ladies, seemed to bring Georgianna no joy. She tried hard to remember how it had felt to love Giles Farnham, but she could scarce recall that young man's face. Then she tried to imagine how it would feel to have a man look at her the way her father had looked at Suzanne Patterson.

But the memory of that picture caused her eyes to sting, and this despite the fact that she had grown to like Mrs. Patterson in the few short weeks since they had first met. "Stop it!" she admonished herself sternly, pulling the brush through a tangled curl with a painful yank. "Why should he not fall in love again and remarry? It is perfectly *natural* that he should do so. He might even . . ."

Her brush faltered, and her eyes brimmed with unshed tears, but she took a deep breath and continued. "He might even wish to have another family. He is quite young enough to do so, and so is Mrs. Patterson."

She put down the brush and stared at her face. A long sigh arose from deep inside her, and when she spoke to herself again her voice was small and thin, the voice of the little girl she had not been for several years. "I *might* be able to live with the thought of a brother," she said. "I don't think I could bear it if he had another daughter."

◄◄[two]►►

THE NEXT MORNING, as Miss Georgianna Pennington was reconciling herself to her decision to fall in love at once, in a street not ten minutes away as the crow flies but rather more if one is trying to maneuver a curricle through the traffic of Mayfair, a discussion of quite a different sort was going forward.

"I've got a century says you couldn't pull it off," said Alexander James Trevelyan, fifth Earl of Kitteridge, to his companion.

"It won't fadge, Alec," replied the Hon. Robert Trevelyan. "I know you think you know me to a nicety, but you're not going to gudgeon me into doing it, so don't think it."

The two gentlemen were strolling down New Bond Street toward Gentleman Jackson's Boxing Saloon, that bastion of upper-class masculinity and athleticism. As brilliant July sunshine poured down upon them, they tipped their hats to a few gentlemen and a good many ladies they encountered on the way, setting more than one feminine heart aflutter and more than one mama thinking hard. It was an effect they'd been having for years.

"Oh, give over, Robin," said Lord Kitteridge. "Why shouldn't you? Got to have some diversion in your life, and

Lord knows I stand in need of some novelty in mine. I'm
bored speechless at the thought of going to Vienna by myself,
but I stupidly promised I'd go. You're just as heartily fed up
with your books and your cozy study at Oxford. And don't
bother saying you're not either because it won't fadge. Know
you as well as I know myself and I wouldn't believe it."

He stopped a moment to admire a showy watch fob in a
jeweler's window and an equally showy ladybird dimpling
down at him from a passing barouche. After tipping his high-
crowned beaver in her direction, setting it at an even more
rakish angle than usual, he returned his attention to his companion.

"And it isn't as if we haven't done it before," he continued.
"We were always covering for each other at Harrow. D'you
remember that time Formsby gave you a caning instead of
me?"

"Which time?" replied Robert Trevelyan dryly. "My memory has always been superior to yours, and I seem to recall
any number of canings I took for you. Old Formsby was such
a twit he never could tell us apart so he just grabbed the first
one who happened by. As you, my dear and craven brother,
were more adept than I at making yourself scarce in moments
of crisis, it was generally me who happened by."

The two gentlemen, both dark-haired and tall, both athlet-
ically built, both with a mere seven-and-twenty years in their
dish, with identical blue eyes and nearly identical, slightly
lopsided smiles, were, as their old nurse was used to say, "as
like as tuppence to a groat." Their mother had been horribly
afraid she would bear twins, for her father was one and her
mother had had twin sisters. "Blood will out," she would
soulfully prophesy, "and how I am to care for *two* babies when
the thought of *one* puts me into a positive quake I cannot
imagine."

In her case, blood did out, and after presenting her lord
with a son and heir, Lady Kitteridge immediately (or rather
some ten minutes later) presented him with another. A second
wet nurse was hired, another cot was moved into the nursery,
and the countess had very little more to do with both her sons
than she would have had to do with only one, which was to
say very little indeed.

"Friday-faced Formsby," said Lord Kitteridge with a
chuckle, still remembering their ill-fated school career. "What
a cabbage-headed clunch the fellow was." They strolled south

into Old Bond Street where the din of traffic was even louder
and the crush of shoppers and strollers greater.

"True," agreed his brother, "and I completely failed to see
his logic in thinking that either of us would do for punishment
whenever *you* got into some scrape. I seem to recall that it was
about then that I took to dressing differently from you. Only
way to avoid his stick." They crossed the street, dodging a
tilbury, a pair of horses, and a dray, and narrowly missing a
potboy scurrying past with a jug of ale for some thirsty shop-
keeper. "But you can hardly blame the fellow for mixing us
up, Alec," said Mr. Trevelyan of the hapless Formsby. "Even
Mama frequently failed to tell us apart."

"Only because she generally didn't care to," said the earl
with a discernible degree of bitterness. "She always thought of
us as a single being."

"Yes," admitted Robert, though he seemed to mind less
than his brother. "I expect it was easier to simply refer to us as
'Alec/Robin' and be done with it."

"Canty never did so," Alec pointed out.

"No, but we could hardly expect to fool our own nurse.
Trying to cozen Canty would have been as useless as going
rabbit hunting with a dead ferret."

"But it was fun to try," said Alec with a grin. "And we did
cozen a good many others, didn't we, Robin?" He was at his
most charming, which was devastatingly charming indeed.

His brother knew when he was being gudgeoned and
wasn't fooled for a moment, but they were so fond of each
other he simply agreed. "That we did," he said and smiled at
the memory almost in spite of himself.

"And could easily do so again. Do it, Robin," Alec
coaxed. "Come with me to Vienna and pull a switch on them
all. You'll be me, and I'll be you. It'll be a lark."

"Surely, Alec, the time for larks is past."

"What a cursed dull dog you've turned into!" mourned
Alec. "If you weren't a mirror image of me I'd suspect you of
being a changeling."

"And besides," said Robert, ignoring his brother's asper-
sion on his character as he always did, "what makes you so
certain *you* could pull it off? What makes you think you could
pass for me?"

"Nothing simpler." Lord Kitteridge laughed warmly. "Stick
a tome under my arm and wander about looking vacant and
spouting Latin."

"I do not look vacant!"

"Well, you don't exactly look bang-up, either."

"If you mean I don't look like a tailor's dummy, I thank you. Besides, I was rather looking forward to your stay abroad. It'd make my life here a deal quieter."

"Not quieter. Duller. Sometimes I think I'm the only thing that keeps you from taking root in Oxfordshire and becoming a potato or whatever they grow up there."

"*Not* potatoes," corrected his brother with a wry smile. "That's Ireland."

Alec disregarded him entirely. "And it ain't as though it would be forever, Robbie. The whole dashed show in Vienna's likely to be over in a few weeks, at most."

"So I've heard, though I fear it's an overly optimistic view of the Congress. Likely to go on for months if I'm any judge of diplomats."

"And there'll never be another like it. Whole of Europe'll be there, don't you know."

"Good morning, my lord," came a cloyingly sweet voice from a landaulet that had stopped just in front of them. A lady in a very large and very grand hat, the "Oldenburg Hat" that was sweeping Town in that season of the grand duchess's visit, inclined her head and her hat toward the earl and, belatedly, toward his brother. "Mr. Trevelyan," she acknowledged.

Robert nodded a greeting to the ladies though he did just chance to wonder how her ladyship had been so certain that he was he and not his brother.

"You both know my daughter Cecily, of course," she added, poking a simper out of the beruffled young lady seated beside her.

"Of course, Lady Adair, Miss Cecily," said Lord Kitteridge with a bow and an elegant lift of his hat, "for I make it my business to know all the prettiest ladies in town." His grin, well practiced and versed in the ways of knocking feminine hearts acock, blossomed across his face. The two gentlemen were treated to three more simpers, two giggles, and a sigh.

"I do hope I shall see you both at my little soiree tomorrow evening," said Lady Adair, her feathers fluttering. "The czar himself has promised to honor us, you know." In imparting this information, the lady, not particularly petite at any time, puffed up remarkably until she threatened to burst from her mulberry lustring edged with teal ruchings and purple ribbons.

"Oh, dear," said the earl. "What a tragedy that we are promised elsewhere. I must hope that Miss Cecily does not lose her heart to the Russian giant before any of us simple Englishmen have a shot."

A strangled sound was heard, but not from the young lady this time. The Hon. Mr. Trevelyan was having a difficult time holding his countenance.

"Of course she won't," said Miss Cecily's mother in a very matter-of-fact voice, "for the czar is already married, you know." On this practical note, she pounded her cane on the floor of the carriage and ordered her coachman to drive on.

As soon as the ladies were out of earshot—or at least Robert *trusted* they were out of earshot—he let out a guffaw. His brother soon joined him. "It really is too bad of you, Alec, to make such a game of her," said Robert when he could speak. "I thought I'd pop."

"I thought *she'd* pop," said Alec. "But she didn't know she was being made game of, y'know. Her type never does." They were still chuckling when they turned into the doors of Jackson's, leaving the cacophony of Bond Street behind them.

Inside they encountered a din of a different sort, one no less lively but considerably more genteel than that of the public street which, after all, allowed every John Doe and Richard Roe to share the pavements with his betters. Here the rooms swarmed with Corinthians, Pets of the Fancy, and Bang Up Swells. Here a mere viscount could plant a leveller at a duke with perfect impunity. The accents were high-born and the side bets for high stakes, but sweat still poured off the backs of the combatants and they still turned purple and blue when they took a drubbing, be they ever so noble.

The brothers headed for the changing room to prepare themselves for a sparring session with the great man himself.

"Lady Adair's put paid to your scheme," said Robert, easing his feet from his well-worn and comfortable boots. "She hadn't the least difficulty in telling us apart, and she's a virtual stranger."

"Well, of course she knew me straight off," agreed Alec, peeling off his gray kid gloves and carefully removing two watch fobs and an onyx stickpin before beginning to strip, "for *no one* in London would look to see me in such a dull rig as that." He gestured to his brother's simple attire. "Last year's coat, for God's sake, and only one crease to your neckcloth! Really, Robbie, couldn't expect anyone to mix us up with you looking sober as a preacher."

Lord Kitteridge, while not precisely in the dandy class despite his brother's aspersions, was undeniably magnificent in biscuit-colored pantaloons, a blue coat of Bath Superfine of Weston's most exacting cut molded to his shoulders, and Hessians that gleamed like mirrors. His marcella waistcoat was subtly stripped, and his neckcloth was high, wonderfully starched, and intricately tied in the "Waterfall."

In contrast, his brother's black coat, while undeniably well made, was cut rather more for comfort than for fashion, his neckcloth held only a minimum of starch, and his top boots had definitely been near a horse or two in their time.

"And those boots!" Alec continued. "When are you going to get yourself a proper valet as I've been telling you to do for donkey's years?"

"I am perfectly capable of blacking my own boots," replied Robin, "and, unlike you, I don't require two strong men to ease me into my coat."

"Unfair. It's only my evening coat that is so tight. The one I wear to Almack's. But I do insist Chevis use champagne blacking on my boots, of course."

"Of course," agreed Robin, turning to a long mirror on the wall to study their twin images. He had to agree that no one who knew either of the Trevelyan twins was likely to confuse the two of them dressed as they were, however much they may resemble each other when stripped. He had always thought his attire appropriate to the quiet, scholarly life he'd chosen for himself, but now he was struck by its drabness. When had he become so colorless, he wondered. And why?

"C'mon," said Alec, knocking his brother's black felt hat to the floor with a laugh. "Let's go show Jackson that two Trevelyans are more than twice as dangerous as one."

A grin crossed Robert's face, suddenly lightening his sober appearance dramatically, and they began to strip. If female hearts had fluttered up and down Bond Street at their passing, there would have been a positive epidemic of swoons could those same females be allowed to see the Trevelyan twins now. Despite his quieter life in Oxford, Robert was a confirmed athlete and presented quite as glorious a sight as his brother. A pair of broad chests, now bared to the warm air, tapered to slender hips and long, strong legs. Both men kept in trim, and it showed.

Soon they had donned athletic clothes and soft boxing gloves and entered the gymnasium proper. The air was redolent with the ripe smells of clean sweat, new rubber, and old leather. It thrummed with the sounds of lightly shod feet on canvas, of leather hitting leather, and of the grunts that followed when leather hit bare flesh.

Jackson was in the ring, instructing a young marquis who would one day be a duke how to keep up his guard. To the accompaniment of a great deal of advice, the young man concentrated fiercely on every word the great man uttered. "Elbows in please, sir," said Jackson in the soft, deferential voice that seemed so much at odds with his appearance.

Jackson had been the undisputed and unbeaten champion of England, and it showed in the confidence with which he handled himself. So formidable an opponent had he been that he had only actually had to fight twice in his career. Each of his opponents left the ring feeling he'd fought at least one too many bouts. "Pay attention to your footwork, my lord," the ex-champion instructed the young marquis.

A short man, Jackson rather resembled a stubby oak tree that had somehow managed to retain the face of a rather ingenuous boy while taking on the grace of a panther, a strange and wholly beguiling combination. It had earned him the respect of the gentlemen of the *ton*. It had also earned him a tidy fortune; the sons of the nobility were willing to pay well for the privilege of being floored by Jackson himself.

Soon after entering the gymnasium, the Trevelyan twins were in the ring with the ex-champion, each taking a turn at sparring with him while the other watched critically from a corner.

"A little less wild, my lord," said Jackson as Lord Kitteridge took a hearty but careless swing. "A little more science, if you please." Alec laughed and swung again, putting all his energy into it. Again he missed. After a few more tries, it was his brother's turn.

"A little less care, Mr. Trevelyan," instructed Jackson, as Robert dodged about, well out of range. "You are thinking too hard. A little more instinct is needed, sir." Robert studied his opponent cautiously, analyzing his every move and planning his responses. He connected a few solid blows and protected himself well, showing good form, but all in all he fought an unimaginative fight.

When Alec came up again, he plunged in like a bull, fighting hard and wild, missing more blows than he landed. "You could do with some instruction from your brother, my lord," said Jackson just before Alec landed him a facer that caused him to stagger, a feat attained by few of the ex-champion's protégés. The entire room fell silent for a moment then erupted in cheers for Lord Kitteridge.

"I think that will do for today, gentlemen," said Jackson, rubbing gently at his jaw. "A good blow, my lord," he acknowledged, "but a sloppy fight. May I suggest that you both spend some time learning from each other? Combined, you would make a formidable opponent indeed."

A good few gentlemen gathered around Alec to congratulate him on popping in a hit over the master's guard. "Never saw the like!" cried a young baronet with what looked like a severe case of hero worship written all over his face. "Aye," another agreed, "but if you ask me, his brother showed the better science." As the brothers headed for the changing room, they left a lively debate behind them about who was the better fighter.

It was quiet in the changing room. They stripped off their gloves, toweled the sweat from their steaming bodies, and washed in silence, enjoying the peace that comes after strenuous exercise and the harmony that comes from being alone with a dearly loved twin.

After a moment, another gentleman poked his head in the door. "Ah, Kitteridge," he exclaimed to Alec as soon as he saw them. "Just the man I'd hoped to see. Hear you're off to Vienna for the party. Got a little proposition for you."

"Afternoon, Creighton," said Alec. "You should know I never discuss business undressed. See me later at the club. We dine there at nine."

"Done," said Lord Creighton and turned belatedly to Robert. "Nice to see you in Town, Trevelyan. Do you go to Vienna, too?"

Before Robin could answer, his brother said, "It is not yet decided, but I hope to coax him into going."

"Must go, y'know. Everyone is. London'll be a wasteland." And with that Lord Creighton poked his head out again.

As Alec brushed his glossy locks before the mirror, Robert came to stand behind him, a thoughtful frown on his face. "He knew us apart," he said slowly.

Alec paused, then said as casually as he could, "So he did."

Dressed as they now were in identical stockinette leggings and soft shoes, with their dark locks damp with sweat and tumbling over their high brows and with the handsome chests bare, they truly were as like as Canty's tuppence. And yet, Robert mused, Creighton had known them apart at once.

He stared at himself a long time, searching for clues. "Have I grown so dull that it shows on my very face?" he finally asked, speaking as much to his own image in the mirror as to his brother.

"I suppose so," said Alec in a suspiciously nonchalant tone. "Imagine you were in the right of it to refuse to fall in with my scheme. Pretending to be me in Vienna while I impersonate you—no, obviously it wouldn't fadge." He reached for his shirt of fine linen, beautifully ruffled down the front.

"Give me that," said Robert suddenly, taking the shirt from his brother's hand. Alec watched with a growing grin as his brother donned Alec's ruffled shirt, Alec's trousers and waistcoat, struggled with Alec's neckcloth before achieving a moderately acceptable version, and eased himself into Weston's masterpiece of a coat.

Alec then put on his brother's clothes with only the smallest grimace of distaste. When they were done and stood before the mirror for the last time, Robert said softly, "A century, you said?"

"I did," agreed his brother.

"Brother, prepare to lose a hundred pounds. I am going to Vienna."

·····❦{ *three* }❦·····

IT SEEMED INDEED that all the world and his wife was on the way to Vienna in that late summer of 1814. The road from London to Dover was jammed; all the packets crossing the Channel were full as they could hold; and the stream of carriages heading across Europe was at full flood. Miss Georgianna Pennington joined the deluge.

Despite the natural eagerness of a young, adventurous spirit and the fact that she had been anticipating the trip to Vienna with unrestrained enthusiasm, when it came to the point, Georgianna found herself reluctant to embark upon her journey. Having taken the firm decision to launch into her search for the perfect husband without delay as soon as she arrived in that glittering capital, she was now loath to go.

Her attitude was not, it must be said, echoed by the bulk of the unattached young ladies destined to be left behind in London. Georgianna Pennington had taken the *ton,* or at least the eligible male portion of it, quite by storm, and the hordes of lesser beauties knocked into relative oblivion by the dash she cut through the Town could hardly be expected not to rejoice at seeing the back of her. To a woman, they breathed a collective sigh of relief the day her heavy traveling carriage rumbled away from the house in Curzon Street and headed south.

She was, much to her chagrin, accompanied not by her father, who had been required to go on ahead and travel with greater speed than she found comfortable, but by Suzanne Patterson. Also by a pair of abigails, a coachman to drive the heavy berlin that would make the long jolting ride as comfortable as possible, and a courier to ride always a day ahead of them to make arrangements and ease their passage. They were also chaperoned by a very large dog of indeterminate parentage (one of whose ancestors was certainly an English sheep dog) on whom Georgianna had bestowed the exalted name of Monsieur de Talleyrand—or Talley, as he was more commonly known.

Georgianna, when informed that she was to travel with Mrs. Patterson instead of with her father, had been stabbed with disappointment. She had lectured herself several times in the past fortnight on her father's absolute right to marry the widow if he wished to. She had reiterated to herself a dozen times and more her own decision to marry as soon as possible, thus making room in her father's home and heart for a new wife. She had recounted over and over how certain she was to find her own perfect gentleman in Vienna. But still she found it difficult to be comfortable with Suzanne.

She had even harbored hopes, ignominious though she knew them to be, that Suzanne was afraid of dogs, or even better, that they made her pretty eyes run and her dainty nose turn red and erupt in constant sneezes. But the bitter truth was that Suzanne adored Talley on sight, and Talley took a liking to Suzanne with an enthusiasm Georgie found difficult to forgive.

"I do wish it hadn't been necessary for Papa to go on ahead," said Georgianna as the two women and the dog stood on the dock in Dover watching their coachman supervise the loading of the carriage and their mountain of luggage onto a ship for France. "I'm never quite comfortable traveling without him."

Glowing pinkly from the invigorating salt air, she stared out at the expanse of water her father had crossed a week earlier, holding one hand to her very fetching chip straw bonnet lest the breeze carry it away and clutching Talley's leash firmly with the other. The dog, still something of a puppy at only two years of age, was sniffing all about and wagging his tail delightedly at the ripe smells of the dock while simultaneously trying to chase a sea gull that insisted on venturing rather nearer than was wise.

"True," said Suzanne. "It is so much more comfortable having a man along." Georgie had to admit, however reluctantly, that the widow looked quite delicious in a traveling costume of cerulean blue marocain trimmed with velvet topped by a matching bonnet. With her rosebud of a mouth, her huge blue eyes, and her fashionable turnout, she might have been peeled right off the page of one of Mr. Ackerman's modish style books. Georgie herself was far from dowdy in a very fetching sprig muslin that sang of summer, topped by a spencer of forest-green velvet fetchingly trimmed with ecru gimp, but she knew she'd have to own several more years before she could compete with Suzanne in élan. "But we shall do nicely without him, Georgianna," Suzanne went on. "Why, with so many of the English on their way to Paris or Vienna, I doubt we shall have a moment alone on the road. We're far more likely to wish for some peace than we are to fear for our safety. And besides, we shall have Talley to protect us, won't we, love?" This last was directed at the dog who wagged his tail contentedly and allowed his new friend to scratch his ears.

"I am not in the least afraid," said Georgie, bridling up as she did so easily whenever she was with Suzanne. She hated herself for such a base reaction, but there it was. "It is merely that Papa is such a delightful traveling companion."

"I am certain he is," Suzanne said simply and smiled what Georgie could only think of as a secret, self-satisfied smile.

In truth, Georgianna was dreading the trip across Germany more than she would admit though her anxiety did not spring from any fear of danger. It was a route she had traveled earlier that year with her father in the wake of the victorious armies approaching Paris. What she had seen in those war's-end days appalled her: dazed soldiers looking worse than scarecrows trudging listlessly toward home, the bloated bodies of dead horses putrefying in ditches, and the fly-strewn corpses of dead Frenchmen staring sightlessly at the sky, stripped of anything usable or salable, their naked bodies rotting in the sun because the Germans refused to bury their vanquished enemies. They looked all the more tragic lying beside the riotously blooming mayflowers and primroses and wild lady's slippers edging the road.

In Hanau there had been the inns full of wounded Russians, hopelessly trying to communicate their pain in a language no one around them understood. Georgianna had felt so helpless and frustrated and unbearably angry at the waste this interminable war had caused. Now, at least, with the great Congress of Vienna to settle once and for all time the proper boundaries of Europe, they could finally rest easy in the thought that there would never again be such a horrid, useless, *wasteful* war.

Haunted by her memories, she breathed deeply of the Dover air, thick with the aromas of tar and hemp and fish and with the taste of salt on the breeze. In Germany, she had feared she would never get the smell of death out of her nose or the screams of the dying out of her mind.

The two women on the dock, each wrapped in her own private thoughts, lapsed into silence—if one could ever describe the cacophony of the busiest dock in one of the busiest ports in England in full roar as silence. All about them stevedores shouted at one another; carts and wagons rolled across the cobblestones under their heavy burdens of trunks, valises, and bandboxes; and vendors plied the waiting passengers with every sort of necessity, delicacy, medicament, and frivolity that a journeyer could possibly require. Masts creaked as ships rocked on the tide. Chatter, yells, oaths and curses, children's squeals, clanking cranes, and the cries of the peddlers mingled into a rich stew of sound that simmered all around them.

The breeze picked up suddenly, blowing Georgie's flowered muslin up around her ankles—to the delight of a number of nearby gentlemen—and tipping Suzanne's stylish bonnet over one eyebrow.

"Let's move inside," Suzanne suggested, having to nearly shout to make herself heard above the din. "It looks to be an hour at least before we may board, and this wind is like to ruin our complexions."

Georgie agreed though she secretly doubted anything, even age, could ruin Suzanne's milk-and-honey complexion. She only wished that something could and berated herself all the way into the inn for such an ignominious desire.

Really, she scolded herself in one of the heated inner monologues she'd been much given to of late, this will not do. You have already decided that Suzanne will make the perfect wife for Papa, and there is no sense in finding imaginary things to dislike in her now.

Tugging a reluctant Talley behind them, they headed up the hill toward the Fox and Two Geese, where their abigails awaited them and where they could be sure of a decent scone and a good cup of tea as well as a shelter against the breeze.

The Earl of Kitteridge and his brother also began their journey that day. They'd spent the past fortnight on the Kitteridge estate in Devon, enjoying the country air, the home in which they grew up, visits to their aged nurse, and each other's company. The drive to Dover had started out well. They'd sent their trunks on ahead so they could tool down in his lordship's curricle pulled by a spanking team of matched bays, perfect to a shade. Both brothers were in high spirits as the sun beat down on the carriage hood and the wind riffled their thick dark hair. It was a beautiful day complete with wild roses in the hedges and robins in the trees; they were driving through a classically bucolic English countryside; and they were young, healthy, and off on an adventure. Even Robin admitted that, having reluctantly accepted the wager, he was looking forward to the trip as something of a lark.

Except for the stroll home from Jackson's the day the wager was made and accepted, they'd not yet stepped into each other's shoes, so to speak. They had decided that should wait until they reached Vienna. They could use the interim to coach each other in their respective roles. Thus it was that Alec spent the first part of the drive to Dover "instructing" his brother in what was expected of the Earl of Kitteridge.

"Give over, Alec," said Robin finally. "Isn't as though I haven't been watching you do it all my life. What is there to it, after all, but parading about in some dandified rig, wooing all the ladies, and regularly making a perfect cake of myself for some trifling wager?"

"Ho! Is that what you think of me, then?" cried Alec. "Knew all along you was jealous, but never thought it went deep as that." He laughed and hardly noticed that his brother did not seem to share the joke.

But for Robin this particular subject was not one for levity. He had, in fact, often been if not jealous at least envious of his brother during their lives. There were times when he could not but consider what a difference a mere ten minutes could mean in the shape taken by a man's life. Had he emerged out of his mother's womb those few minutes ahead of Alec . . . Or had their father been a Scot—though the mere idea was laughable, for the last Lord Kitteridge had detested his brethren to the north—how different the twins' lives would have turned out.

In Scotland, the second born of twins was considered the heir on the theory that he was the first conceived. A sort of first in, last out view of the situation.

But Robin hated these thoughts as much as he loved his brother, which was a great deal indeed. He knew as no one could how painful it was to envy someone even while you would go to almost any length to save him from hurt. It was the very reason he had chosen the quiet, scholarly, and alto-gether predictable life away from London that he had.

Since he couldn't *be* Lord Kitteridge, he had decided, there seemed little point in tagging along in Alec's shadow, as he had been wont to do as a child, aping everything his brother did. He was always going to come off a poor second to his more noble twin, and the resultant rivalry could only pain them both, for Robin knew that Alec loved him as much as he was loved.

So Robert Trevelyan had purposely chosen a life for him-self as different from his brother's as he could possibly make it. And on the whole, it was a life that suited him very well. He had his books and his friends and his animals. He loved good conversation—not necessarily witty or fashionable, but sensible, involving, even challenging. He rode and he fished, often with a friend and always with a dog or two for company. He even played cricket with a local team on the village green. He was satisfied—or at least he had been until Alec proposed this absurd scheme and he'd discovered how ready he was for a change. The idea gave him pause.

His life had for many years been so well ordered. Since the one event that colored every other in his life, his birth, had been so totally beyond his control, he had developed a deep-seated need to control everything else that happened to him. He did not like surprises and he didn't like things that chal-lenged the order he had created in his life. Why, then, his agreement to this harebrained stunt of Alec's?

There had been, he had to admit, one factor other than a simple desire for change involved in his decision. His brother, as always, hit it square on. "This caper is going to be very good for you," said Alec as they tooled along the road to Dover.

"You make it sound like some sort of medicament."

"And so it is. This little lark will definitely be good for what ails you."

"And what is that?" asked Robin with a grin.

"What you need in your life, my boy, is a little dalliance. Kick up a little dust. Set a few feminine hearts fluttering. You could easily do it, you know, if only you would."

"You know I'm not much in the petticoat line. I leave that sort of thing to you; you're so good at it."

"Yes, I am," Alec admitted without false modesty. It was, after all, only the truth. "And I'm heartily glad to know that you, my boy, will now be forced to act the part. It's time and past that you had a taste of those particular joys."

"I'm not precisely a monk, Alec," Robin averred.

"No, you ain't. But you are giving yourself short shrift. Why, if I hadn't taken matters in hand we'd have seen you shackled to that gawky girl you introduced me to last winter. What's her name? Evergreen? Everdull?"

Try as he might to summon up a suitable indignation, Robin could not completely suppress a smile. "Miss Everbright is a very amiable girl," he said.

"I'm certain she is, but she is not to be your wife. I won't have it. Why, you'd turn into an absolute stump of granite out there in Oxford, stuck in your own dullness like an oak tree in the ground. Never get you to Town at all, or anywhere else."

Actually, Robin had already begun to have his own doubts as to the suitability of Miss Evelina Everbright, for all her amiability, to be his wife. In truth, the questions about her that had taken root in his brain had quite taken him by surprise, for he had made up his mind to do the thing at last. Put his fate to the touch, so to speak. She was ideally suited to the situation. Clever, sensible, healthy, a good manager—that was Evelina Everbright. She had every quality to be a fitting wife for him except for one.

Robin, on the very verge of offering for her, had realized he could never love her. He had tried, he really had, but it just wouldn't fadge. Now he must decide if he was willing to marry without love for the sake of order, comfort, and a life that would be eminently predictable.

The problem was that he had not the leisure to ponder the question in private so long as he remained at home in Oxford. Mrs. Everbright had made it abundantly, oppressively clear that she was in daily expectation of a proposal of marriage from Mr. Trevelyan for her daughter's hand. She also made it quite clear that her permission and that of her husband would not be tardy in following on the heels of such a proposal. Though Mrs. Everbright's family was genteel it was not

noble, and she was not about to whistle an earl's son down the
wind, even if he was a younger one. Nor had she any intention
of letting him slip through her, or her daughter's, fingers. All
Robin had to do was ask the question, and the banns were
likely to show up on the church door within the week.

But he, usually so firm at knowing his own mind, could
not seem to bring himself to the point, and the situation had
become increasingly awkward. Robert could not deny that it
had aided and abetted his unwonted impulsiveness in taking
the decision to join his brother in Vienna on this ridiculous
lark. The thought of not having to face Mrs. Everbright for
several weeks could not but make him feel lighthearted, even
giddy with his newfound freedom.

Robin, who had been berating himself for his foolishness
ever since accepting his brother's wager, discovered the farther they journeyed from Devon (and from Oxford) the
younger and more carefree he felt.

Alec's mood, on the other hand, darkened as they drove
farther and farther south. His carefree humor began to take on
a hard edge, almost as if it were forced. There was a nervous
quality to his laughter.

The problem was a simple one. The Earl of Kitteridge and
boats of any kind had never made good companions, and the
prospect of the coming sea voyage could not please him. His
propensity toward *mal de mer* was an acute embarrassment to
him. A Channel crossing was the very last thing he was looking forward to. Though the weather was fine and the sharp
breeze was like to make the journey a short one, he knew his
treasonous stomach was liable to unman him. The thought was
not a pleasurable one.

By the time they finally trundled into Dover, Alec was
positively irritable.

Robin ignored his brother's odd humor, understanding its
origins and his brother's embarrassment over it. He refused to
be drawn into an argument no matter how much Alec baited
him.

"Keep telling you you ought to swallow a dose of powdered ginger," he said calmly as Alec carefully steered the
curricle through the dense traffic of the port town. "Never did
understand how you could be such a terrible sailor when the
sea doesn't bother me in the least."

"And powdered ginger does not help me in the least," Alec

growled. "I've tried it. I've tried everything. Just have to stay below till it's over."

"That you will not," said Robin decidedly. "We will remain on deck. Best possible thing—fresh air, y'know, and then, too, you can see the shore approaching instead of just rolling about blind in a stuffy bunk. Walk up and down a bit, too, that's the ticket."

"You sound for all the world like Canty," Alec complained.

Determined to pull his brother up out of the mumps, Robin said in a tone that faithfully mimicked their old nurse, "Now you'll do as I say, Master Smart Alec, and no more roundaboutation."

Alec managed a small grin. Robin made another joke; Alec's smile grew; and by the time he tooled the curricle into the busy innyard of the Fox and Two Geese, they were both laughing easily again.

If there was anything better calculated to charm every female within sight than one of the Trevelyan brothers laughing it was two of them in whoops. Georgianna was not proof against that charm, for all her ill temper with herself. The two women were just emerging from the inn, eagerly led by Talley and with their maids trailing behind them, to return to the dock. They had managed to devour—albeit with perfect good manners and breeding—a substantial tea, and Talley had been given a marrowbone on which to gnaw.

Georgie was wondering who the remarkably striking pair of gentlemen, as perfectly matched in every feature as the superb horses that pulled their curricle, may be when Suzanne smiled at them as they alighted from their dashing equipage. "Kitteridge!" she cried in recognition. "And Mr. Trevelyan. Do you sail today as well? The *Caroline*, I hope."

"Hallo, Suzanne," Alec replied casually as he jumped down with an easy grace. Over his shoulder to the ostler he added, "See they're well rubbed down, mind, and give them an extra ration of oats and an apple apiece."

The young ostler touched his forelock, mumbled an "Aye, my lord," winked at Georgianna's abigail, and led the magnificent bays off to the stable. Georgie, who had a sound eye for fine horseflesh, watched them go with an admiring look. Robin watched her watching them go with an admiring look.

"Yes, we're sailing on the *Caroline*," said Alec, managing to keep a grimace at the thought of that coming ordeal from his handsome face.

"How do you do, Mrs. Patterson," said Robin more formally than his brother as he took the prettily gloved hand she offered.

She introduced the brothers to Georgianna, adding, "Now our stay in Vienna is guaranteed to be a success, Georgie. No party can be boring with even one Trevelyan in attendance. I should imagine two will be diverting indeed."

"Don't think it, Miss Pennington," said Alec with a wicked gleam of amusement in his eye. "My brother's a dull dog, don't y'know. Goes all prosy whenever he gets the chance. Just wait, you'll see," he added with a grin, knowing full well that it was he, Alec, they would be seeing when they thought they were seeing Robin. "He'll be spouting Latin at you in a trice if you let him."

"Then we shall reply in Greek," Suzanne teased with her lilting laugh, "and you, my lord, will not have the slightest notion of what we are talking about."

"She's got you there, Alec," said Robin. "Never were much a linguist. And shall you understand us then, Miss Pennington?" he asked Georgianna, looking down into lovely brown eyes. He found himself wondering what sort of voice would match such a pretty face.

"Yes, I'm afraid I shall," she replied with a smile that suddenly made Robin truly glad he had come. "My parents, you see, never believed that girls should not be as well educated as boys. Perhaps they would have felt differently had I not been their only child, but as I was, education was positively lavished on me, whether I would or no."

Suzanne, her eyes holding an arresting gleam as she noted the admiration on Mr. Trevelyan's face at sight of Georgianna, added, "Let me tell you, sir, that she would also understand you perfectly were you to speak German, Spanish, or Italian."

Georgianna glared at her companion's lack of subtlety, but Robin was clearly impressed, just as Suzanne had hoped he would be. He smiled even more warmly and said, *"Français aussi, naturellement,"* with a questioning cock of his head.

There was something about the warmth of the young man's smile that Georgianna found appealing. *"Naturellement, monsieur,"* she agreed, and his smile grew until it reached deep into his eyes.

"Est-ce que c'est votre première visite à Vienne?" Robin continued, that warm smile holding her gaze.

"Oui, la première," she agreed. *"Et vous?"*

"Here, enough frog talk," interrupted Alec. "We did win the war, y'know." He was suddenly acutely uncomfortable over his deficiencies as a linguist. Robin was so damnably good at all that sort of thing. And how the devil was he to enact that part of the charade, he wondered? For the first time since having the brilliant idea that they should trade identities, he felt a twinge of doubt about his own ability to pull the thing off.

"True," said Robin, allowing his smile to turn on his brother and crinkle up until it was positively devilish. "But since French is the language of diplomacy as well as the lingua franca of most of Europe, it is bound to be the language of the day in Vienna." He knew it was unchivalrous to tease his brother, but he couldn't help it. "I expect we will all be using French right and left. Don't you agree, Miss Pennington?"

"Oh, yes," Georgie readily acknowledged. "When we were in St. Petersburg, we found that nothing but French was spoken. It was disappointing, actually, for I had hoped to learn at least a bit of Russian while we were there. But the Russians use their own language only with their servants and their peasants, I'm afraid."

"St. Petersburg! Tell me . . ." Robin began, and soon they were off on a dialogue discussing her various travels. Never terribly at ease with the fair sex, he was amazed at how comfortable he was talking with Georgianna Pennington. Suzanne and Alec began chatting together of parties they'd recently attended and of mutual friends they thought likely to be in Vienna, and the conversation carried the entire group, Talley in the van and pulling the others in his wake, down to the dock.

Luggage and servants, carriage and dog, they were all soon aboard the *Caroline*. The tide began to turn; the ropes were cast off; the wind filled the sails; and Lord Kitteridge began to turn vaguely green.

⤛ four ⤜

GEORGIANNA LOVED THE sea. She loved the sight of it, the smell, sound, and taste of it, its cleanness and the possibilities for adventure it seemed always to offer with such tantalizing promise. And now it was leading her into a new adventure as well, one she had misgivings about, to be sure, but one that was bound to prove interesting, at any rate. Her spirits began to soar.

Soon after the enormous white sails had bloomed with the westerly winds, pushing the ship at a spanking pace away from Dover's gleaming cliffs, Suzanne went below to the cabin they had bespoken. Not for her the dangers of sea air, well known for its propensity to ruin a fine complexion. But Georgianna couldn't bear the thought of being cooped up in a stuffy, tiny cabin when she could be exhilarating in the taste of salt air on her tongue and the feel of it on her skin, when she could be letting the seaborne breezes riffle her hair and pinch her cheeks to a rosy pink.

She stood in the bow of the ship, her face turned to the sea and her bonnet hanging by its ribbons from one hand, caring not a fig for the impropriety of such informality, while her hair blew about her in glorious abandon. Talley lay on the deck at her feet, his shaggy mane blowing about just as hers did, and seeming to love the wind in his face, flattening his ears against his head, just as much as she did.

All around her the ship teemed with activity. Seamen scurried about doing all the mysterious things seamen do—climbing ropes, furling and unfurling sails, adjusting, watching, sniffing the wind, and shouting incomprehensibly to each other. A few passengers sat or strolled about the deck though most, like Suzanne, had opted for the more familiar comforts of their cabins or a soothing cup of tea in the common room. A few, like the Earl of Kitteridge, were feeling not quite the thing, but they, unlike him, were doing it below and in private.

Robert Trevelyan, pacing endlessly up and down the deck with his brother while he sternly informed Alec that he was *not* to be seasick, could not stop his eyes straying often to where Georgianna stood in the bow. She stood immobile, and he thought she looked like nothing so much as a classical figurehead—Helen of Troy, perhaps, or a fitting decoration for Jason's *Argo*.

He laughed silently at his own whimsy, for though a classicist he'd always considered himself the most unpoetic fellow imaginable. He did just happen to notice an arresting thought wafting across his mind—he found Miss Pennington as different from Miss Evelina Everbright as it was possible for two females of the same species to be. Chalk and cheese, Canty might have said, and Robert was afraid he hadn't the slightest doubt which was the chalk and which the cheese.

Georgianna glowed. The breeze that had been pleasantly brisk in Dover was much stronger out on the open water. The ship fairly danced and flew over the waves, up and down, up and down, lulling her into happiness as surely as a cradle. Forgetting temporarily any and all troubles, challenges, or demands to be made on her talents in Vienna, she was content to be exactly where she was at that moment.

But the same regularity of movement that made Georgianna glow with pleasure was having quite a different effect on the Earl of Kitteridge. Up and down, up and down went his stomach as he was led inexorably around the deck by his brother who, in Alec's opinion, was talking in a disgustingly hearty and condescending manner. "Keep breathing deeply," said Robin cheerily. "That's the ticket. You'll be right as a trivet in no time."

"*Mrfgrgl,*" muttered Lord Kitteridge, who was trying to

say something very pithy indeed but who was afraid to open his mouth for fear he would be well and truly sick. He was having as much difficulty hanging on to the dignity he felt his title required as he was hanging on to his lunch.

"Wouldn't want to make an ass of yourself in front of the others, would you?"

Alec stopped pacing and faced his brother, managing to speak through gritted teeth. "S'why I took a cabin. Can very well make an ass of myself in private." Maintaining his delicate hold on his dignity was a primary concern of the young earl, for there were several people on the ship he knew well. With half the *ton* going abroad at just that moment, it would have been wonderful indeed had there not been.

"Sit in a dingy cabin for several hours?" said Robin. "And be fagged to death for a week afterwards? No, no. Thing is to breath it out now and enjoy the rest of the trip." And up and down they continued pacing.

Georgianna was not long alone in her lookout from the bow. Before disappearing into the relative safety of her cabin, Suzanne had introduced her young protégée to several of their fellow passengers. One of these new acquaintances, a bulky gentleman with a military air and magnificent side whiskers of which he was clearly enamored, joined Georgianna now on deck.

Captain Bloomfield was a personable gentleman, she thought, with a hearty manner and a ready smile. In his early thirties, she estimated, he was a good-looking man in a substantial sort of way. He was dressed in a well-cut civilian coat of brown kerseymere, but he wore it as if it were a set of scarlet regimentals, and he tended to speak as if addressing troops in the field. Old habits died hard, she supposed.

"Lovely day, what?" blustered Captain Bloomfield with a huge smile that seemed perfectly at home on his ruddy face.

"Perfectly lovely," she agreed.

"Off to Vienna, then, what?" he added.

"Yes, we are going to Vienna," she replied, stifling a giggle and an urge to add "what?" "We plan a short stay in Paris first, however. His Grace of Wellington has invited us to visit at the embassy."

"Yes, yes, good man the duke."

Again Georgianna had to stifle her merriment, for to use the term "good man" in reference to the Duke of Wellington was carrying understatement to the point of absurdity.

"Paris," the captain continued. "Like Paris, the ladies do. Never could understand it myself, this passion for Frenchie things. After all, just spent dog's years knocking them into line, didn't we? But there. Full of frills and furbelows, I understand Paris is. Ladies like to be up on all that sort of thing, what?"

"Yes, I fear we do, sir. And Paris has been denied us for so many years, you know."

"No, no. Quite right. Paris, it is. Pretty you all up a bit. Not," he added hastily, "that you need any of that sort of thing. No, no, not at all, what?"

"I thank you, sir," she said with a smile that turned his ruddy cheeks an even more vivid red and puffed out his whiskers.

Georgianna found she liked Captain Bloomfield despite his somewhat overblown manner. The fellow was so amiable it was difficult not to like him. She did, however, wonder if she could tolerate spending any great amount of time with a gentleman who ended every pronouncement in such a fashion. Of course, she *might* be able to break him of the habit if she really chose to, but she could not but wonder if it would be worth the effort.

With her new determination to find the perfect husband without delay, Georgie had begun to look quite differently at every gentleman she met, weighing them, she would have to admit if questioned. It was amazing how different a gentleman looked to one when one was considering him as a potential husband, something she had not done with any gentleman in many years. To spend a half hour in pleasant conversation was one thing; to contemplate a lifetime of a gentleman's unbroken company was quite another.

She had, of course, had her share of offers since breaking off with Lieutenant Farnham. She was a very pretty, lively girl; she came from an excellent family; and she would have a respectable fortune from her father one day. But she had taken the promises of undying affection from her many suitors with a large grain of salt. Her lively manner coupled with her total disinterest in anything more serious than a *very* mild dalliance had earned for her a reputation as a heartless flirt.

Fortunately, no hint of this epithet had reached her ears. She would have found it grossly unfair. It was simply that she could not take seriously any of the young men she met, or their offers of marriage.

Georgianna did not deny her own charms, but she was also a realistic young woman with a very good understanding of the emotions young men away from home are prey to. Traveling with her father, she had frequently been the only eligible female for miles around among a group of gentlemen young enough to be easily impressed and in the middle of a war besides. She knew better than to take any proposal made under such circumstances seriously even had she been interested.

Then there was the undeniable fact that not one of her erstwhile suitors had touched her heart even slightly. With her father as the pattern card by which she judged all men, her beaux all seemed either too frivolous, too gauche, or too young. And, too, she had not been in the least concerned with finding herself a husband. She was quite content to have things go on just as they were.

But her father was no longer content that they should. It might pain her, but she could not deny it. And so she would act, she must act, to rid him of her care. Because she loved him, she must elicit a proposal she *could* take seriously from a gentleman she could take seriously. She wondered what that gentleman would be like as she peered up into the undeniably genial face of Captain Bloomfield.

"First trip abroad, Miss Pennington?" he asked.

Aha, she thought, I've already managed to get a sentence out of him without a "what?" She laughed lightly. "Quite the contrary, sir. In fact, I have spent very little time in England in the past few years." She explained her father's position, and described some of her travels with him.

The captain frowned very slightly; it seemed an expression at which he'd had little practice. "No place for a young girl, a battlefield," he said. "Shouldn't think it was at all the thing, taking you along like that, what?"

Oh, dear, thought Georgianna. A relapse. "I shouldn't think, Captain, that a battlefield is a fit place for anyone, man or woman." His frown grew, causing his side whiskers to droop alarmingly. It was clear to Georgianna that she had severely disappointed the man. "Of course, I do see," she said, trying to recoup, "that we had no choice. We certainly could not allow Bonaparte to have his way and simply ride roughshod over the whole of Europe, could we?"

"No, no, couldn't do that," he said. His whiskers shot up again in pleasure. "Of course, never was any danger of his winning. Fellow's a bit of a bounder, what? Corsican, don't you know."

"Yes," she said and chuckled lightly despite herself. "I had heard."

"Well, mean to say, what could you expect? Not as though he was even French and they're bad enough. Couldn't really expect to beat Englishmen, now could he, what?"

"Or even Russians," she replied and realized her attention was beginning to fade. Her eyes wandered along the deck and alit upon the Trevelyan brothers, still pacing though at a less frantic tempo than earlier. Lord Kitteridge even managed a grin as they passed her, and Georgianna was captivated by it. He really was a charming fellow, she thought. And his brother's sincere smile, while not quite as boyishly engaging, made her feel warmed in the cool breeze.

For his part, Robert Trevelyan was beginning to tire of energetically pacing his brother about and jollying him out of the notion that he was going to be sick. He had much rather be up there in the bow talking to Miss Pennington. Three times in the last quarter of an hour they had walked past where she stood chatting to that military fellow. And three times he had caught a glimpse of the smile he thought so delightful and a note of the laughter he found so musical. Whatever could the fellow be saying to her, he wondered, to bring such a charming smile to her face?

And so he was more willing than his brother might have expected when Alec finally dug in his heels and called a halt to their endless constitutional. "Not another step," Alec proclaimed with a mulish look at his brother. "Wear out my new boots at this rate. Then Chevis would desert me. Just because you ain't got a valet don't mean I should have to lose mine."

"Oh, very well," said Robin, leaning against the railing to face his brother in a position that just happened also to allow a particularly fine view of Miss Pennington's profile. "Got to admit, though, you do feel more the thing. Not likely to lose your lunch now."

"I had rather you'd given me some of Canty's powdered ginger."

"We'll get some in Vienna for the voyage back home," said Robin.

"Aaargh," moaned Alec at the thought that in some weeks' time he would be forced to go through this dreadfulness all over again. "Why the devil does England have to be an island, anyway?" he asked the sky.

Robin simply laughed and lit a cheroot. The smoke trailed off on the wind, and the two brothers relaxed in companionable silence, Robin looking completely at ease, Alec looking distinctly less comfortable than his brother but also less green than he had earlier.

Finally Captain Bloomfield took himself off below for a cup of tea out of the wind, and Mr. Trevelyan was emboldened to approach Georgianna. His brother, perhaps out of habit from having followed him about the deck all afternoon, followed him.

"May we join you?" asked Robin with punctilious correctness.

Georgianna, who had been staring up into the fluffy white clouds hanging over the sea, turned and smiled. "Of course," she said. "I have just been looking for sky animals."

"Sky animals?" asked Alec.

"In the clouds. There's a camel off to the right there. See it? And I *think* that's a kangaroo lower down. Of course, I have never actually seen a kangaroo except in picture books, but it does look as though it has a baby in its pouch and is gathering its forces to bound off toward the horizon, does it not?"

"By Jove," said Alec, shading his eyes and following her pointing finger. "Dashed if it don't."

"Perhaps it is eager to join the elephant over there to the left," said Robin, pointing and causing two other sets of eyes to shift.

"It is an elephant!" said Georgianna with a delighted laugh. "With quite wonderful tusks. And he is most definitely headed toward my kangaroo. Oh dear. I'm not at all certain an elephant and a kangaroo are likely to become friends, are you?"

"Well, perhaps that is only because they have never had the chance," said Robin.

"Course not," added Alec. "No elephants in Australia. Any clod knows that. That *is* where kangaroos live, isn't it? No, no, your kangaroo had much better become a hyena or some such, Miss Pennington. Same continent, y'see."

"Not at all," she said firmly. "As my kangaroo appeared first, it is for Mr. Trevelyan to change his elephant. A wallaby, perhaps, thought I am not at all certain what a wallaby looks like."

"Nothing at all like an elephant, I assure you, Miss Pennington," said Robin.

"Oh, I was afraid not," she replied and smiled at him so charmingly that he had a quite irrational notion to jump up into the clouds and change their shapes with his own hands just to elicit another such smile.

Alec, grown bored with the game, said, "Going to be quite a party in Vienna. Everyone will be there."

"So I've heard," said Georgianna. "They say there will be upwards of two hundred putting up within the Hofburg Palace itself. I hope the empress can manage. She's so young, and I'm told she is ill, poor thing."

"Can't expect much help from the emperor, either," said Alec. "I understand the fellow's favorite hobby is making toffee in his private kitchen." And he laughed derisively.

"It sounds like a very pleasant pastime to me," said Robin. "Especially when one has so many affairs of state weighing on one's shoulders."

"I met him once," said Georgianna, "in Frankfurt. I found him a kind, rather wizened old man and not at all worldly. This Congress must be something of a trial for him, for he hates public occasions, you know."

"And you?" said Alec, feeling well enough to grace her with the famous Kitteridge smile. "Do you care for public occasions?"

"Of course, my lord," she said and the smile she gave him back was fully as charming. "For how else could I show off all the new gowns I intend to purchase in Paris?"

"I shall look forward to the show," he replied.

Robin, feeling totally outshone by his brother's dazzle, said nothing more.

It was shortly afterward that Suzanne Patterson finally decided to brave the elements and reappear on deck. She had wrapped a pretty blue and green paisley shawl about her shoulders and carried a parasol the exact shade of her dress and with the same blue velvet trim. Stepping lightly over coils of rope, around barrels, and under spars, she approached the trio in the bow.

"Gentlemen," she said with a pretty smile. "It happens that several of the passengers have brought food hampers aboard. Captain Bloomfield, for one, and Mrs. Alderstunt, and a few others as well as Georgianna and myself. And I have had the most splendid idea! Why not combine them for a feast at sea? I have asked some of the crew to clear us a spot on deck and set out barrels and such. It will be a very dashing picnic!"

"What a famous idea, Suzanne!" said Georgianna, completely forgetting her unease with her future stepmama.

"We should love to have you gentlemen join us, wouldn't we, Georgie?" added Suzanne.

"Oh, yes, please do," said Georgianna and clapped her hands with enthusiasm. She thought that, too, was a perfectly splendid idea.

"I thank you, ma'am," said Robin with a pleasure enhanced by the fact that Miss Pennington would make one of the group. "I admit I should be glad of a bite. The sea air always makes me sharpset."

Suzanne looked at Alec. "Kitteridge?" she inquired. "I can promise you some chicken in aspic, and I understand there are jellied eels."

Alec did not reply, could not reply, in fact. True, he had been feeling very much better, but the mention of food, the eels in particular, was playing havoc with the tenuous control he had gained over his rebellious stomach.

"I think not, ma'am," Robin replied gently in his stead. "My brother made a hearty meal on the road, you see."

Alec smiled faintly at this. Suzanne, who was not stupid and was truly kind-hearted besides, looked at him with understanding and nodded. "You might just wish for a cup of tea, my lord," she said gently. "I understand the purser has prepared some in the common room."

"Tea," managed Alec. "Yes, tea. Just the thing." He made his hurried excuses and gratefully went below at last.

The other three walked around to the port side of the ship to join their fellow passengers. Crewmen bustled about, moving coils of hemp aside and setting out barrels for the ladies to sit on, spreading some unused sails over the sun-bleached decking, and generally bumping into the servants trying to unpack the hampers and lay out the repast in the shade of the big mainsail.

There was a feeling of gaiety in the air, a feeling of being daringly casual, that affected them all. "La, Mama," said Miss Alderstunt, a whey-faced girl with a mouth full of teeth. "I declare being at sea is better than a masquerade." She turned her large, toothy smile on Robert Trevelyan, who had just approached, then she tried, with indifferent success, to flutter her almost nonexistent eyelashes for his benefit. "One can be ever so daring with no thought to the consequences. Don't you agree, Mr. Trevelyan?"

"I suppose," he said as he seated himself on the sail-covered decking, "that one must always be aware of the consequences of one's acts, but it is certainly true that there is something liberating about a sea voyage."

"La, yes," she went on, fluttering as fast as her eyelashes could go and twirling a beruffled parasol into a positive churn. "I for one wish never to arrive at Calais. I declare, I should like to sail right around the world."

"No, no, dear lady," said Captain Bloomfield. "Shouldn't think you'd like it at all. Bound to be damp, what?" Then, turning his attention to the food being unpacked, his whiskers smiled hugely. "I say! That looks a bit of all right, what?"

Georgianna chuckled softly; Robin looked down at her and smiled, and they shared a moment of amusement.

The hampers proved to be generous indeed, filled with thick slices of ham and roast beef and fresh bread and butter. In addition to the promised jellied eels and chickens in aspic, there was a cold pigeon pie and one of mutton, several pasties, some salmon croquettes, and a half dozen Scotch eggs.

As Georgianna settled herself on a barrel, spreading her skirts daintily about her, Robin could not help but notice how delightfully her cloud of dark hair curled in wild tendrils about her face and how brightly her eyes sparkled with her high spirits. "Oh, I do adore Scotch eggs!" she exclaimed, and he filed the fact permanently in his memory.

Captain Bloomfield's hamper contributed a pair of spit-roasted pigeons and a wheel of Stilton, while Mrs. Alderstunt's overflowed with seed cakes, damson tarts, macaroons, and gingerbread nuts, a clear indication that her massive girth was lawfully come by. "My cook does do a nice cream cake, my dear," she said with an indulgent smile toward Georgianna. "Do try one and you shall see."

"Thank you, ma'am. I shall," Georgianna replied and placed one of the sticky confections on the plate someone's footman had just handed her.

Even Robin was not to be left entirely out of the generosity. He had brought aboard a basket-wrapped jug of cool lemonade which was now offered to the assembled company. A bottle of champagne also appeared from somewhere.

Chatter flowed as easily as the champagne; laughter hung in the salty air. Talley bounded about, sniffing everywhere and generally getting in the way until Rose, Georgianna's abigail, discovered the pair of rib bones, a good deal of charred meat still clinging to them, that the landlord of the Fox and Two Geese had thoughtfully included in their basket. With such a treasure in his teeth, the big dog was content to settle onto the deck at Georgie's feet and gnaw happily away.

Sir Grevesby Jamison was another member of the party. A mere scrap of a man, he was hardly larger than Talley and possessed considerably less hair. He was dressed in an old-fashioned, full-skirted coat of rusty black with knee breeches, stockings that showed a sad tendency to sag around his scrawny ankles, and square-toed shoes that looked too big for his feet.

Sir Grevesby fancied himself something of an expert on matters of international law—and on nearly every other matter, if it came to that—though no one in the government seemed to require his opinions in the great matters of the world soon to unfold in Vienna. He would not dream of letting such a momentous event as the Congress pass him by. Those dullard diplomats might give away the whole show and let Europe fall apart altogether if he was not by to prevent it with his clear-eyed assessments of the situation.

"Far too much salt," he muttered as he bit into a Scotch egg. "One pinch per pound of meat, that's what is needed." No one paid him the least heed. "This Stilton is not ripe," he said a few moments later to Captain Bloomfield. "It must be served at the precisely correct moment, you know." The captain, having been mildly acquainted with Sir Grevesby for years, paid him no heed either. "Pasties, eh?" the baronet then said. "From Cornwall? No one but the Cornish, you know, can make a proper pasty, and I don't imagine these have come all that long way. Bound to be inferior."

Every item that emerged from one of the hampers must be commented upon by the baronet, and none of it was entirely to his liking. He grumbled and advised and complained until Georgianna muttered, "Our own Momus."

Robert Trevelyan looked at her, startled into an appreciative smile at her knowledge. "Indeed," he said for her benefit alone. "I believe every such gathering needs one disciple of that ancient god of fault-finding."

"Oh, yes," she agreed cheerfully enough in a voice only he could hear. "And really, I quite like old Momus. So different from most of the gods—so much more human. His irascibility, like Sir Grevesby's, takes the burden of complaint from the rest of us. We are free simply to enjoy our meal in complete confidence that he will root out every flaw for us."

"What an unusual young lady you are, Miss Pennington," said Robin.

"Why, thank you, Mr. Trevelyan," she answered with a pert smile. "That *was* a compliment, I hope?"

"Indeed it was," he said with conviction, and they both joined the general conversation and enjoyed the next hour very much indeed.

·••❧[*five*]❧••·

IT WAS LATE afternoon when they arrived at Calais, a bustling transit port with little else to recommend it but its convenience, a town designed for those passing through. As such, it provided all the amenities necessary to a comfortable brief stay and few of the things that give a place charm and character and cause the traveler to wish either to linger or to return.

The Reine de Bourgogne was the finest hostelry in town, where travelers could be assured of a good meal and fresh linen on the beds. Here rooms had been bespoken for Georgianna and Suzanne as well as for the Trevelyan twins, and to this hostelry they all repaired as soon as they were once again on dry land.

It seemed the most natural thing in the world that the two duets should become a quartet—a quintet if one included the dog, something Talley was determined that they *should* do—and stroll together up the hill toward the hotel.

Lord Kitteridge's spirits soared as soon as his feet could feel something beneath them that did not sway and lurch about in an odiously discomforting fashion. He suffered still from the headache as well as from a degree of embarrassment—he truly hated the damage done to his dignity whenever he was forced to travel by sea—but he was so grateful to be off that damned ship that he could even contemplate the idea of facing dinner—in several hours' time and after a bit of a lie down.

"The Reine lays a good table, I'm told," he commented to Suzanne as they walked along.

"So I am led to understand," she replied and turned to him with a mischievous but not unkind twinkle in her eye. "And I imagine you shall do the chef justice this night, Lord Kitteridge."

"Lord, yes," he said, even able to laugh at himself a little, for he and Suzanne had been friends for ages. "Not just yet, I shouldn't think, but I'm bound to be devilish sharpset by dinnertime. Join us, why don't you, both of you?"

"I must say, my lord," she replied with a chuckle, "the formal elegance of your invitation overwhelms me. How could I refuse such a prettily phrased request?" He grinned, but before he could reply Robert and Georgianna caught up with them and Suzanne added, "Georgie, Lord Kitteridge has most kindly invited us to join him and his brother for dinner. What do you think?"

"Please say you will," put in Robert with an enthusiastic smile. "You were so kind as to invite us to join your picnic on the ship. You really must give us the pleasure of returning the compliment."

"Very prettily put indeed, Mr. Trevelyan," said Suzanne and turned to Alec. "You should take a leaf from your brother's book, Kitteridge. *That* was an invitation to coax a lady."

"Well, will you?" asked Alec with an unrepentant smile. "Join us, I mean?"

"What think you, Georgianna?" said Suzanne.

Georgie smiled at both gentlemen. "Of course, we should enjoy it of all things. We thank you, sirs." And she dropped them a pert and pretty curtsey.

"Famous," said Robert. "Eight?"

"Seven," corrected Alec who had not, after all, eaten any lunch.

Seven was agreed upon as the entrance of the hotel was reached. The genteel bustle of introducing themselves to the landlord and being assured that their rooms were ready was accomplished, and they parted company, each ascending the elegant carved and gilded staircase with a very interesting and agreeable set of thoughts, hopes, and speculations with which to wile away the few hours remaining until dinnertime.

As it happened, neither Georgianna nor Robin was destined to wile those hours away in solitude. After a brief toilette to refresh herself, Georgie realized she hadn't the least desire to remain cooped up in her room for several hours, especially when the sun was shining, the war was over, and there was a new place to be explored. Likewise, Robert Trevelyan.

Thus it was that scarce a half hour after parting company they encountered each other once more in front of the Reine and agreed to stroll about the town together. Robert, though somewhat disappointed that she had given into propriety and tucked her hair, which had blown about so gloriously aboard the ship, under a bonnet, even if it was a quite fetching one, was nonetheless delighted to have her company. She had donned a very becoming pelisse of orange bloom lustring that gave an even prettier glow than usual to her cheeks. There was no hiding the fact that he was delighted to meet up with her again.

Her dimpled smile showed clearly her own pleasure in once again having his company, and she agreed with alacrity to his invitation to see something of Calais together. "And no, Talley, you may not come with us," she said sternly as the big dog came bounding across the stableyard toward her at that moment.

"Sorry, Miss Georgie," said Tom Coachman who came running after him, making a grab for the dangling rope trailing from the dog's neck. "He's that hard to hold onto, the great beast." He managed to grab the rope and dampen the dog's enthusiasm sufficiently to keep his great muddy paws from dirtying Georgie's pelisse. "Sit, oaf," said the coachman, and the dog did as he was told, panting a smile, his tail heartily thumping the ground and raising a cloud of dust.

Robin casually reached down and scratched the dog's ears; Talley not only allowed it but wagged his tail even harder and looked hopefully up at this new friend who might be persuaded to take him for a walk. So patent was the desire, and so comical the big shaggy smile that covered Talley's face, that Robin threw back his head and laughed warmly. "No, you hopeless brute," he said, unable to make his voice sound sufficiently stern. "You heard your mistress."

"Yes, you did," she agreed, laughter bubbling like music just beneath the words. "Go back to the stable now where you belong and chew on a saddle or something."

Robin laughed all the harder, but Talley, head drooping, trotted reluctantly back to the stable since Tom Coachman was exerting an undeniable tug on the other end of his rope.

"I really must begin teaching him some manners," said Georgianna as they went off, chatting almost as easily as old friends do.

Despite Georgianna's extensive traveling, she had never been in Calais. The seemingly endless war with the French had made travel through that country impossible for years. She was, therefore, eager not to miss a single sight worth seeing. She had even prepared herself for her foray by tucking a guidebook neatly into her reticule.

In truth, there was little enough in the way of sights to intrigue an inquisitive mind, but Robert Trevelyan, from a curiosity about the world he'd never had an opportunity to satisfy, and Georgianna Pennington, from a curiosity about the world that was never fully satisfied no matter how much of it she saw, were far from bored with what Calais did have to offer. And what the town itself failed to provide, the company more than made up for.

"How do you find it here?" asked Robert as they strolled back down toward the sea. "I mean as compared to the many other places you have seen."

"Well, it cannot be compared to Paris, of course, or even to Boulogne from what little I have seen of it as yet. I find myself wondering what the *Calaisoix* must think of it." She stopped a moment to study the faces of a ruddy-skinned woman peering out a nearby window and a man in *sabots* clomping over the cobbles under a load of faggots. "Perhaps they do not see its shortcomings and limitations so clearly as we might. I rather suspect that everyone, no matter where they may be from and however dull it may be, must find a certain beauty in their own town that escapes the rest of us."

"I have never thought of it in just those terms," said Robert, struck once again by the perceptiveness of her mind, "but I imagine you are right. I know I shall never cease to think of Devon as my home no matter how long I may live in Oxford."

"There, you see? While we may all suspect the grass of being sweeter on the other side of the hill, we always seem to long for the peculiar taste of our own particular grass once we have been away from it a while, do we not?"

He laughed. "How well you put it, Miss Pennington. I fear, however, that I can agree with you only from speculation rather than from experience. I have traveled very little, you see, and that never terribly far from home. I should have toured the Continent had Boney not mucked things up so badly. Alec and I thought of traveling to Italy anyway, but the notion of getting there was a little too daunting." His eyes smiled as he added, "We would have had to travel by sea, of course."

She smiled knowingly and sympathetically. "Yes, I should imagine it would be daunting . . . to at least one of you. Did you never consider going on your own, Mr. Trevelyan?"

He looked a little startled, for, in truth, the thought of traveling without his brother had never seriously occurred to him. And it should have, he realized. Damn, he suddenly thought. He should have gone, and whyever had he not? And why was he so loath to admit to this young lady he scarcely knew that he hadn't had the bottom to do so?

She saved him embarrassment by cutting into his thoughts. "I don't imagine it would be a very pleasant trip for you without him. You seem to be quite close."

"Yes, very," he replied, for it was the truth. They were as close to each other as two people could well be for all they were in some respects polar opposites.

"I must admit," she went on as they strolled along the quai overlooking the strand, "that I shall be glad when the Congress is over and we may return to England. I know Vienna will be gay and exciting and certainly very important to the peace of the world, but Papa and I have been traveling for such a long time. I long so to unpack every trunk I own and plant myself like a tree in a perfectly unexceptionable English house."

"But you must be glad for the opportunities you have had," he said.

"Oh, yes, I am terribly grateful and very much aware that few young ladies have been given the chance to see as much of the world as I have seen. But there is something to be said, I feel certain, for knowing with complete confidence that your gown shan't be too mussed from traveling to wear to dinner and that you have not left your favorite book behind in a drawing room a thousand miles away. *And* that you need not worry how you shall find English tea in Frankfurt when your current supply is exhausted."

"Still, I'll wager your father never went without his tea and you never appeared for dinner in a mussed gown," he said with confidence. "I hope you shall not think me impertinent, Miss Pennington, but you seem to me to be a young lady with a remarkable degree of aplomb for one so young."

"Well, I thank you, sir," she replied prettily, dimpling up at him even more prettily, "but I can scarcely take a great deal of credit to myself. It would have been remarkable indeed if I should have remained a simpering schoolroom miss—which I must say I *never* was—after what I have seen these past few years." Her smile faded as she added, "I can assure you that there have been many sights not fit for a young lady's eyes."

"Nor anyone else's, I shouldn't think." His tone was suddenly as sober as her own.

"Exactly," she replied, inordinately glad that he seemed so instantly to understand.

"An ugly thing, war," he went on softly, "and such a useless, needless one."

They walked on some little while in silence, both of them content with each other's company. Near the end of the quai they came upon a street vendor selling something from a large cart and stopped to watch him.

"*Frites!*" he called. "*Pommes frites très chaud ici!*"

"Oh!" exclaimed Georgianna with delight when she saw his wares. A rich aroma and a hearty sizzling sound wafted toward them as the vendor's fat wife dumped a pail of fresh-cut potatoes into a vat of bubbling fat. "Have you ever eaten *pommes frites,* Mr. Trevelyan? No, of course you haven't and you must! I promise you, you shall never forget them."

A number of children had crowded around the cart. As his wife lifted the golden potato sticks from the bubbling oil with a slotted spoon, dumped them into paper cones, dusted them liberally with salt, and topped each with a dollop of thick yellow mayonnaise, the vendor collected a coin from each grubby little hand and replaced it with one of the cones of *frites*. The delighted children scampered off with a round of happy squeals.

Robert was enchanted by the look of anticipation on Miss Pennington's face, as eager as that of any of the children had been. He quickly purchased two cones of potatoes, still sizzling hot, and handed one to her. Big-eyed and with a very pretty, dimpled smile she thanked him.

Burning their fingers and their tongues, then happily licking salt and mayonnaise from their fingertips and laughing like schoolchildren, they continued on their way. Robert smiled to see how Georgianna relished the treat. He had a sudden image of Evelina Everbright faced with a greasy paper cone full of fried potatoes. He doubted she would know what to do with it. He was certain she would not eat them. To be fair, she might wish to, he would say that much for her. But her mother would definitely not approve, and Miss Everbright seldom did anything of which her mother did not approve.

"I don't imagine it is at all the thing to eat something so messy, and with one's fingers, too," said Georgianna, echoing his thoughts.

"Definitely not good *ton,* as I am certain my brother would point out," he agreed, licking a crystal of salt from one finger with relish.

"It is certainly unladylike," she said. "But, oh, they are delicious, are they not?"

"That they are," said Robert, dipping into the cone for another.

"Did I not tell you so? We had them in Brussels last year, and I quite fell in love with them. Papa adores them as well, even if they are so hoi-polloi. The Belgians devour them by the thousands, I am told, but I did not know they had traveled into France as well."

"I am not surprised," he replied. They finished the *frites,* and he handed her his handkerchief to wipe her fingers. When she handed it back with a pretty thank you, he grinned, took it, and dabbed at a spot of mayonnaise on her cheek. "You look like a ragamuffin," he said softly as he wiped it off, surprised at his own daring but even more surprised at how natural he felt in Miss Pennington's presence. She did not answer but smiled at him in a way that might have caused him to dare even more had they not been on a very public quai.

He turned quickly away, startled at the strength of the pull she exerted on him, a young lady he hadn't known above a few hours. He who had so recently and accurately described himself to his brother as "not at all in the petticoat line" had come very near to kissing Georgianna Pennington!

They walked on some few minutes in silence, each very much occupied with private thoughts, but he felt the need to say something, to reestablish that light camaraderie they had been so enjoying. "I should think it is experiences like eating *pommes frites* from a cone that are among the chief joys of traveling. Do you not find it so, Miss Pennington? Completely new things to be discovered and tried, I mean."

"Exactly," she replied, delighted that he had finally spoken. For Georgianna, too, had been somewhat shaken by the intensity of that one brief moment, of the look in Mr. Trevelyan's eyes and the warmth she felt as she basked in it.

She went on lightly, feeling that she was chattering but unable to do anything else, "I have never completely trusted people who have no curiosity at all about what lies beyond their own backyard." Almost immediately, she warmed to her topic, and soon felt as easy with him as before. "I *detest* travelers—and the English are the worst, I promise you—who try only to re-create their own surroundings wherever they go. Hanging on for dear life to a bit of old England no matter the weather, the beauty, the delights they could see if they would only open their eyes and their minds. They never eat anything new or wander off into an unmarked lane, and they cannot see the beauty in anything that is different from the way they think things ought to be arranged."

Her eyes had lit with her zeal, and he smiled into them. "I imagine they are merely afraid of the unknown."

"Oh, I know, and I suppose I ought to be more charitable, for, of course, most of the English travelers I have met have had little or no choice in the matter, what with the war and all. They have simply been sent somewhere to do a job when all they truly wish is to be at home again. And traveling *can* be so unsettling. Much as I love it, even I admit that I am always relieved to go home again."

"And where is home?" he asked.

"Somerset," she replied with the delightful smile that word always evoked. "We have the loveliest house there. Not grand, at all, and not an estate, which is just as well, for who would tend to it with Papa so often away? But so very comfortable. It is full of odd angles and quirks and steps in strange places. And it has a really enchanting garden, full of wildflowers and trailing vines and altogether disorderly. I love it dearly."

There was some imp of mischief in her eyes that seemed to Robert to imply a "However..." and he picked up on it immediately. "And every time you return to this delightful house with its delightful, disorderly garden," he said with a grin, "you pretty soon find yourself itching to be packing up your trunks again and setting sail for some foreign parts. Do you not?"

She laughed delightedly, pleased more than she would have

thought at being so transparent to him. "Of course! Though
how you could know it I cannot guess. You who have so
seldom traveled. But it is true. I love returning to Somerset. I
potter about in the garden and exclaim over how much the
trellis roses have grown. I reacquaint myself with the horses in
the stables and the books in the library. I blow through the
house like a positive whirlwind, checking linen closets and
choosing new hangings for the front parlor and, I am certain,
making poor Mrs. Bunting, our housekeeper, long avidly for
my departure again. But barely are all the wrinkles hung out
of my gowns and the new hangings ordered than I find myself
wondering where we shall go next and how I shall like it. Is it
very spoilt of me never to simply be satisfied with where I
am?"

"I think it is merely very human. Though my circumstances have been such that I have done little traveling, I long
to do a great deal more. I am filled with curiosity about what
the world has to offer. And though I know several people who
profess to have no desire to go farther than their own backyard, I find I seldom believe them. And the ones I *do* believe
are those I find boring beyond belief, for I, too, am mystified
by such a lack of curiosity."

"How well you have put it!" she exclaimed, feeling inordinately pleased that Mr. Trevelyan should so perfectly mirror
her own thoughts on a subject dear to her heart. "How anyone
could be content to see only his own neighborhood, to walk
only over his own hillsides, however beautiful those hillsides
may be, I shall never comprehend. Not when there are new
towns and hillsides to explore and new neighbors to be met
with!"

"I think you must be something of a writer, Miss Pennington. You must certainly pen a book about your travels. Can
you not see it on the shelves at Hatchard's? It would be placed
next to the works of Lady Hester Stanhope. We must settle on
a title. What think you of *The World as I See It,* by a Lady?"

Her lovely laugh tinkled again. "I think it sounds delightfully arrogant. I must ask Aunt Jane to haul out all my old
letters to her when I return to England. They are ridiculously
long and prosy, you know. Than I shall lock myself up in the
study and scribble away at it. It shall be terribly erudite."

"Oh, certainly," he agreed.

The conversation went on in this somewhat inconsequential
vein as they continued their stroll. For two people who pro-

fessed to be so intrigued by new surroundings, Miss Pennington and Mr. Trevelyan seemed to be paying scant attention to the world around them. Georgianna's guidebook reposed untouched in her reticule.

They might have been walking along a typical English country lane for all the notice they took of the crowds of strollers, the bright kiosks selling winkels and mussels, the bathers in the sea, or the ships bobbing in the harbor some little distance farther along. The scents of fish and seaweed seemed to strike them as no more exotic than a simple English daisy, and the babble and chatter of a half dozen languages swirling about them seemed to strike their ears as no more unusual than village gossip at home.

What Robert Trevelyan *did* notice was how prettily the breezy air caused her cheeks to glow, and how merrily her eyes danced when she laughed. What Georgianna Pennington noticed was how broad were his shoulders and how well he carried himself, with a sense of quiet confidence that was not at all arrogant or show-offish like so many town beaux.

Neither was at all dissatisfied with the sights they were enjoying.

The only note of disappointment came when Robert happened to ask after the route Georgianna and Suzanne planned to follow to Vienna. When he learned of their plans to spend at least a fortnight in Paris, he was ready to kick himself. Alec had thought to do the same, but Robin had insisted that they should make straight for Vienna.

But perhaps he could change his brother's mind. . . .

". . . because I don't wish to go to Paris!" said Alec to his brother an hour later. "I hear the roads are a mess now. We'd be jolted about beyond bearing."

"We could ride."

"For days and days on end? Not me, I thank you. And if we go south, it'll mean going over the mountains or coming back north again before we can go on. No, no, you were absolutely right, Robbie, when you convinced me we should make direct for Vienna." He turned to his valet who had just entered the room to dress his master. "Which of my coats do you think my brother should wear for dinner, Chevis?"

Before the valet, who disapproved remarkably of the scheme his young master had got himself into but who had little choice but to go along with it, could answer, Robin broke in.

"Oh, no, Alec. I will not begin our little charade this evening, and that's flat. I may have agreed to the cork-brained notion of impersonating you in Vienna, but we are not in Vienna yet. For tonight, I remain myself." He thrust his hands in his pockets and leaned against the mantel, looking for all the world like a stubborn little boy refusing to do what he's told.

"But why?" asked Alec. "Don't you remember Canty's favorite dictum? 'Always start as you mean to go on.' What better time to begin the charade than now?"

"Because . . . because I don't wish to," said Robert with uncharacteristic reticence. "Deuce take it, Alec. It's going to be devilish difficult pulling the thing off at all, and I'm not about to jump into the fire without first picking your brain clean as a whistle on what and who I ought to know to turn the trick."

"Well, that's true enough," Alec agreed, running a silver-handled brush through his dark locks while Chevis began laying out his master's evening clothes, his face set in lines of disapproval.

"And," Robert continued, "I'm not about to be made to look a perfect fool in front of Miss Pennington and her friend, either." He paced before the fire, waving his hands about in a most uncharacteristic display of emotion. "Bound to if I showed up tonight as you. I spent the whole afternoon with the girl, after all. She'd know in a trice sure as check. And if she didn't guess, *you'd* be bound to make her think me a regular dolt if not a complete coxcomb."

"Oho!" said Alec with a slow whistle and a large smile. "Blows the wind in that direction? Just met the chit this morning and smitten already? Really, old boy, I'm proud of you. Didn't think you had it in you."

"I am *not* smitten, as you chose so indelicately to put it," lied Robin, his pacing suddenly stilled. "But Miss Pennington is very far from being a fool. I cannot think she is unlikely to find me somewhat changed should you try to gudgeon her into thinking you are me tonight. Suppose she should make some comment on our conversation of this afternoon? You'd be made to look nohow."

"And she, of course, thinking me you, would lose interest. Is that your fear, brother?"

He leaned back against the mantel, trying with only limited success to look unconcerned. In truth, he was uncertain just what exactly he *did* fear. Did he wish to make a push to gain Miss Pennington's notice? he asked himself. Perhaps, but he was certainly not ready to admit as much to his brother when he was so unsure of his feelings himself. After all, he'd only just met the girl. Alec was looking at him searchingly, and he felt the need to say something. If only his brother didn't have the damnedest way of reading his mind! "I merely wish not to be made to look foolish. And not to have *you* looking foolish for me."

"I," said Alec, sliding his arms out of the gorgeous brocade dressing gown he had been wearing and stepping into the canary yellow pantaloons Chevis had handed him, "never look foolish."

His brother laughed. "No, never, except every day and twice on Sundays."

"Shows what you know," said Alec with something akin to a smirk of satisfaction as he allowed his valet to drop a snowy shirt of exquisite silk over his head. When his glossy head emerged again, he added, "I *am* all the crack, you know. Still, I agree we should remain in our skins for tonight. Just as well we ain't headed to Paris, though. We'd never pass her muster by the time we got to Vienna. Or Suzanne's either. She's fly to the time of day, Suzanne Patterson is. The fewer people who see us in our true guise from here on out, the better." He adjusted the lace at his cuffs with a slight tug. "And tomorrow we begin school."

"School?"

"School." He stood up straighter and put on the dignity of his earldom as surely as he had just put on the waistcoat Chevis had handed him. "I shall school you in the behavior and attitudes proper to the Earl of Kitteridge."

"Oh, Lord," muttered Robin.

"And you shall begin to instruct me in the deportment, somewhat less taxing, I am certain, of a classical scholar and Oxford gentleman."

"Oh, very well," said Robin as he moved toward his own room. Just at the door he stopped and turned back to his brother. "By the bye," he said casually. "Do you think I might borrow your marcella waistcoat tonight? The striped one?"

"No, I do not," said Alec with a small shudder. "Not at all

the thing with that brown coat I know you mean to wear, is it, Chevis?"

"No, my lord," the valet agreed and turned to his master's brother. "If I might suggest, Mister Robin," he said with the familiarity of a lifelong servant, "your own cream-colored pique would be quite unexceptionable."

"And besides," added Alec, "you shall be in my clothes soon enough, y'know. No need to push the thing."

"Oh, very well," Robin said again with a laugh. "The cream pique it will have to be." And he strode out of the room.

Dinner was a gay affair with many extravagant compliments from Alec on the beauty of his guests, much sensible conversation from Robin, and a good deal of laughter and pleasure on the part of everyone concerned. Robin directed most of his conversation to Georgianna or at least as much as could be considered polite in so small a gathering, for his manners were very good. He found her replies lively, animated, and intelligent, buttressing his already favorable opinion of her. It was clear that Georgianna enjoyed her dinner thoroughly.

The gleam in Suzanne Patterson's eye as she and her young friend took their leave was marked. "You seemed to enjoy Mr. Trevelyan's company, Georgie," she remarked casually when they reached the privacy of their own suite. "He is a most respectable *parti,* you know, though not, of course, nearly so eligible as his brother."

"He is a pleasant companion," said Georgia noncommittally as she stripped off her gloves, "and extremely well informed."

"So I've been told. Kitteridge, on the other hand, never opens a book. I sometimes wonder if he ever has." She kicked off her satin slippers and wandered aimlessly about the room in her stocking feet. "Of course, few people know more about the inner workings of the *ton*. If you wish to know of the most recent fashions or whose horse is expected to win at Newmarket or who was dallying with whom at Lady So-and-So's rout, then Kitteridge is the man to ask. But on any more substantive subject, he's quite hopeless."

"I found them both delightful," said Georgie.

"Oh, certainly," Suzanne agreed, plopping into a striped satin chair and tucking her feet under her in a manner that surprised Georgianna with its casualness. "Kitteridge is something of a scamp, but a charming one. But I shouldn't think one would wish to be married to such a fellow, for all that he has a fabulous fortune and Kitteridge Hall is one of the grandest estates in Devon."

Georgie did not reply but sat opposite Suzanne with studied nonchalance, mirroring the older woman's relaxed position.

"No," Suzanne went on, "Kitteridge is something of a bee, I think, needing to flit from flower to flower to make sure he hasn't missed out on the choicest bit of nectar. Robert Trevelyan, I feel, is a different matter altogether, however," she added with a thoughtful look. "Of course, I do not know him at all well. He spends but little of his time in Town. And without the title he is naturally a less desirable match than his brother. But he seems to me to be the superior man in many respects. There is more . . . I cannot say precisely. More substance, I suppose. He, I believe, will require only one flower to satisfy him so long as she is the right flower. A woman of sense could do worse, I should think, than to align herself with a man like Mr. Trevelyan."

Georgie knew an unpleasant warring sensation in her mind. On the one hand, she found every word Suzanne was saying to be of consuming interest. But she resented what seemed a patent attempt to interest her in matrimony. It was one thing to decide for herself that she would find a husband at once so her father would be free to marry Suzanne. It was quite another to have Suzanne trying to marry her off, and literally to the first presentable gentleman they had met.

Then, too, there was the undeniable truth that Suzanne was right. Even on such a short acquaintance, Georgianna had the definite feeling that Mr. Trevelyan would make a delightful husband. With her newfound determination to fall in love, she had been probing at her heart all evening, rather like a child who daily touches a scraped elbow to see if it still hurts.

But what she was looking for was a rather different sensation. What did it feel like to be falling in love, she tried to remember? And was she feeling it now?

She frowned as she looked at the elegant widow. Much as she might *wish* to dislike Mrs. Patterson, as the usurper of her father's affection, Georgianna was finding it extremely difficult to do so with any success. She wished she did not admire her so very much.

But she absolutely would *not* fall in love at her would-be stepmama's whim. She might be reluctantly willing to jump out of the nest, hoping to fly away on the wings of love, but she was not about to be pushed. Not even for her dear papa.

It was a considerably confused young woman who crawled under the down comforter an hour later and willed herself to sleep only to dream of a handsome gentleman in a sober coat with a serious face that lighted brilliantly when he smiled. In her dreams, she smiled back.

·••◄[six]►••·

VIENNA WAS THRONGED. Indeed, the word might have been invented to describe the crowds, hordes, and mobs of people milling about the narrow streets and lanes of the old city, ambling along the ramparts, or strolling through the leafy paths of the Prater.

The heavy berlin that had so faithfully and comfortably carried Georgianna and Suzanne (and, less comfortably, Talley) to Vienna, and all the delights that city held in store for them, had been forced to slow to less than a crawl as it wove its way through the narrow streets toward the house hired by Sir Richard Pennington. Horses, carts, and carriages of every description vied for each inch of the narrow roadways that had never been designed with such traffic in mind. Pedestrians darted between the wheels, venturing forth, jumping back at the last moment, trying again, then finally scurrying across when they saw the least chance of making it across the street unharmed.

"More than one hundred thousand visitors already," Sir Richard told the ladies when they were finally ensconced in the drawing room of the tall, narrow house in the Schuler-strasse. He had greeted them with enthusiasm, a bear hug for Georgie and a kiss on the hand and a glowing smile for Suzanne, together with a hearty "Now we shall be more comfortable." Talley, much to his indignation, was sent off to the stables where he was to sleep under the watchful eye of Tom Coachman.

The rest of the party was soon cozily seated in the drawing room, sipping sherry—brandy for Sir Richard—and trading tales.

"I must say the streets did seem uncommonly congested," said Suzanne. "Worse even than Paris, and far, far worse than London."

"So I should think, my dear," said Sir Richard. "The population of Vienna has swelled by fully a third, and more arriving daily. The emperor has ordered more than three hundred imperial carriages just to carry the Royals and their entourages about, and the empress needs must set forty tables for dinner each night at the palace."

"Forty!" exclaimed Georgie. "I shouldn't have thought there were so many Royals in all of Europe."

"But there are, my love, and I heartily wish there were not," said Sir Richard. "We are being honored with the presence of no fewer than two hundred German princelings alone, a veritable Teutonic avalanche, not to mention a rather large handful of Poles and Serbs. Then, of course, the Queen of Etruria has sent her agents. And the Pope. Of commoners, we have the Swiss, who have insisted on sending a representative from every single canton, and every Italian city-state must add its tuppence worth of argument."

"But if that is so, Papa, how will the Congress manage to agree on anything?"

"Oh, I shouldn't think it would," he said genially. "Not the entire Congress, anyway. But in truth, it will only be we British with the Russians, Prussians, and Austrians who will make the decisions that matter. Of course we may have to give a sop to Talleyrand for the French now that the Bourbon's back on the throne."

"Will the drawing of new boundaries be the principal concern, do you think?" asked Suzanne.

"Yes, and deucedly trickly it'll be, too," he said, running his fingers through his thick hair, "what with Prussia claiming the whole of Saxony, Austria wanting to put one of her princes on the throne of Sardinia, Naples without a ruler, and the Poles without a country. Devilish sticky, that one," he continued, sipping his brandy with a small frown. "Nobody can tolerate this having Poland partitioned right out of existence, but what's to be done with it? The Prussians aren't ready to give up their claims. The czar says he wants to give the Poles their country back with a liberal constitution, but what he really wants is to keep them firmly under his thumb. And none of the rest of us think that's an improvement over the current nonexistence of the place."

"Isn't Lord Castlereagh anxious that the slavery question be addressed as well?" asked Georgie. It was a subject she found particularly interesting.

"Adamant. Declares he won't return to England until the slave trade is abolished entirely."

"I hope he sticks to his word on that," said Georgie.

"It does seem," said Suzanne thoughtfully, "that we are about to witness an occasion of earth-changing proportions, does it not? I've heard it said that the goal of the Congress is nothing less than to ensure the peace of Europe for the next hundred years."

"Yes, God willing," said Sir Richard. "As I see it, the primary goal must be to ensure that no one country comes out of this unholy debacle of war with enough power to threaten the rest of Europe. Balance is the key."

"Well," said Georgie finally, "it shan't be boring, at any rate."

"Not the least worry of that, my pet," said her father with a chuckle.

"I should think," said Suzanne, "that such a plethora of the bluest blood in Europe has drawn any number of others in its wake."

"How perspicacious of you," said Sir Richard, showing her his warm smile. "You would scarcely believe the numbers of portrait painters, musicians, jugglers, tailors, opera dancers, servants and cits, not to mention pickpockets and every other sort of rogue, that have poured into town in the past fortnight."

"But where will the Viennese put them all, Papa?"

"The question on many a lip, my love," he replied, swirling his brandy in the glass and taking a sip. "How relieved I am that we made our arrangements to hire this house so far in advance. Vienna has become very much a seller's market. Families that have been living comfortably in a dozen rooms are suddenly finding they can make do very well instead with two and hire the others out at a ridiculous profit." Just then a

servant entered with a heavily laden tea cart and soon everyone was munching happily on tea sandwiches with rich liver
paste, buns sticky with crystallized sugar, and pastries thick
with cream. "By the bye, Suzanne," said Sir Richard as his
daughter handed him a cup of tea, "I've been over in the
Burgherstrasse only this morning, just to see that all was in
order with your rooms there. You'll find them to be quite
spacious and well appointed."

"Why thank you, Richard," she replied warmly. "That was
kind of you. You have such excellent taste that I know I shall
be comfortable there if you approve them."

He beamed back at her. "We shall deliver you there after
you've had your tea and allowed me to look at you a while
longer." He smiled at her in that special way of his that made
Georgianna's heart hurt just a little. What was worse, Suzanne
smiled back just as intimately. Georgianna felt a strong need
to change the subject.

"Shall we find Vienna very gay, Papa?" she asked brightly.

"Oh, very. Indeed, my dear, I find myself wondering when
the work of the Congress is to be conducted. There is a pile of
invitations on my desk at this moment that I am persuaded
even you will find satisfyingly high."

"Oh, famous!" she exclaimed, sounding very much the
young girl she really still was. "Tell me!"

"Well," he said and put down his teacup, the better to enu-
merate the coming treats. "On Friday, Princess Bagration
holds a ball at the Palm Palace, rather select, only some two
hundred guests. I wonder if I ought to take you, for to tell the
truth, the princess isn't *quite* the thing, but I hear the Castlereaghs will be attending so that's all right and tight. Monday
morning there's to be a military fête, a sort of review I suppose, outside the city walls. Later in the month we are called
to attend a masked ball at the Hofburg. Three thousand have
been invited, though I daresay hundreds more'll find their way
in." He gave his daughter a teasing smile. "I hope you've got
a masquerade costume somewhere in that mountain of luggage
I saw the footmen struggling under."

"Of course," she said with the same teasing smile. "I got it
in Paris. But I shan't tell you what it is. Not yet."

"No, don't, Georgie," said Suzanne. "But I'll wager, Sir
Richard, that you'll not be displeased with your daughter."

"Oh, Papa is never displeased with me," said Georgianna.
"Are you, sir?"

"Oh, never," he agreed with an alacrity belied by the twinkle in his eyes. "Except when you are being a saucy baggage, which is nearly all the time."

She laughed delightedly. How she had missed him! "What else shall we do, Papa? Tell us."

"Well, the Metternichs have two hundred fifty people to dinner at the chancellery each Monday, and they give a ball at least one night a week. There are informal dinners at the Castlereaghs' several nights a week at the embassy. Then, of course, there are bound to be numerous balls and routs and dinners at the Prussian and Russian embassies and military parades in the Prater—that's the gardens, delightful really, on an island in the Danube. Every theater and concert hall holds a performance every night. Every restaurant and café in town fills every table. And hostesses by the dozen vie with each other to hold the most glittering *salon*. Does that sound gay enough for you, my love?" he concluded, the twinkle in his dark eyes even more pronounced.

"Oh, my," Georgianna answered on a sigh, not sure whether to be pleased or dismayed. She wondered when she would find time to sleep.

But one thing was certain. There would be no shortage of opportunities for a lively, pretty, and *determined* young lady to meet and choose a perfectly suitable husband in Vienna in this fall of 1814.

"By the bye," Sir Richard added, seemingly as an afterthought, "you've had a pair of callers already."

"Really?" she said, trying not to show her quickened interest. "Who?" she added, hoping she knew the answer.

"The Earl of Kitteridge and his brother have called twice to see if you'd arrived yet. In fact, they were here not an hour since." He beamed at her. "Pleasant sort of chaps, both of them, though myself, I'd say the earl's got the edge on his brother. Well, stands to reason, doesn't it?"

"Did you think so?" asked Georgie. "How odd. I found Mr. Trevelyan much the more interesting of the two and would have thought you would also."

At that, her father was somewhat taken aback. "You did, did you? Odd, that. Myself, I should certainly have said it was the earl that would have caught your fancy." He looked at her hard. "He certainly showed the keener interest in when you'd arrive. Fairly knocked me over with his eagerness. Trevelyan hardly had two words to say on the subject."

Georgie, confused and even a little hurt, said nothing to this. In truth, she didn't know what to say. She had hardly spoken to the earl on the ship and exchanged only pleasantries with him over dinner in Calais. But she really had thought Robert Trevelyan displayed a considerable interest in furthering their acquaintance. It was an interest she shared, for she had liked him very much. The sense of disappointment she now felt seemed out of all proportion to the amount of time they had spent together.

"Well now," Sir Richard went on. "Let me show you the house. Unless, Suzanne, you're anxious to get to your own rooms? I'm convinced you must be weary as a dog, even if you do look pretty and fresh as an English rose."

"Probably more weary," Suzanne replied with a laugh, "since Talley did not seem at all discomposed by our journey. Indeed, I have never seen an animal look less tired. His energy is quite awesome. But, please, I should dearly love to see your house. It seems so charming. Then you may escort me home, if you will."

"With very great pleasure," he said warmly and reached for her hand. "Come."

He led them all over the house. It was charming, spacious, and well appointed, and Sir Richard had been very lucky to engage it. It was the town home of a Count von Hohenstalt, a gentleman who loved comfort and hated people, especially when gathered in crowds greater than two or three. Not for him the mobs of Vienna this fall. The count had waited about only long enough to reassure himself that this Englishman to whom he was entrusting his beloved house was a suitable gentleman to have the care of it. Then, satisfied, he retired to his country estate for the duration.

"What a charming room," exclaimed Suzanne as Sir Richard led them into the music room. "You will be able to practice in comfort here, Georgie."

"Oh, yes," she agreed, pleased beyond measure by the room. Georgianna was a gifted soprano and had been sorely missing an opportunity for daily practice. She ran her fingers lightly over the keys of an elaborately painted harpsichord. It was in perfect tune.

"How I look forward to once again hearing you sing, Georgie," said her father with a fond smile.

"You shall have your own private concert this very evening, Papa," she promised.

Drawing rooms and studies, morning rooms and an exquisitely appointed library, they went through them all. Finally on the uppermost floor but one they reached the bedchambers. Georgianna felt uncommonly embarrassed when they all stood in the doorway peering into the master suite. The room itself was not the problem, for it was a straightforwardly elegant and masculine room filled with large but simple mahogany furniture of good quality and fine hangings of brown and gold brocade.

No, it was not the room that bothered Georgie. It was the looks on the faces of her two companions. Suzanne let her eyes rove slowly over everything in the room, from the comfortable wing chair in front of the fire to the sturdy rolltop desk near the window, before allowing them to alight and linger on the large four-poster bed. "Yes," she said softly. "I can see you in this room." It was almost as though she were talking to herself.

Sir Richard did not reply. He just gazed down at her fondly.

"Which room is mine, Papa?" asked Georgianna suddenly, turning back into the hall.

"Just next door," he replied, tearing his eyes away from Suzanne's. "Here." He led her to the next chamber and threw open the door with a flourish.

"Oh, Papa, it's perfect!" Georgie cried. She wandered all over the flower-pretty chamber, exclaiming over the dimity hangings embroidered with cherry-red flowers and birds, over the French doors with their balcony overlooking the street, over the satinwood furniture that was so light and airy that the room might have been a garden. Just outside the windows stood a fine old chestnut tree, its branches growing right up to the house. "Isn't it perfect, Rose?" she said to her maid, who was already unpacking her trunks.

"Oh, yes, miss, that it is. And just right for you, too."

"That it is," agreed Sir Richard, beaming at his daughter.

"Papa, what are these metal things?" she asked, going to stand on a sort of grate that was flush to the floor next to the fireplace. "I've seen them in several of the rooms."

"All of them," he corrected. "They're one of the wonders of the modern age, my dear. Hohenstalt considers himself something of an inventor, you see. He's put in quite a unique system for heating the rooms. There's a great furnace in the cellars and ducts that carry heat to every room in the house.

This is a grate to let the heat in. Daresay we shall be glad of it in another month or so."

"How terribly clever," said Suzanne, "and what a luxury. To have heat whenever you wish it and never have to worry about a smoky fire in the fireplace. I must have one put in my house in London, for I swear I am like to freeze to death every winter in that big barn of a place."

"We mustn't have that," said Sir Richard and gave her hand a squeeze. "And the mention of heat leads me to think that I should get you over to the Burgherstrasse. I'll wager you're anxious for your own fireside by now."

"With my shoes off," she readily agreed with her lilting laugh.

Sir Richard left to escort her home. His daughter watched them leave with a frown creasing her delicate brow. By the time he returned some two hours later, Georgianna had fallen into a troubled nap.

"No, no, try again," said the Earl of Kitteridge that evening to his brother.

They were preparing themselves for the evening ahead, a bachelor party with some dozen other young Englishmen currently enjoying the festivities of Vienna. Many of the gentlemen were friends of Alec and were at least acquainted with Robin. Though they'd been instructing each other in their respective roles in the game for weeks—halfway across Europe and for the fortnight they'd been in Vienna—neither was letter perfect in his part.

They'd been under a bit of a strain trying to pull it off, but they had managed well enough so far since many of those who knew them had not yet arrived. But tonight would be a truer test, and they knew well that things would get decidedly trickier in the next few days. Hordes of English were pouring into the city daily; they'd have to be constantly on their mettle.

It was only here, in the sitting room of their suite at the König von Ungarn, a delightful small hotel not a hundred yards from the Penningtons' house in the Schulerstrasse, that they could truly relax.

"It must be done with the lightest possible flick of the thumb," Alec went on, demonstrating with exaggerated nonchalance the correct manner of opening a snuff box, the manner decreed by Beau Brummell himself.

"But I can never get the thing to open that way," complained Robert Trevelyan, trying it once again. "Damned thing always seems to stick. And who the devil cares anyway?" He was beginning to grow more than a trifle irritated with the seemingly endless rules he must learn if he hoped to live up to his brother's fashionable image.

"I do," said Alec bluntly. "I have a certain reputation to uphold, y'know. And so should you care if you hope to pull off our charade." He reached out and stopped his brother's hand just as it headed for the edge of his fashionably knotted neckcloth. "And stop pulling at your knot! Took Chevis an hour to get it right since you refused to hold your head still."

Robert Trevelyan's neckcloth was, indeed, a veritable monument to the valet's art. In fact, every inch of his person, from his dark, glossy locks carefully pomaded and brushed into the Windswept style to the toes of his gleaming Suvaroff boots, was perfectly calculated to convince any beholder that he was none other than the Earl of Kitteridge. The only thing missing was the mischievous twinkle that so often decorated the earl's eye.

Robin let his hand drop and gave his brother a reluctant grin. "And you thought it was I who lived the boring life," he said. "At least I don't have to sit immobilized on a hard chair in a dashedly uncomfortable position while a disapproving servant fusses over me for hours at a time trying to make me presentable."

"With me, it does not take hours," Alec pointed out smugly. "Now here, watch me again." With a languid grace, he lifted his left hand which held the elegant little enameled snuff box. With the lightest flick of his thumb, he opened it. He removed a tiny pinch with his right hand, placed it on his left wrist, and sniffed it delicately. He then withdrew a fine linen handkerchief from his pocket and flicked a stray grain or two from the sleeve of the subdued brown coat he wore, Robin's coat. *"That* is how it is done," he said finally and handed the box to his brother.

Robin made a sound rather like a snort, but he took the box and tried again. This time he performed the maneuver acceptably if not with quite the polished grace of his brother.

"Well enough," said Alec. "At least you won't again make the mistake of opening it with two hands as you did with Sir Richard this afternoon. Good thing he was looking away at that moment. May not be part of my set, but he dashed well knows the Earl of Kitteridge ain't cow-handed with a box!"

At the mention of Sir Richard, Robert frowned. Since meeting Georgianna Pennington, his view of this little lark of theirs had taken on an entirely different cast. He no longer found anything to interest him in the idea of pretending to be his brother. For how could he then press his own suit on Georgianna? And he had not the slightest doubt, though he had spent but one day in her company, that that was precisely what he wished to do.

Still, a bargain was a bargain and a wager was a wager. He'd said he would go through with it and he would. But he couldn't like it, not anymore.

"And now for the quzzing-glass," said Alec, looping the long black ribbon of an ornate glass around his brother's neck.

Robin steeled himself for his next lesson in dandydom.

The whirl began for Georgianna and Suzanne. Vienna at this particular moment in history was a spectacle such as had never been seen before and, many instinctively felt, might never be seen again. Such lavish hospitality, such determined gaiety, such an incredible show of pomp and circumstance and wealth—it was a heady experience even to one who had seen as much of the world as Georgianna Pennington.

After giving them a day or two to get themselves acclimated, to meet their servants and learn the intricacies of their new households, and to let the wrinkles hang out of their wardrobes and their travel-weary minds, Sir Richard took his two ladies for a ride in the Prater. The weather had been uncommonly fine for so late in the year, so they ventured forth in an open carriage, the better to see and be seen which was, after all, one of the primary reasons for riding in the popular park that sat on an island in the Danube.

So genial was Sir Richard's mood, he even consented to allow Talley to accompany them. The big dog sat on the seat beside Georgianna with the breeze riffling his shaggy mane and with his tail thumping the leather upholstery whenever he saw something of particular interest—a squirrel perhaps or another dog on a leash; once he took exception to a very large black crow decorating the wide-brimmed hat of an Austrian lady, but Georgie managed to soothe him before he could leap out of the carriage to kill it.

They turned into the Hauptallee, the three-mile-long, perfectly straight main road that ran through the park. A long stream of carriages, riders, and fashionably dressed strollers passed happily under the bronze leaves of the chestnut trees, their wheels, hooves, and feet crunching on the glossy brown nuts that littered the road and the gravel paths. Children scampered nearby, chased by nursemaids. People of all classes sat at the rustic outdoor tables of the many cafés the park sported, sipping syrupy Viennese coffee in the shade of the trees. A hundred and more voices arose all around the carriage as it rolled along, a veritable Tower of Babel in this, the most cosmopolitan city in the world at this moment.

Sir Richard was kept busy introducing his two lovely ladies to his many acquaintances. Georgianna had not quite resigned herself to the now obvious fact that Suzanne Patterson was to be her companion virtually every time she went out in public with her father. Still, she smiled a greeting at everyone they met.

Some of them Georgianna already knew from her travels, and these old friends she greeted with open delight. They happened upon Captain Bloomfield, trotting along on a fine bay mare and looking far more comfortable on a horse than he had on a ship.

Georgianna introduced the captain to her father. The two men shook hands, and Sir Richard managed to wince only slightly as he pulled his mangled fingers from the captain's crushing grip. "And who's this fine fellow?" he inquired, gesturing at Talley as his habitual smile bloomed all over his ruddy face. The dog was then introduced as well and Captain Bloomfield roared with laughter when Talley, at Georgie's soft command, solemnly offered a huge paw to be shaken. "Pleased to make your acquaintance, sir, there's a good fellow," he said, and they all laughed. "Quite a party, what?" Captain Bloomfield then bellowed. "Dashed if I ever saw such a show."

"And are you enjoying all the frivolity, Captain Bloomfield?" asked Georgianna with a slightly saucy smile.

"Oh, yes, yes, to be sure. Dashed well earned it, haven't we? All that mucking about all over the Peninsula and chasing Boney across half of France. Time to relax a bit, what? Kick up a lark, don't you know."

"To be sure," she agreed.

The two gentlemen fell into conversation for a few moments before the captain turned back to Georgie. "Um," he began. "Er, you wouldn't . . . I mean," he muttered, then fell silent. His side whiskers had drooped alarmingly and his genial face had turned redder than ever.

"Yes?" she said helpfully.

"That is, don't suppose you'd, uh, care to give me a dance at this Hofburg do they're planning, would you? Not the waltz, of course. I'm too big and oafish by half to pull the thing off. But I can manage a respectable country dance."

"Of course, Captain Bloomfield. I should be delighted to dance with you," she said, then added with a twinkle, "if you can recognize me."

"Recognize you?" His eyebrows, which were almost a match for his side whiskers, shot up in puzzlement.

"It is a masquerade, you know," said Suzanne with a saucy tilt of her head, a tilt that showed to perfect advantage the dashing green shako perched atop her lovely golden waves. "We are all to be in disguise. Even you, Captain, or you shan't be allowed in."

"Uh, oh, right, what? A masquerade. Devilish things, masquerades."

"Why, sir," protested Georgie. "They are not at all devilish. Only very great fun."

"Right, right," he said. "Ladies like that sort of thing." He fell silent a moment while his whiskers and eyebrows worked furiously in thought. "But how the devil am I to dance with you if I can't find you, what?"

Suzanne laughed delightedly. "Well, Captain," she said. "I shall give you a little hint if Georgie won't." She dropped her voice, a conspiratorial imp in her eye. *"And* if you promise not to tell a soul."

"Oh, er, never, ma'am. Soul of discretion, assure you," he managed.

"Well then, you shall look for her in a red gown."

"Red gown," he muttered as if memorizing the words.

"And feathers," Suzanne added solemnly.

"Feathers," he repeated like an obedient student.

And with that the ladies nodded, Sir Richard, hard pressed to stifle a laugh, touched his hat, Talley barked, and the carriage rolled off again.

They met with Sir Grevesby Jamison and with the Alderstunts. They encountered their old friends Lord Castlereagh and his dumpy, amiable wife, strolling arm in arm and smiling contentedly at each other. They even had the dubious pleasure of being acknowledged from a distance by Monsieur de Talleyrand or, as he was more properly and formally known (Sir Richard informed them), Charles Maurice de Talleyrand-Perigord, Prince de Benevent, Grand-Dignitaire de France.

"So, Talley," said Georgianna with the hint of a giggle in her voice. "What do you think of your namesake? Myself, I find you far handsomer than the French prince."

"Definitely," Suzanne agreed. "He has eyes like a dead fish," she observed as the Frenchman gave them his cool nod. A minute later she added with a chuckle, "And they go down like the shutters on a shop window, do they not?"

Georgie couldn't help but giggle, so apt was the description. She had to admit that Suzanne was a clever woman. Georgie even admitted that she had quite admired Suzanne before she knew that Papa had grown so enamored of the beautiful widow. She was, in fact, the perfect sort of woman to make Sir Richard happy, and Georgie knew it.

She gave her parasol an agitated twirl and looked off across the lawns and trees. She would not hate Suzanne. She *would not*. But she was not yet quite able to love her. The carriage rolled on.

The Trevelyan twins had also chosen to enjoy the Prater's sunshine and company that afternoon. They had called twice more on the Penningtons since the ladies' arrival, but each time they had found Georgianna not at home.

It was a close thing to know who was the more disappointed. Georgie railed at her stupidity for choosing precisely the wrong time to venture out in search of extra linens, a pair of carpet slippers to replace the ones Talley had chewed to limp ribbons his first night in Vienna, and those special English delicacies that made her father's life so much more comfortable when he was abroad.

Robin veered between disappointment at having called when Miss Pennington was out and a deep anxiety that she was actually at home but chose not to see him. He didn't yet wish to think about why the possibility of rejection from a young lady he had known such a short period of time should bother him so greatly.

And so this day, when the Penningtons' butler had informed the brothers that his master and mistress had gone driving in the Prater, they decided to turn their own horses in that direction. They rode under the trees, nodding to some acquaintances, stopping to chat with others. They were al-

ready feeling quite at home in Vienna. Even Robin had begun
to relax.

He was, however, more than a bit nervous this afternoon.
It seemed a certainty that they would run across the Penningtons, and it would be the first time he'd seen Georgianna
while he was in the guise of his brother. He'd been doing
passably well in the role so far, he thought. He'd even fooled
Lord Creighton whom he had last seen in the changing room
at Jackson's Boxing Saloon in London. Then, his lordship had
known the twins apart even undressed, but here in Vienna he
had accepted completely that each of the brothers was exactly
who he said he was.

But Georgianna Pennington might well present a more
rigid test. Strangely, he wasn't sure whether he wanted to pass
it or not. Well, he was playing Alec, right down to the champagne shine on his fashionable boots, and Alec never worried
about anything. He just accepted life as it came to him. Robin
would do the same, he decided. Or at least he'd try.

"By the bye," said Robin to his brother as their horses
ambled along, "I've made a wager with Wartszewski. Last
night at that embassy dinner. Said I could best him in a fenc-
ing match. Bet him a pony on it."

"Lord, why'd you go and do that?" asked Alec. "Know
very well you ain't a dab at that sort of thing. Hate to say it
against my own brother, and you know I don't hold it against
you, but fact is, Robbie, you're ham-handed with a saber, and
you know it, too."

Robin grinned. "Yes, but he doesn't. Besides, told him my
brother'd been giving me a pointer or two. Can he beat you,
d'you think?"

"Me? It's your wager, your fight."

"Yes, but you're going to fight it. Where's the harm? It's
you he thinks he's going to fight, anyway."

Alec looked at his brother closely. "What's got into you?
Never would have thought of such a start till you came here."

"That's true," answered Robin with a thoughtful look. "But
I am learning all sorts of things about my character while I
plumb the depths of yours. Can he beat you?"

"Oh, I shouldn't think so. Saw him practicing one day.
Fellow's more wind than action. Can't let him win, at any
rate, can we? A Pole, after all. Honor of Britain, and all that."

"Right," said Robin. "In any case, I imagine you can stand
the nonsense if you lose."

"A pony? Well, it won't bankrupt me," said Alec with a grin, "though at the rate you're going, dear brother, you'll have me washed up the River Tick in no time."

"Always had a fancy to help you spend your money," said Robin, grinning hugely.

"A feat at which I excel sufficiently all by myself, thank you," replied Alec.

"And you really couldn't begrudge me the money for some new boots, Alec. You wouldn't let me wear my own. . . ."

"I should think not! Those raggle-taggle things'd give us away in less than no time."

". . . and yours are too big. Had two blisters before I'd worn 'em an hour. How'd you let your feet get so out of hand?"

"You know my tastes run to excess," said Alec with a laugh. His brother joined in and they rode along chuckling, having no idea how many female hearts fluttered wildly inside delicately heaving breasts at the sight they made.

Well, perhaps they had *some* idea.

The little trio in the Penningtons' carriage (a quartet if one counted Talley) was nearly decided to leave the Prater and return home when the Trevelyan twins spied them and quickly approached. Sir Richard ordered Tom Coachman to stop the carriage once again.

"Good afternoon, Kitteridge," said Suzanne with her friendliest smile. "I see you had a safe journey."

Robin, rigged out perfectly as the earl, bowed easily to the three people in the carriage. "Afternoon, Suzanne. Pretty as a picture as always, I see," he said with a practiced smile, as practiced as hours spent in front of the mirror accompanied by his brother's tutelage could make it. His manner was smooth, almost as smooth as the real Alec's would have been, but inside he was quaking horridly.

He'd been acting the part of the earl for nearly a fortnight now and had even begun to feel he just might be able to pull the thing off after all. Certainly no one had questioned the accuracy of their claimed identities as yet. But now, seeing Georgianna Pennington for the first time while in his brother's guise, Robert Trevelyan's uneasiness returned. And he had enough self-awareness to know, suddenly and completely, that at least part of his discomfort arose from the fact that he hadn't the least desire to pass himself off as his brother in front of this particular young lady.

Robin had thought often of Georgianna since departing from her in Calais. Many times the image of her piquant pixie face had floated unbidden into his mind. Now he could see, though he would scarce have believed it possible, that she was even lovelier than he remembered. In a lustring carriage dress as blue as a summer sky and a villager hat framing her ebony curls and tied in a jaunty bow at one ear, he thought she was the prettiest thing he'd ever seen. "Miss Pennington," he said as he tipped his brushed beaver hat to her. "I trust your journey was pleasant."

"Very, my lord," she replied with a smile. "It is a pleasure to meet you again. And you, Mr. Trevelyan," she added, turning to Alec. Her smile grew a trifle more brilliant, a fact not lost on her companions. Alec had so far remained silent though he was grinning hugely. He was soberly dressed in Robert's coat of dark gray merino over gray breeches, the whole ensemble restrained, quiet, unlike the emerald-green coat and tan buckskins his brother wore.

"No more a pleasure than it is to see _you_ again, Miss Pennington," said Alec with a twinkle in his blue eyes as he doffed his hat. His brother's interest in the diplomat's daughter had not gone unnoticed, and he thought it would be no bad thing to foster the budding romance if he could. At least it might scotch any possibility of Robin marrying the hopelessly inadequate Miss Everbright.

The two gentlemen greeted Sir Richard, and they all chatted comfortably for a few moments, commenting on their respective journeys, the lovely weather, the crowds, the dog. Georgianna, normally such a sparkling conversationalist, said surprisingly little. She watched the twins, marveling once again at how very alike they were even though they dressed so differently as to make identification of them quite simple.

Her gaze lingered most often on gray-garbed Robert Trevelyan. There seemed to be something subtly different about him from the man she had shared _frites_ with in Calais, though she could not think precisely what it was. He certainly looked exactly the same. Her eyes flitted back to the more flamboyant earl. He, too, she thought, seemed somehow changed. He certainly seemed to be paying more attention to her than he had when last they met. Of course, he had been quite unwell on the ship, she remembered. But when they had all taken dinner together at Calais, though he had been pleasant and flattering, she definitely did not recall his eyes lingering on her face with such warmth as they seemed to do now. And her father *had* said he had asked after her. Most particularly, he'd said.

"Do you go to the Princess Bagration's ball tomorrow?" asked Suzanne after a few moments of conversation.

"Do you?" asked Robin, sounding surprised.

"Why, yes," said Suzanne. "I know she has something of a scandalous reputation, but everyone goes to her parties, I hear. I am quite longing to meet her."

"Then we shall most certainly go," Alec put in. At his insistence, the brothers had put in an appearance at one of the princess's *salons* at the Palm Palace the previous week, and an invitation to her ball rested on their mantel at the hotel at this very moment.

"Famous," said Georgianna before she could stop herself. Then she wanted to bite her tongue for her unwonted show of girlish enthusiasm.

"Am I too late to claim the first waltz, Miss Pennington?" asked Robin.

Georgianna, thinking him the earl, felt a tiny stab of disappointment. She had hoped his brother would claim the honor of the first waltz. She had nothing against Lord Kitteridge—in fact, she found him rather a charming fellow in a roguish sort of way—but she had been wondering for days how it would be to waltz with Robert Trevelyan. However, she put on a warm smile. "I should be honored, my lord," she replied.

"Unfair, Alec!" cried Alec with a look of mock despair. "You are too fast for me. It seems, Miss Pennington, that I am to spend the whole of my life following my brother, for I always seem to be just a trifle too late." His blue eyes twinkled with merriment. "But I hope you will honor me with the second waltz."

Her smile grew unmistakably brighter. "Of course, Mr. Trevelyan. I should be delighted."

A few more words were exchanged, Suzanne was solicited for a pair of dances, and the carriage finally rolled out of the park toward home.

By the time they delivered Suzanne to her rooms and returned themselves to the house in the Schulerstrasse, Georgigianna had to proclaim their first outing an unqualified success. They had accepted no fewer than a dozen invitations for the following fortnight. It was clear that the new Parisian gowns hanging in her wardrobe were apt to prove insufficient to the task at hand.

Once back in her bedchamber, she began rummaging through the exquisite gowns, tossing creations of amber lace and peach blossom sarcenet, of satin and spider gauze and fine Indian muslin in every color of the rainbow onto the bed with abandon, trying to decide exactly which fatally lovely concoction she would wear to the Princess Bagration's ball the following night. Though she didn't stop to wonder why, she was determined to look more beautiful than she had ever looked in her life. She felt inordinately happy.

So, too, did Robert Trevelyan. He had not missed the extra glow that seemed to light Miss Pennington's smile whenever she looked on his brother in the Prater. And, of course, she could not know that it was Alec she was gazing on so warmly rather than himself. She likes me! he thought, the real me, and a bubble of giddiness he'd never felt before rose within him. Me, Robert. She likes me better than Alec!

Oh, Lord, he then thought. Was ever there a more devilish coil?

·····❖[*seven*]❖·····

THE NEXT MORNING, Sir Richard Pennington, temporarily
freed from the heady matters of state which were the reason
for the convening of the Congress, took his daughter on a tour
of Vienna. They climbed once more into their hired but quite
acceptable barouche, pulled by a capable if uninspiring team
of chestnuts. Georgianna unfurled a beruffled mauve and
white parasol that perfectly complemented her sprig muslin
gown topped by a mauve spencer of cut plush velveteen. Purple ribbons at her waist and on her parasol rustled delicately in
the autumn breeze.

"Ah," she sighed audibly as the barouche rolled out of the
Schulerstrasse. She felt absolutely happy. It was almost the
very first chance she'd had to be alone with her father since
he'd left London, and she intended to enjoy every moment of
it. She did just happen to wonder why Suzanne Patterson had
not been invited to join them, but she was not about to ask the
question that hovered on her lips. It was enough that the dashing widow was not present.

The streets pulsated with people, scurrying hither and yon,
going about their various tasks with the industry of a particularly feverish hive of wasps. It was like London, and yet unlike, thought Georgianna.

"How comes it about, Papa, that Vienna seems somehow ... I don't know, older than London?"

"Older? I don't know that I should put it just that way, Georgie. Rather say more gracious. I think it comes from our actually being what Bonaparte accused us of being—a nation of shopkeepers. We are, you know. True, we have a king, God rest his poor troubled mind, but London has ever been a business capital rather than a royal one. But Vienna—ah, Vienna." He sighed hugely and looked out on the graceful baroque swirls of an arch they'd just passed, on the delicate tracery of a balcony gracing a window nearby, on the late autumn flowers blooming gaily around the base of a tree. "Vienna has always been a royal playground and therefore designed specifically to be a thing of beauty."

"Well, the designers have certainly succeeded," she acknowledged.

"Yes," he agreed and shifted his gaze to his daughter. He smiled at her fondly. "As have I."

She smiled back at him but seemed confused. "Papa?"

"I, too, have created a thing of extraordinary beauty," he said softly. "Of which, I should add, I am extremely proud. Of course, I really ought to give some credit to your mother. More than to myself, I fear, if I am to be truthful, for you are the image of her, Georgie."

She laughed delightedly. "Well, I am pleased you are proud, Papa, but I should hope it is for more than merely my beauty. You have, after all, gone to rather extraordinary lengths to educate me far beyond what most girls are lucky enough to receive."

"Yes," he said with a hearty laugh, "but it is not the brain that attracts the bees, puss. It's the honey coating the surface. And I'll wager the very masculine bees currently swarming about Vienna shall be highly attracted by your honeyed smile. I look forward to the show, I do indeed."

"Well, I shall endeavor not to disappoint, sir," she said and gave him a saucy smile. But it was a little forced. Here was more evidence, she thought, of his eagerness to have her find a husband. Well, she thought, he is no more eager than I am myself. She gave her parasol a determined twirl and turned to watch the show rolling past the carriage.

They enjoyed this most beautiful of cities as well as each other's company for more than an hour, chatting brightly about everything and nothing, as was their wont. "And now, my dear," Sir Richard finally said, "I am taking you to lunch at Sperl's. You shall enjoy it. They have the best food in Vienna. And," he added with a twinkle, "the most beelike of clienteles, a veritable hive, I think you'll find." Even as he spoke, they turned into the Gumpendorferstrasse and alighted in front of the charming café.

Sir Richard was certainly right about the clientele. As they enjoyed a light luncheon, acquaintances by the score approached their table. While savoring her liver dumpling soup, Georgianna must be introduced to a stiff-backed Polish count with a sad tendency to click his heels together every time he had something to say—which was a great deal and none of it terribly interesting. While tucking into a tasty plate of thick-cut sauerkraut spiced to perfection with juniper berries and caraway, she had to chat with a German princeling and his exceedingly fat mistress (the princess, of course, had been left at home to tend to her children and her sense of ill-usage). And while trying valiantly to pay attention to a very deserving portion of wild hare simmered with herbs and mushrooms and accompanied by a salad of cabbage and celery root flavored with mustard and freshly grated horseradish, she needs must meet two Russian, three Austrian, and at least a half dozen young British officers, their gold and silver-gilt buttons and epaulets nearly blinding her (though not so completely as her brilliant smile blinded them).

"Buzz, buzz, buzz," Sir Richard murmured into her ear with a chuckle as he made swatting motions with one large hand. She shushed him determinedly, but grinned all the same.

By the time the poppy-seed strudel arrived, Georgie despaired of giving it the attention it deserved. And with good reason. For just at that moment, Suzanne Patterson floated into Sperl's on the arm of none other than Prince Metternich himself. The young men buzzing about the Penningtons' table drifted off into the woodwork with a good deal of bowing and murmuring.

Suzanne was her usual vision of loveliness in a Tyrolean cloak of garnet levantine edged with black chenille and draped with perfect negligence over a walking dress of smoke-gray book muslin embroidered in garnet silk. Her golden hair was set off to admiration by the pair of glossy coq feathers that graced a sporty red shako. Her escort was his always dashing, handsome, and perfectly turned-out self, smooth and shiny as a piece of Viennese crystal.

For a fleeting moment, Georgianna allowed herself to hope that there might be a romance brewing between the beautiful English widow and the dashing Austrian prince. Everyone in Vienna knew he had very little to do with his long-suffering wife. But her hopes were quickly dashed when Suzanne looked at Sir Richard Pennington. Her already lovely face took on an almost magical brilliance as she smiled at him, her love plain for every diner in Sperl's to see.

The elegant couple glided across the parquet floor and approached the Penningtons. "See who I have brought to see you, Georgie," said Suzanne in her slightly husky voice and her charmingly accented French. The foreign minister of Austria stepped forward and bowed elegantly over Georgianna's hand. "Clemens was complaining to me just this morning that he had not set eyes on you since London. I promised to rectify the situation at once."

"How do you do, Prince Metternich," said Georgianna in perfect French. "How good to see you again."

"The pleasure, Mademoiselle Pennington, is mine, I assure you," replied the prince. He shook Sir Richard's hand and they chatted a few moments of the gaieties of this city the prince loved so well. "You will both come to a little soiree I am planning, I hope. We are all to wear ethnic costume. With so many nationalities in Vienna at present, it should prove to be diverting."

"Of course we shall come," said Sir Richard. "I intend that Georgie shall not miss a single party that Vienna has to offer."

"Papa! If I do that I shall never get even a wink of sleep and shall turn into a positive hag," she said lightly.

"Ah, no chance of that, puss, is there, Prince?" said Sir Richard.

"Not the slightest," agreed Metternich.

Georgie smiled her acceptance of the compliment, but she did take a moment to wonder, however, if her father's eagerness to make her so popular in Vienna might be caused by an equal eagerness to get her off his hands. She chatted some little while longer with the so-charming prince while Sir Richard and Suzanne conversed together in low voices. Georgianna could not hear their words, but she had no need to. It was clear from their faces that they were exchanging lovers' nonsense.

After a few moments, the prince eyed the untouched pastry in front of Georgianna. "But we interrupt your lunch. One should never divide one's attention when eating Viennese strudel, you know. Such a creation of heaven deserves total concentration."

Georgianna laughed. "I am certain it does, sir."

And with that Suzanne tore herself from her conversation with Richard, laid one smartly gloved hand on the arm of the prince, and together they floated away.

Georgianna finished her strudel without gusto, retrieved her parasol, nodded to the numerous young men still lounging about in a manner guaranteed to keep her well within their sights, and left Sperl's on her father's arm.

She smiled and nodded and showed great interest as her father continued her first real sight-seeing outing in the city, but her mind was otherwise. She knew as no one else could that this time in Vienna was the watershed of her existence. Once this lovely, lively capital was left behind, her life would never be the same. Even more important, her relationship with her father would never be the same.

Had she been back in the Schulerstrasse, alone in her bed-chamber, she would have had a serious conversation with her mirror. As it was, she must discuss herself silently as the carriage rolled through the autumn streets.

It is time, Georgie, she admonished herself. Every bird must leave the nest, no matter how comfortable that nest has been, and it is time and past that you learn to fly. Yes, it's true that the popular wisdom is that it's the parent who is usually reluctant to see the bird make its first tentative attempts at wing-flapping. But you mustn't mind it that in your case the parent is particularly eager to see you soar. Papa is hardly pushing you over the edge, after all. It is just that the nest is not really big enough for three. And you would find it ridiculously uncomfortable if it were. You know you would.

So, she continued her monologue as the cobblestones rolled by under the carriage wheels, you will fly. And the nest, a very comfortable and cozy nest filled with a loving papa and a delightful Suzanne (who, if you are truly honest with yourself, you must admit you like and admire very much indeed) will always be there to welcome you warmly when you wish to visit. He will never stop loving you, you know.

But it will be *their* nest. And you will have your own to return to. Now all you have to do is find the properly plumed companion with which to furnish it (or at least decide which one you want, for Lord knows Vienna is filled to bursting with exactly the right sort of exotic creatures you seek).

Sir Richard's hearty voice rose and fell in the tones of an enthusiastic guide as he drove her about the town, pointing out the Belvedere, the ramparts with their green walks and cafés, the Hofburg Palace, the pencil-slim spires of St. Stephen's Cathedral, and all the other sights for which Vienna was deservedly famous.

But Georgianna saw very little of it.

Back in a suite in the König von Ungarn the brothers Trevelyan were having yet another friendly argument.

"No, dash it, Robbie, you can't send her those," said Alec, gesturing to a white florist's box on a table before him. "No one who knows a thing about me would expect me to send a lady violets. Withering little things."

"D'you really think so?" asked Robin. He looked at his planned offering with an uncertain eye. "I thought them rather pretty." He lifted the nosegay from its nest of silver paper. Delicate hothouse violets clustered into a ruche of Alençon lace, the whole tucked into a prettily carved ivory holder.

"Well, perhaps," conceded Alec, "in a simpering sort of way. But not at all the thing the Earl of Kitteridge sends a lively girl like Miss Pennington. No dash to them. Now this," he said with something of a flourish as he reached into an identical white box sitting next to the first, "is something like!" He pulled out a spray—it was too grand to be called a posey—of flame-red and butter-yellow rosebuds mingled with glossy green leaves and tied with golden and scarlet ribbons.

Robin eyed the roses skeptically. "I don't think they look much like her."

"Of course they do! All women love roses. She'll be proud to carry these at the princess's ball tonight."

Robin looked again at the violets—they were his favorite flower—then back at the flamboyant roses. Then he conjured up an image of Georgianna Pennington's face—not a difficult feat since he'd been doing it at least two dozen times a day for some time now. Then he grinned. "Very well, Alec. We shall send her both. And *I* think she'll prefer the violets."

"Rubbish!" said Alec.

"Care to make a small wager on it?" asked his brother.

Alec, never one to turn down a bet, laughed. "Done. What stakes?"

"If I win, you'll promise to sit still for a few lessons in Latin and mythology so as not to make me look quite so foolish in Miss Pennington's or anyone else's eyes."

"And if she prefers the roses?"

"I will promise not to complain about the tightness of your coats and the ridiculous height of your neckcloths and will even let you finally instruct me in the proper method of damping all pretensions with a quizzing-glass. Agreed?"

"Latin, huh?" said Alec with a rueful expression.

"And mythology."

"Lord, she had better prefer the roses." With that Alec pulled an elaborately chased and gilded card case from the pocket of his coat, being worn just now by his brother, and drew out of it one of his engraved visiting cards. He walked to a tiny buhl desk by the window, dipped a quill in a standish, and scribbled on the card, "To one who outshines these poor roses." He signed "Kitteridge" with a flourish and waved the little card about to dry the ink. "We'd better stick one of your cards in with the violets. They have to come from somebody, y'know."

"Naturally. I do, after all, want Miss Pennington to know which of us has the better taste." On one of his own visiting cards he wrote simply, "I look forward to our waltz." The signature "Robert Trevelyan" didn't have quite the panache as that of the Earl of Kitteridge, but it was all he had.

The cards were dropped amongst the blossoms which were dropped back into the boxes and dispatched at once by a footman.

When Georgianna and Sir Richard returned from their expedition it was to find two gleaming white florist's boxes awaiting them on the marble-topped table in their entrance hall.

"Oho," exclaimed Sir Richard at sight of them. "More conquests, puss? I cannot think of any gentleman currently in Vienna who is likely to be sending *me* posies."

Georgie, despite the headache she'd been nursing the past hour and more, charged at the boxes and tore them open. From the first she pulled an impressive and elegant spray of rosebuds.

"Pretty," murmured Sir Richard, looking over her shoulder in an attempt to read the name of the sender.

"Yes, aren't they," his daughter agreed, fishing for the card. "They're from Lord Kitteridge," she finally announced with an enigmatic smile. "How kind of him."

"And these?" asked her father, gesturing to the other box.

She opened the second box. "Oooh!" she breathed softly as she lifted the violets tenderly from their silver paper. "Aren't they *lovely!*" She pushed her nose deep into the flowers' heart and breathed in their delicate scent while her father retrieved the sender's card.

"Trevelyan," he said and began to chuckle. "Well, well. If we're not careful, miss, we shall see the beginnings of the next war right in our drawing room."

"Don't be silly, Papa. They are brothers."

"That, my dear, is precisely what I mean. Messy things, family squabbles." He chuckled softly, gazing fondly at his very beloved daughter, then looked again at the two boxes of flowers. "Lord!" he suddenly exclaimed, hand on head. "I've forgotten to order flowers for Suzanne. Thing to do, you know. Can't ask a lady to a ball and not send her a posey. I must go and do so at once."

"At once, Papa," Georgianna agreed with a warm smile, suddenly realizing that her headache had entirely evaporated.

"Problem is, what kind do I get her? You seem to like those violets. Think she'd like some, too?"

"Absolutely not, Papa. Suzanne is not at all a violet sort of lady." An impish smile overspread her features. "Roses, Papa. By all means, roses," she said. And the two of them went off into peals of laughter, neither quite knowing why, but enjoying it immensely all the same.

·····≫{ *eight* }≪·····

"YOU *MUST* FLIRT with her," Alec said discreetly to his brother over the punch cups that evening.

"Why?" said Robin with a look on his face that suggested the punch he was sipping might be sour.

"Everyone flirts with the Bagration. You'll offend her if you don't." His statement was clearly true. Amid the select crowd gathered in the Palm Palace, a circle of admiring gentlemen, including the czar, two grand dukes, and a half dozen princes, surrounded the pretty little blond princess who was their hostess. Her round face glowed pinkly from the heady combination of their flattery and her own excellent champagne; her lithe body swayed provocatively beneath its nearly transparent gown, typical of the style that had earned her the nickname "The Naked Angel."

"From what I've seen," Alec continued, "she ain't a woman who takes snubbing lightly, and she could make our lives in Vienna devilish uncomfortable. Besides, if you don't flirt with her, Robbie, no one'll believe you're me. Everyone knows *I* flirt shamelessly, and with every pretty lady in the room." He said it proudly, rather like a peacock showing off his fine plumage, but not without a self-mocking smile that brought an answering grin from his brother.

"Don't I know it," groaned Robin. "Wish I'd known earlier what a hey-go-mad reputation you had, Alec. I'd never have gotten myself into this."

"Yes, you would," said Alec confidently.

"Dash it all, Alec," said Robin. "You know I'm not an accomplished flirt. You may find this easy, but I find it devilish tricky. Puts me to the blush every time. What the deuce do I say to her?"

"Offer her snuff. She likes it, thinks it makes her distinctive to dip snuff. And you've learned to handle a box tolerably well at last. I dropped a particularly pretty one into the pocket of that coat you're wearing. Got a reclining lovely painted on the inside looks a bit like her. She'll like that. Just be sure you hold it open so she can see it but no one else can. Then give her a wink." Robin took out the snuff box in question, opened it, and closed it again quickly with a look of vague alarm. "She'll probably ask to have it," Alec continued. "One of her favorite tricks, I hear. Might as well give it to her."

"I shall do so with alacrity," Robin replied and gave his brother an almost comically prudish look. He dropped the box back into the pocket of the midnight-blue coat he wore. "D'you do this sort of thing often? It must get devilish expensive."

"It does." Alec grinned and set down his punch cup. "But what can one do? It is expected. Go on now, it's why I wanted you to come. The little Bagration and her ilk will be good for you. Just the thing to bring you out a bit."

"If I survive her," said Robin. He shook out the exquisite lace at his (or rather his brother's) sleeves. "You'd best come stand behind me, Alec, to cover up my gaffes which I am bound to make, y'know."

Alec patted him on the back and began steering him toward their hostess. "My dear brother," he said with a hearty chuckle that made Robin want to hit him, "I have every confidence in your acting abilities. Just try to forget you speak perfect French and remember your smile."

"And you try to smooth out that abominable French accent of yours. It's a disgrace to the name of Trevelyan," Robin retorted. He had not the confidence in himself his brother seemed to have, but he plunged into the fray, game as a pebble, the proud Alec might have said.

"My lord," twittered the princess as he bowed low over her hand. Remembering his lessons, he did not offer her the usual chaste salute that would hang in the air an inch or two above her dainty fingers. Instead, he turned over her hand and brushed his lips against her palm, a liberty that felt decidedly unnatural but which the princess seemed to accept quite naturally. He willed himself not to color up like a schoolboy and give the game away, attempting instead to cover his face with a rakish smile.

"My princess," he murmured as he rose again. "The very stars over Vienna must be crying from jealous rage this night so eclipsed are they by you." He'd read that in a book somewhere once. He'd almost become nauseated at the time, but the princess seemed more than a little impressed with his eloquence, despite the broad English accent with which he had overlaid his perfect French.

"You see," she said to her companions with a delighted giggle and a wave of her fan. "Have I not told you these Englishmen they are poets?"

"Ah, yes," said a tall Russian count who dripped gold braid and medals from a scarlet tunic. "But anyone can conjure up fine words. In love, it is actions that speak most loud, is it not so?"

"Very true," Robin replied smoothly, flicking an imaginary bit of lint from his perfectly lint-free sleeve, "but there is surely room for both, is there not? After all, our own very English Shakespeare, while undoubtedly one of the finest poets the world has ever known, had also a reputation as a gifted performer." And where on earth did *that* come from, Robin asked himself. He cast a suspicious glance at his beaming brother wondering for a moment if Alec was capable of silently putting words in his mouth merely by thinking them.

Everyone in the circle chuckled appreciatively, the princess loudest of all. At a surreptitious cue from his brother, Robin chose that moment to offer her snuff, which she accepted with a pretty twist of her wrist. She did indeed ask for the snuff box after she had batted her golden lashes at him provocatively, tapped him playfully with her fan, calling him a "naughty boy," and given him a look that a lesser man might have fought a duel for but which only made Robin blink twice at her.

By the time he'd spent nearly half an hour in conversation with the princess and the other distinguished members of her group, he actually began to *feel* like the Earl of Kitteridge. Alec's voice, gestures, wit, and charm were beginning to feel almost natural. In fact, he actually began to enjoy the unaccustomed freedom that came with wearing another's identity.

But then he looked across the glittering room and saw Georgianna Pennington chatting with the Castlereaghs. Suddenly he felt like the veriest schoolboy unable to think of the right answer (or any answer at all) to a question the master had just asked.

She was dressed in one of the gowns she'd had made in Paris, a floaty, dreamy concoction of blue China silk. It drifted about her in a half dozen layers, each an inch or two shorter and a shade paler than the one beneath it so that it shaded from a deep sapphire nearest her skin to a topping of cool ice blue that shimmered in the candlelight. When she moved, as she did almost as soon as he noticed her, he thought the dress made her look like a water sprite. The silk flowed about her in soft waves, the white lace across her bosom seeming like the foam at the wave's perfect crest.

But the thing which came most clearly into focus—after her exquisite face, of course—was the lovely nosegay of delicate violets she carried in one gloved hand. His heart danced to know that he had guessed aright her taste, despite his brother's confidence that she would prefer the roses. But even more gratifying was the knowledge that the divine Miss Pennington had chosen the offering of a mere Mr. Trevelyan over that of the far more exalted Earl of Kitteridge. Surely it must mean she cared for him at least a little.

His mood, already elevated with the princess's fine champagne and his success at his masquerade, soared quite to the elegantly gilt and chandeliered ceiling.

All unknowingly, Robert had stopped talking in mid-sentence at the sight of Georgianna, his gaze riveted on her. With his silence, all conversation in the group clustered around the princess ceased; all eyes turned toward the newcomer. Several gentlemen were so unwise as to murmur aloud their appreciation of the picture she presented.

"Who is that?" Princess Bagration finally asked. It was clear from her tone that she was none too pleased to have such a vision of loveliness suddenly appear in her ballroom. "I am quite certain I did not invite her." Before anyone could answer, she turned to the czar. "Cousin Alexander, go send her away at once."

"No, my little cat, I shall not," said the Czar of all the Russias, giving her a chuck under the chin. "She is Pennington's daughter and a good friend. *And* I am certain you did invite her though you would not have done so if you'd known how pretty she is, would you?"

"Do you find her so?" the princess pouted, flicking her fan in perfect imitation of a mifty cat flicking its tail. "*I* do not."

"No," agreed Alexander. "I am sure you do not. Now pull in your claws and stop glowering at her. It does not become you at all."

This conversational exchange was lost on Robert—all his attention was on the Penningtons—but it was not missed by his brother. They may have been in Vienna only a fortnight, but Alec had seen that look on the Bagration's face before, and he knew it boded no good for Georgianna Pennington. The princess wasn't fond of competition in any guise. Already it was rumored that she and the Duchesse de Sagan, who lived in the other half of the Palm Palace, had had a hair-pulling fight over Metternich. The princess would bear watching, he decided.

Georgianna had no idea of the roiling emotions and speculations she had already set in motion on arriving at her first Viennese ball. She was perfectly prepared to enjoy herself hugely. After only two days in the city, the carnival atmosphere of the place had infected her. She felt almost giddy with it.

Almost immediately after the Pennington party entered the brilliantly lighted room, the musicians lifted their instruments for the first dance of the evening. Georgianna instinctively turned toward her father. She had never in her life been to a ball that she did not begin by dancing with him. But as she stretched out her hand toward Sir Richard and opened her mouth to say "Shall we, Papa?" he offered his arm to Suzanne Patterson. And Suzanne, quite a vision herself in a Grecian gown of gold tissue set off with rubies at her ears and throat and Sir Richard's blood-red roses twined into her hair, took it with that warmly intimate smile of hers.

Looking over his shoulder almost off-handedly, Sir Richard said, "You don't mind, do you, Georgie?"

"Of course not, Papa," she said quickly past the lump in her throat, adding as flippantly as she could manage, "I daresay I shall find a partner somewhere in this crowd."

But she did mind. She minded horribly.

A moment ago she had felt pretty and powerful and giddy with happiness; now she felt like sinking into the floor and crying like a child. But Georgianna Pennington did not cry—certainly not in public. And Georgianna Pennington did *not* feel jealous—certainly not of her own father. Why, the idea was worse than absurd.

She watched her father move onto the floor with the woman he loved. Nothing could more clearly have proclaimed that a torch had been passed. Georgianna's hands felt achingly empty.

But she was still Richard Pennington's daughter, and she was, as her Aunt Jane would say, made of good stuff. The creamy white shoulders so prettily bared by the water sprite gown squared themselves. The pert chin raised itself with determination. All right, little sparrow, she told herself sternly. Start flapping your wings. It is definitely time to start flying.

She was surrounded by an eager group of gentlemen begging for her hand in the waltz. Her eyes, only half seeing, scanned the group, wondering idly which of them she could love, *would* love, for she was determined to fall quite thoroughly in love this very night.

She barely heard the solicitations being poured upon her head, most of them in French or German. But one, in English and seemingly quieter but clearer than the others, she did hear. "Miss Pennington," said Robert Trevelyan, trying hard for the fashionably detached air of his brother. "It is the first waltz. My waltz, I believe."

She turned to him with a dazzling smile she didn't even know she wore. She was more grateful to him than he could know or she could have imagined, for here, at least, she felt she had a friend. "Of course, Lord Kitteridge. I have not forgotten." She offered her hand and they took the floor.

She wanted desperately to let her eyes follow her father, but she would not. She forced herself to focus all her attention on her partner. He was a less polished dancer than she would have expected of such a stellar member of the *ton*. Oh, he was certainly graceful enough, but he moved as though strangely unused to waltzing, and she could almost fancy that the hand encircling her small waist was trembling. Almost as if he were nervous.

She brushed the thought away; it was too ridiculous. The Earl of Kitteridge was a well-known flirt with a glib tongue and a grin that could charm a cat away from its cream. He would certainly not be nervous waltzing with a mere Miss Pennington.

But Robert was nervous. Terribly so. Though he had never held anything more delicious in his arms, he had also never been more sorry that he'd agreed to come to Vienna in the guise of his brother. He might be able to pull it off with such as the Princess Bagration and her friends. Even the Czar had accepted him unquestioningly. But he'd never be able to fool Miss Pennington, he told himself as he twirled her about the floor. And what was worse, he didn't want to. Damn Alec and his harebrained schemes!

He gazed down at her, holding her brown eyes with his own blue ones. He could smell the delicate scent of the violets that she held in her right hand, now resting so deliciously on his shoulder. Even more delicious, he could feel the warmth of her body through the layers of thin silk of her gown. And he realized that in all the many times he had danced with Evelina Everbright at the local Oxford assemblies, he had never felt the heady intoxication he experienced with this delightful girl in his arms.

Despite her smile, he sensed that she was unhappy about something. For a tiny moment, as she had watched her father and Suzanne Patterson take the floor, she had looked positively stricken. He couldn't imagine why that should be, but he was astonished at how desperately he wanted to make the pain go away. The thought that Georgianna might be unhappy was one he found unbearable.

So he smiled. It was not precisely his brother's smile. It was not quite flirtatious or challenging or mischievous enough, but it was an altogether heartfelt smile that started at the corners of his mouth and traveled up his face to rest deep in his eyes. And it seemed to do the trick. He could feel her relax in his arms, and some of the hurt that had been imperfectly concealed by her smile went out of her eyes.

Georgianna smiled up into his handsome face. She didn't know why, but she suddenly felt very much more comfortable. Except for his grander and more colorful clothes and a slight variation in the way he combed his hair, he was so like his brother that looking at him was an eerie experience. Even the warmth of his smile was exactly as she remembered Mr. Trevelyan's smile that day they had walked along the quai at Calais. If she had not at that moment been able to see that very Mr. Trevelyan across the room chatting with Lady Castlereagh, she would have thought she was dancing with him rather than with the Earl of Kitteridge.

Though inordinately pleased to have elicited a truer smile from her, Robin felt distinctly uncomfortable under such close scrutiny. Suddenly the silence between them seemed to reverberate louder than the violins sawing out the waltz. He had to say something. "You should always carry violets," he said unthinkingly then wished he had bit his tongue first. It was, after all, supposedly his brother who had sent them to her.

She blushed slightly. "I do hope you are not offended, my lord, that I am not carrying your roses. They were exquisitely beautiful, and I do thank you for your thoughtfulness, but as you can see I would have chosen them at the peril of my ensemble. Red and yellow roses and blue silk do not, I am afraid, make a charming combination."

"You would be beautiful carrying ragwort," he said with his brother's glinting smile. But this time the words were all his own.

"And you, my lord, are an accomplished flirt."

"Of course," he replied. "It's a requirement for earls, don't you know."

"But of course," she agreed with a tinkling laugh. "I understand that they take your ermine and strawberry leaves away if you do not break at least a dozen female hearts each Season."

"Two dozen." He chuckled and pulled her ever so slightly closer to steer them on an elegant diagonal across the room. They didn't speak for some moments, each feeling quite content with their present company and activity.

"How are you finding Vienna?" he asked after a few moments.

"Busy," she replied. "And dreadfully crowded. But that was to be expected, of course."

"It is certainly not Somerset."

"True. Nor Oxford. I imagine your brother is a little overwhelmed. Do you think he is enjoying himself?"

"What?" he asked. He had once again forgotten who he was supposed to be. Miss Pennington had a way of sending all thoughts that did not center on her straight out of his head. "Oh, Robin. Oh, uh, yes, yes. He's quite liking it." He would have to be more careful around her, or he would be certain to give himself away. He put a bit more Alec into his voice. "Been trying for years to pry him out of his fusty study, y'know. Thought Vienna would be good for him."

"Good for him?"

"Yes. Give him a bit more town polish. He's kept himself buried away long enough." Even as he repeated his brother's words, he knew they were true. Robin felt certain he would never again be content with the simple life of an Oxford scholar facing the prospect of a marriage with the likes of Miss Everbright, or any other of her ilk.

Georgianna let her eyes wander back to Robert Trevelyan (or so she thought) on the other side of the room. He had not danced, but stood watching her and his brother. When he caught her eye, he nodded and grinned, a grin quite unlike any she'd seen on his face before, a grin very like his brother's. And she was almost positive that he *winked*, though she told herself she couldn't possibly see it at such a distance.

She also saw a petite blonde hanging on the arm of the Czar, scowling at her. Though she had not yet been introduced to her hostess—the princess hated the fusty practice of receiving lines—she guessed that this was the infamous Princess Bagration. Georgianna wondered what she could possibly have done wrong to warrant such a dagger glare from the woman.

She and her partner waltzed on in silence, garnering a number of glances both admiring and envious. They were quite a vision in their varying shades of blue. There was something about the way the earl held her that made Georgianna feel completely comfortable. Actually, *safe* was the word that went through her mind, but she dismissed it as being ridiculous.

"Did you manage to find a supply of English tea?" Robin suddenly asked.

"Tea?" she said with a blank look.

"Yes, you said—" He cut himself off, wanting to bite his traitorous tongue. This was getting to be ridiculous! It had been to *Robin,* not Alec, that she had talked of tea. "My, uh, brother mentioned that when you travel you . . . you sometimes have trouble finding English tea." The words sounded lame in his own ears.

"Why, yes, I found some. With so many English in Vienna just now it presented little problem. I imagine the merchants have laid in all sorts of stores they might not normally need."

"Good," he said. "Good." He twirled her into a heady series of turns that allowed no more opportunity for conversation. The music built to a crescendo, and a few moments later he returned a rather breathless Georgianna to her father and Suzanne.

Anyone in the room who happened to be watching—and there were more than a few—then saw Robert Trevelyan, perfectly coiffed and attired as the Earl of Kitteridge, head straight for the punch bowl where he quickly swallowed a large cup of the strong concoction the princess had provided for her guests.

Georgianna moved on to other parties. Indeed, her dance card was entirely filled by the time the second dance, a stately polonaise, began. True to her word, she had saved the second waltz for the other Trevelyan twin.

"The waltz, Miss Pennington," said Alec as it was announced. "My brother has had his chance and now it is my turn." He grinned and offered his arm; she grinned back and took it.

Georgianna was surprised to learn that he was a much more accomplished dancer than his brother. He turned her effortlessly around the floor, belying the soberness of his dress of black and gray with the dash of his footwork.

"How do you find Vienna, Miss Pennington?" he asked. He couldn't know he was exactly parroting his brother, but he did think it sounded like the sort of banal, nonflirtatious thing Robin would say.

"I like it vey well," she replied, then added with a grin, "and I find myself wondering what the Viennese think of it. But of course, Vienna is not Calais."

He looked at her blankly. He hadn't the vaguest notion what she was referring to, but though his mind might be less quick than his brother's, he was quick enough to see from her grin that he *ought* to know what she was referring to. Damn Robin for taking that solitary walk with her in Calais while Alec recuperated in his room. He had to say something. His mind clicked madly like a slightly out-of-sync clock.

"No, it is certainly not Calais," he said, still trying for a clue as to the subject under discussion. "For which I can only think the Viennese must be eternally grateful."

"Yes, certainly," she said, "even though they do not have *frites* in Vienna."

"*Frites?*" he said weakly, whisking her into a heady turn while he wondered furiously. What the devil was *frites?*

"At least I have not seen any as yet," she said after the turn was completed. "Do you not long to taste them again?"

Aha! A clue, he thought. Food. "Yes. Oh, yes. They were, uh, delicious." He hoped they really had been delicious and were not some ghastly French thing like smoked eels or, worse yet, snails, for God's sake.

"Delicious," she agreed and seemed to mean it. "Grease and all." She was grinning like a conspirator.

Feeling emboldened by her help, he smiled heartily. "Grease and all," he agreed and swung her into another turn. He would have to have a *detailed* conversation with Robin about Miss Pennington and particularly about that solitary walk on the quai.

"Have you encountered Mrs. Alderstunt or Sir Grevesby since you arrived in Vienna?" she asked a moment later.

Here he felt on safer ground. At least he knew to whom she was referring, for he remembered briefly meeting them on the ship from Dover. "Yes indeed. Saw her sailing back and forth in front of St. Stephen's yesterday with a guidebook in her hand and her chitty-faced daughter trailing in her wake crying 'La, Mama!' every other second. As for Sir Grevesby, we encountered him on the ramparts the other morning sitting in one of the cafés. He was complaining about the quality of Viennese coffee, if you can imagine such a thing."

Georgie laughed delightedly. "But of course he was! It is part of his Momus nature."

"Momus nature," he murmured, confused once more and strongly suspecting that he *ought* to understand her.

"Yes. Do you not find it interesting to note how like the society of the ancient gods is to our own, Mr. Trevelyan? We, like they, have our Momuses and our Silenuses, our curious Pandoras and, of course, our Bacchantes."

Mythology. *That's* what she was talking about, and he knew just about enough on the subject to fill a thimble made for a baby's finger. "Our Bacchantes, of course," he replied noncommittally. Well, he'd lost the bet over the flowers so he suspected he'd soon have at least some idea to whom, or what, she was referring. Mythology lessons. And Latin! Ugh, he thought.

"And our own Aphrodite—or Venus, if you prefer," she added with a sideways glance at their hostess. "Venus who beguiles all, gods and men alike, and steals away even the wits of the wise."

Here, at least, was a name he recognized, for no self-respecting English gallant could be unacquainted with the goddess of love. "Venus, yes. She'd like to hear you call her that. The princess is most conscious of her own beauty."

"Deservedly so, I should think. She is lovely."

"But not half so lovely as one of her guests," he replied, giving her a devastating Kitteridge smile and feeling at last on safer ground as they turned into a final set of twirls.

He bowed over her hand as the dance finished. "Thank you, Mr. Trevelyan, for a most pleasant dance," said Georgie with a smile that could melt the polar ice cap. "And thank you very much for the flowers. How could you guess that violets were my favorites?"

Score one for Robin, he thought and had the grace to blush. "Oh, they just seemed . . . right, somehow. I am glad you like them."

"Very much, indeed, sir." She put her nose to the violets, and when she looked up again it was to be greeted by an Austrian major bowing at her.

"My dance at last, Miss Pennington."

"Of course, Major von Traunstein," she said and willingly offered him her hand. But she smiled back at Alec as she passed him.

The rest of the evening progressed in a haze of swirling skirts and lilting music. Georgianna danced every dance, including a waltz with the czar, a polonaise with the Polish prince Adam Czartoryski, and a country dance with the jovially round Count Pozzo di Borgo, all gentlemen she knew well and liked. She was introduced to a dozen others, each of whom begged for and won a dance, and she gave in once more to the importuning of Major von Traunstein, a most persistent suitor.

As the evening was drawing to an end, she stood quietly for a moment and looked at all the gentlemen in the room. Do I love any of them yet? she asked herself and giggled at her own fancy. She knew she was acting like a child feeling her own forehead for a fever and disappointed to discover she had none and so would not be given the day off from her studies. No, she admitted, I am not yet in love. But I *shall* be.

Her eyes, without any conscious direction from her brain, drifted to where the Trevelyan twins chatted with each other at the punch bowl.

⊷⊶❋[*nine*]❋⊷⊶

A WEEK PASSED; the Congress of Vienna was in full cry. Georgianna attended no fewer than six balls, three routs, five formal dinners, a half dozen *salons,* and a military review. She could see that she would indeed need to visit one of the plethora of *modistes* that had set up shop in the Austrian capital, for she had been right in her fears. Her supply of Parisian gowns, elegantly fashionable though they may be, was proving sadly insufficient to the demands of such an exalted society. She simply needed more clothes.

By the end of that first week, the number of her suitors had already grown to a pleasantly large flock. Major von Traunstein was among the more persistent. She was charmed by his Teutonic gallantry and flattered by his constant attention. He was clever and witty, was a graceful dancer, and flattered her only as far as she wished to be flattered. He did have an unfortunate tendency to click his heels at the least encouragement, but surely that could be forgiven in an Austrian. She allowed him to drive her twice through the Prater and promenaded with him once on the ramparts (with the faithful Talley tagging along behind them or, more often, pulling along before them, the perfect chaperone). The dog did not seem best pleased with the major's company.

A young English officer by the name of Smythe-Burnes was also satisfyingly attentive and regularly sent her reams of overblown poetry that left her in whoops but could not help but flatter her vanity a little. He also filled the house with flowers on so continual a basis that she began to feel as though she were living in a florist's shop.

There were also a pair of Italians—the best of friends since childhood—who were close to coming to cuffs over the lady. She quickly realized she must treat them guardedly, since she knew very well that neither of them would later forgive her, nor would she forgive herself, should she be the cause of a permanent rift between them.

But the gentlemen who clearly brought the brightest light to Miss Pennington's pretty brown eyes were the Trevelyan brothers. They were in almost constant attendance at the house in the Schulerstrasse whenever she was receiving. They each demanded and received the maximum allowed two dances with her at every ball—waltzes whenever they were quick enough to get them. Alec even managed to cut his brother out on at least one occasion.

"Very 'Kitteridge' behavior, Alec," Robin scolded him after he'd stolen a march and carried Georgie off in the waltz, "which is simply another way of saying high-handed. You're forgetting yourself, or rather you're forgetting you're me. Robert Trevelyan would never have done such a thing."

"No, and you wouldn't have had the waltz with the prettiest girl in the room, either," said an unapologetic Alec. "If I'm to be swathed in these depressing duds of yours, least I can do is get some fun out of it." It was true that he looked uncomfortable in his brother's sober black, like a peacock that had just molted. "Besides, I waltz better than you."

"You *did*," said Robin, brushing a nonexistent speck of lint from the elegant sleeve of the exquisite coat of cerulean merino wool that closely fitted his form. It was the coat his brother had had from Weston not more than a fortnight before leaving London, and Robin found he was enjoying very much the wearing of it. "I have been practicing."

"I have noticed," said Alec with a grin.

One or the other of the twins sat beside Georgianna at most of the dinners she had attended, and they always spent some time riding beside her carriage when she and her father took the air in the Prater. She had gone riding once with the earl and once with his brother and had enjoyed both outings immensely.

There was, however, a growing problem. Though Georgie, being so carefully tuned to every tiny flutter of her heart that might signal she was falling in love at last, would not deny that she found her greatest pleasure in their company, she could not decide which of the brothers she preferred.

At first, Robert Trevelyan had clearly taken the palm. They seemed to have such a great deal in common, and their discourse, as exampled by that delightful walk along the quai in Calais, was so easy and relaxed. But he seemed somehow changed now that he was in Vienna. Though she sometimes fancied she discovered a glint of amusement in his eye that almost implied a shared joke, at others he was so prosy and pompous that she wanted to scream—or run off and dance wildly with his lighter-minded brother.

Lord Kitteridge, on the other hand, had turned out to be much less of a loose screw than she had thought he would be. True, he was lighter-hearted than his brother, but she found she enjoyed his lively sense of humor. And he seemed to have as fine a mind as his brother had earlier shown. There was certainly nothing to choose between the two gentlemen from a physical standpoint. They were probably the two handsomest men with whom she had ever been acquainted—excepting, of course, her father.

All in all, Georgie was quite satisfied with her first days in Vienna.

The Earl of Kitteridge was equally satisfied with Vienna. Though not the scholar his brother was, he was far from stupid. Also, he knew his twin very well indeed. It was clear that Robin was deep in the throes of love—even though he might not recognize it yet himself. Alec was delighted with such a state of affairs and was determined to do whatever he could to forward the match between his brother and the lovely, lively Miss Pennington. She was precisely the sort of girl Robin needed to uproot him from his cozy Oxford cottage and his dull Oxford existence and to turn him outward to face the world.

Robert Trevelyan's judgment of his stay so far in the Austrian capital was less clear-cut. His mood seemed to vacillate wildly in a manner wholly unlike his usual calm approach to the world. He found himself feeling more and more at home in the elegant clothes of his brother. Alec's breezier approach to the world, his lighter sense of humor, his wit, were becoming second nature to Robin; he actually began to enjoy the ruse. Whenever he was dancing at a glittering ball, savoring the delicacies of an embassy dinner, or riding with Miss Pennington, he felt certain that God was in his heaven and all was right with the world.

However, when he returned home again, a blackness would often descend on him suddenly, and he was unable to pinpoint the reason—or loath to plumb the depths of his own feelings to ferret it out. But more and more often as he drifted off to sleep a pair of speaking brown eyes in a delicately carved face framed by dusky waves glittered at him, and he fell asleep with a smile on his face.

It was when they'd reached this odd sort of equilibrium with their unusual situation that disaster struck. Just when Robin seemed to be getting the hang of the thing at last and was actually feeling as though he just might make a better Earl of Kitteridge than Alec did himself, the tragedy occurred. Well, perhaps "tragedy" was coming it a bit too strong, Robin admitted later. But it did seem as though the hand of doom had suddenly clenched hard around them and decided not to let go.

It was at a dinner at the Castlereaghs' that it happened. Robin, as Alec, had been chatting pleasantly with Georgianna, Suzanne, and Sir Richard as they sipped sherry in the drawing room and waited for the remainder of the guests to arrive. He had just excused himself and left their side to join his brother, feeling a desperate need to remove himself from Suzanne's informed gossip about their supposedly mutual friends in London.

"Who the devil is Sally Pinchik, and what am I supposed to know about her unorthodox marital arrangements?" he asked his brother *sotto voce* as they stood lounging in a fashionably negligent manner at the fireplace.

"Sally? Prettiest little ladybird you ever saw," replied Alec, the leer in his eyes at odds with the soberness of his attire. "Daughter of a viscount, married to an earl, and keeps house with a butler while the earl shares a bedroom with his housekeeper. The earl acknowledges his wife's children by the butler (fortunately all of them girls), and she pretends that the housekeeper's son is hers. Very interesting menagerie, y'see."

"I'd say shocking, rather," said Robin, pokering up in a very un-Alec sort of way.

"Nonsense," said Alec. "The girls get to call themselves Lady Rose and Lady Dinah, and the earl gets his heir. Besides," he added, "word is that Sally's father was himself the son of a butler and her husband's mother was a housekeeper so it all comes out rather neatly, don't y'see."

Robin laughed in spite of himself, almost choking on his sherry. He had to set the delicate glass carefully on the mantel to keep from dropping it.

Quite suddenly, however, his chuckle trailed off into nothing and his face, turned toward the door, paled to the color of ashes. "Good God," he said on a sort of croak.

"What?" said Alec, looking alarmed.

"By the door."

Alec turned to see that a small group of newcomers had just entered the drawing room. There were a pair of gentlemen he knew to be attached to the Prussian embassy accompanying a young lady and her mama. Unexceptionable, thought Alec, and wondered what had set his brother off. Then he noticed a trio of guests entering on the heels of the Prussians. The threesome was comprised of an elderly, dignified-looking gentleman in rusty black with two ladies, obviously his wife and daughter.

At first, their faces registered not at all on Alec. Then he, too, turned the grayish tone that was decorating his brother's face. "Good God," he parroted. "It's Miss Everdull."

"Everbright," Robin corrected without thinking.

"What the devil are *they* doing in Vienna?"

"How the devil should I know?"

All this "deviling" notwithstanding, both young men had a tolerably accurate idea of exactly why the Everbrights had come to Vienna.

"It's my belief they're chasing after you," said Alec finally.

"Don't be ridiculous," exclaimed Robin, though he feared his brother was right. "Why should they do such a thing?"

"Daresay the mother is desperate at the thought you might slip through her fingers. You have been squiring the girl about for dog's years. She don't mean to see her only daughter whistle an earl's son down the wind."

"But to come here!" said Robin, feeling more and more like a trapped bear and conveniently forgetting that it was, in fact, his brother, dressed as Robert Trevelyan, who should be feeling the trap's jaws closing on his leg.

"Makes perfect sense," said Alec. "The girl's on the shelf. Daresay she's three-and-twenty if she's a day."

"Twenty-four," Robin corrected.

"Well, there you are then. Definitely on the shelf, and the mother's looking to you to haul her off again."

"I cannot think it," said Robin.

"Told you, she's desperate. Stands to reason. Must be to tow the girl and her father all the way to Vienna. She can't have thought it through very clearly, though, or she wouldn't have subjected them all to this. Bound to find themselves so far out of their depth they won't even be able to dog-paddle to shore."

"Well, as to that, Mr. Everbright may be only an Oxford professor, Alec, but he's a good friend of Lord Castlereagh and a noted expert on the Philosophy of Nations. I imagine the foreign secretary invited them."

"Well, I don't see that it makes a ha'p'orth of difference *why* they're here," said Alec with an unwontedly practical view of the situation. "Fact is, they *are,* and I'd just as soon play least in sight till we can think what to do about it." He turned, desperate for a place to hide before the Everbrights could spot him.

"Too late. She's seen us," said Robin in a grim voice.

Alec looked back across the room. "Good God, the woman's waving her fan at us like a Persian slave on a hot day," he said, glancing around in the hope that no one had noticed her gaucheness. "Very bad *ton.*"

The lady in question, a rather spindly, tall woman in a dress as gray as her hair, waving an oversize ostrich fan, and smiling past a mouthful of large teeth, was approaching them through the colorful group. To say that she looked somewhat out of place would have been charitable. She looked like nothing so much as a gray heron in a room full of birds of paradise.

In her wake came her daughter, a tall, broad-shouldered young woman in an unfortunate dress of vermilion silk that made her golden skin look yellow and turned her hair more mouse-brown than anything.

"What the devil am I to say to her?" asked Alec. He seemed to remember for the first time that it was *he,* the supposed Robert Trevelyan, who would naturally be the goal of the lady's progress across the room.

"Ask her how her geraniums go on. She is very fond of her

garden," said Robin with a smile. He had finally realized his reprieve; *he* was not to be Mrs. Everbright's prey. All he had to do to come off clean was play his role as the earl to the hilt. It might even be amusing to see Alec nonplussed for once in his life.

"Then what?" asked Alec in a voice that was beginning to sound desperate.

"I think you can safely remain mute for most of the rest of the ensuing discourse," explained his brother. "Mrs. Everbright is quite capable of maintaining a conversation with little assistance from her listener. Just nod and agree whenever you think appropriate."

There was an undeniable note of mirth in his tone now, and Alec seized on it. "Devil! You are enjoying this."

"Of course I am," admitted Robin. "Is it not the very reason you talked me into coming with you on this lark in the first place? You said it would be fun, and you were right."

"Didn't expect to encounter someone who knew you so well," grumbled Alec. He had, in truth, thought the most "fun" of this lark was to come from watching his brother trying to act an unfamiliar part.

"Oho! So all the discomfort was to be on my part, was it? Well, brother, here's a taste of your own sauce. I hope you like the flavor." And he was laughing outright when Mrs. Everbright reached them, her daughter in tow.

"Mr. Trevelyan!" said the woman in a voice that seemed both too loud and too low for her spindly frame. "It is Mr. Trevelyan, is it not?" she added with an arch little smile. "For how you two gentlemen can expect us poor females to tell you apart is beyond me. Like two peas in a pod, are they not, Evelina? Except, of course, that dear Mr. Trevelyan is always the more soberly dressed. Not, of course, that you are not all that is proper, my dear sir, and quite right, too, that you should not attempt to eclipse your brother, the earl, in your choice of raiment. Black is somehow so eminently suitable to an Oxonian as I am forever telling Mr. Everbright." She fluttered her fan so briskly that a pair of gray feathers detached themselves and slowly drifted to the floor.

Alec, in something of a daze, watched them fall. He couldn't speak, but there wasn't the least need to do so. Mrs. Everbright was perfectly capable of continuing without the least encouragement. "But how surprised you must be to see us in Vienna, sir!" she ran on. "And just when we had thought ourselves so firmly fixed in Oxfordshire, too. Was it not *too* kind of Lord Castlereagh to invite us? He *would* have it that he simply *must* have Mr. Everbright's advice on these weighty Matters of State. So much hanging in the balance, you know. The entire future of Europe to be decided. And how do *you* do, Lord Kitteridge?" she plunged on, scarce pausing for breath. "So lovely to see you again. You remember my daughter Evelina, I am certain." She finally paused long enough to push her daughter forward.

The young woman seemed composed, but a small frown creased her too-wide brow, and her face had flushed slightly with the mortification she must be feeling. She offered a curtsy to Robin, thinking, of course, that he was the earl.

Robin bowed over the hand of the young woman he had been more or less courting for close on two years and twinkled her a Kitteridge smile that was almost as charming as his brother's at its most devastating. "Of course I remember, ma'am," he said smoothly. "How do you do, Miss Everbright?"

"Very well, I thank you, my lord," she replied. "It is a pleasure to see you again," she added in a low, almost husky voice and looked hard at his face. Then she turned to Alec and looked hard at him, and both brothers felt distinctly uncomfortable, as though they had suddenly become transparent as water.

"Uh, tell me, ma'am," said Alec to Mrs. Everbright, "how do your geraniums go on?"

"Splendidly, Mr. Trevelyan! Splendidly. So kind of you to ask. They are in blooming health," she said and tittered at her own joke. "I have decided to try quite a new ratio of sand and loam in the mix, you see, and the blooms are . . ." And Mrs. Everbright was off and running.

Robin turned to the daughter. "Do you stay with the Castlereaghs, Miss Everbright?"

"No, my lord," she replied in the calm way he knew so well. "We have taken rooms in the Herrengasse. A house was impossible at such short notice even if we could have paid the rent, which you must know is astronomically high in Vienna now."

"True," said Robin, casting about in his mind for a picture of how Alec would act with her. "It is too tedious how the Viennese have let things get so out of hand." He reached into the pocket of his, or rather his brother's, coat and withdrew an exquisitely enameled snuff box. He pried it open and took a pinch of snuff as small as he thought he was likely to get away with. Then he sneezed into a lace-edged handkerchief, rather harder than he would have liked, and smiled at her languidly. "Horrid place, Vienna, but what can one do? One could not, after all, miss the biggest party of the century, could one?"

"I suppose one such as yourself could not," she said in a tone that led him to think that she would much have preferred to miss it herself. But she did smile, softening the effect of her words. Miss Everbright's smile was quite her best feature.

Her fondness for her geraniums notwithstanding, Mrs. Everbright suddenly seemed to remember just why she was here and left off her horticultural discourses. Across the room, she spied the Castlereaghs' butler stooping to whisper in his hostess's ear; Lady Castlereagh nodded. Clearly, dinner was about to be announced. "Ah, I believe we are about to be called to dinner," she said heartily and tapped Alec's arm playfully with her huge fan. The action caused two more bits of ostrich fluff to detach themselves from their rightful place and go to join their fellows on the Aubusson carpet. "How fortunate that we are here beside you, Mr. Trevelyan. You may escort Evelina in to dinner. Such a pretty couple you will make."

"Mama!" gasped her daughter not quite under her breath.

At that very moment the butler intoned the words that sealed Alec's fate. "But of course," said Alec with less eagerness than a hopeful mama might have wished for. He turned to the daughter and offered his arm. "I should love to escort you, Miss Everbright. Shall we?" She nodded, her mouth a little pinched, and placed her gloved hand lightly upon his arm as they turned toward the dining room.

As they walked away, they heard Mrs. Everbright say, "Why thank you, Lord Kitteridge. I should be flattered by your escort. Tell me, my lord, do you care for geraniums?"

As Robin and Mrs. Everbright headed for the dining room in the wake of the others, he glanced longingly at Georgianna Pennington. She was smiling prettily up at Major von Traunstein as that gentleman offered his impeccably tailored arm. Robin felt his mouth clench involuntarily, and he cursed all Austrians.

Once in the dining room, Alec found that Mrs. Everbright had been even busier than he had supposed. She had somehow convinced Lady Castlereagh to place the elegantly penned card that read "Mr. Trevelyan" directly to the right of that which read "Miss Everbright." He would have to converse with the chit all through dinner, and he hadn't the faintest notion what to say to her.

"May I say, Miss Everbright," he tendered as a tureen of turtle soup was being dished up, "what a delightful, uh, surprise it is to find you in Vienna." His mind was spinning with trying to think what the devil he was to say to this girl whom supposedly he knew quite well but whom, in fact, he had met only once in his life and then very briefly.

"It is good of you to say so, Mr. Trevelyan, when I know you must be wishing us all at Hades," she said in her calm, matter-of-fact voice as she delicately spooned up her soup. "Coming here was an *odious* trick to play on you and so I told Mama, but she would have it that you would be delighted to see us."

"Have I not just said so?"

"Yes, you have, because you are a gentleman and could hardly say otherwise. But I cannot suppose you truly mean it, sir, and so I wish you will not say it again. You need not, you know. I am only sorry if our appearance has discomposed you in any way, and I do most heartily beg your pardon for it."

Now Alec was altogether flustered. The one time he had met the girl her mother had so dominated the conversation that the daughter had hardly been able to say a word. Now that they were face to face in a situation that required they converse directly with each other, he discovered she was not at all what he had supposed.

"No, no really, Miss Everbright," he blustered. "What do you take me for?"

"Why, for a gentleman, of course, as I have just said." She drank another spoonful or two of her soup, then put down her spoon and looked him directly in the eye. "Mr. Trevelyan, we have been used to speaking rather more frankly together than a lady and a gentleman often do. May I be frank with you now?"

Oh, Lord, thought Alec in a panic, slurping his soup in his agitation. What the devil has my brother said to her? But he turned back to her, smiled brightly, and answered, "Of course, Miss Everbright."

She seemed to gather up her courage, then hesitated. He saw her wringing her linen napkin a moment in apparent anxiety. "Oh, dear. These sorts of things are always more difficult than one thinks they ought to be. I have been wanting to tell you this age, but the moment never seemed to be exactly right. Of course, a formal dinner party is as far from the right spot as possible, but I *must* tell you now, mustn't I?"

He put down his spoon and said with unusual gentleness, "Tell me what, Miss Everbright?"

"That you need not offer for me. I never really expected you would, you know, and you mustn't feel compelled to do so now merely because my mother has had the odious nerve to chase after you across half a continent," she said all in a rush, then colored up in a way that made her almost pretty, thought Alec.

Well, here was plain speaking indeed. It was a very fortunate thing that the footmen chose that moment to begin serving the baked carp in a truffle sauce. Good manners required that they turn away from each other to converse with their other dinner partners. For Alec, who could not remember the last time he had been left at *point non plus* by anyone, particularly a mere countrified female with neither exceptional looks nor fortune to recommend her, could not think of a single thing to say.

His brother, on the other hand, to whom the gods had granted the double felicity of being seated besides Miss Pennington and of seeing his so-smooth brother discomposed for perhaps the first time in his adult career, enjoyed his meal hugely.

ten

ROBERT TREVELYAN SMILED into his mirror. He really did look rather well in blue. Funny he had never known it before. But then, he'd never given himself the chance to know it. Blue was, after all, an Alec color, and Robin had spent much of his life being as determinedly unlike Alec as possible.

Now he needs must do just the opposite, and the effect in his mirror did not displease him. More importantly, it did not seem to displease Miss Pennington. During the thoroughly delightful two hours he had spent beside her at dinner the previous evening, she had seemed to be enjoying their conversation almost as much as he.

Not wanting to seem too "Robert-ish," he had made good use of the various *on-dits* he'd picked up since arriving in Vienna, at least those he could relate without blushing, which seriously diminished the number of stories in his arsenal. He reiterated a lively story about a Spanish grandee and his Prussian fiancée with sufficient wit and style to keep her chuckling, even as she turned to her other dinner partner, that damned von Traunstein fellow. And had he detected a slight but distinct note of reluctance that she must, in good manners, share her attention with the Austrian officer? Yes, he was certain he had.

When his well of amusing gossip ran dry, he regaled her with tales of Alec's more hair-raising romps through the hallowed halls of Harrow (told, of course, in the first person and with a charming degree of self-deprecating humor). But the highlight of this, his most memorable meal in Vienna (and perhaps ever), occurred over the glazed veal olives served with stewed cardoons and Spanish onions.

"Do you ride, Miss Pennington?" he asked.

"Oh, yes, my lord. I was hoisted onto my first pony when I was three, and Papa claims he couldn't pull me off again until I reluctantly fell asleep in the saddle. When I woke to find myself tucked up in my bed, I demanded to be taken to the stables so I could sleep beside Celery."

"Celery was the pony, I take it?"

"Of course. She foaled a few years later, a ghastly orangeish filly whom I insisted on naming Carrot."

He chuckled appreciatively. "And who do you ride now, Cucumber?"

"Oh, no," she replied with a twinkle. "That is not at all an appropriate name for a lively horse, and I couldn't bear to ride the slug for whom it *would* be proper. No, my mare in England is a most elegant and lively lady so I have named her Artichoke."

He laughed so suddenly he nearly choked on a bite of veal. "You are bamming me, Miss Pennington."

"Am I?" she teased. "You may ask my papa, if you wish, my lord. He will tell you she is out of Mushroom, sired by Asparagus."

This time his laughter drew more than one speculative look from the other guests at the table. "I see your stable is a regular Spanish Olio, ma'am."

"Yes, but I seem to be running out of vegetables. Artichoke will be foaling in the spring, and I cannot in good conscience bring myself to name a horse Turnip or Leek."

"Definitely not," he agreed with a mock frown. "How about Potato?"

"Worse!" she cried. "No, I think I must switch to fruits. Gooseberry, perhaps. What do you think, my lord?"

He frowned a moment more as though giving the question serious thought, then pronounced, "Marmalade."

"Marmalade! Of course," she agreed with delight then had to turn back to the Austrian usurper, as Robert was beginning to think of Major von Traunstein.

When she turned back to him as an eschalot of apples and water ices were set before them, he finally asked the question he'd been leading up to in the first place. "Might I hope that you will come riding with me one day soon, Miss Pennington? I cannot promise you a Spinach or a Parsley, but the stable I use has a spirited little black mare that might suit you. She might even answer if you call her Licorice or some such."

"Why thank you, Lord Kitteridge. I should love to. I have been longing forever to get back on a horse and have been bemoaning the fact that it was not possible to bring Artichoke with us."

"Would tomorrow be too soon? If we make an early start, we might ride up to the Vienna Woods. I am told there are superb views of the city as well as some lovely trails." The words flowed out easily enough, gilded with just the right amount of Alec's polish, but Robin found he was holding his breath waiting for her answer.

"In fact, tomorrow would be perfect. Papa will be in meetings, and I feared I would be left to amuse myself all day."

"I doubt that, Miss Pennington, for the gentlemen of Vienna are not blind, you know."

She gave that light laugh he was learning to love. "I thank you, sir, both for the compliment and the invitation. I shall be ready by nine if that is early enough."

"Nine is precisely the right hour, Miss Pennington," he answered with a smile that nearly melted the lemon ice she was spooning up.

Just that easily and naturally had the invitation been offered and accepted, as easily and naturally as if he really were his brother instead of the inelegant and sober-minded Robert Trevelyan. And now here he stood, checking the set of his brother's royal-blue riding jacket on his broad shoulders and the smoothness of his brother's fawn-colored buckskins over his strong thighs and the intricacy of a cravat tied in a perfect Mathematical by his brother's valet.

I think I'll do, he said to himself as he positioned a black topper on his curls. With a riding crop in one gloved hand, he tipped the hat to a jauntier angle and strode from the room.

Alec Trevelyan, Earl of Kitteridge, scowled into his mirror. How he hated wearing brown. Or gray. Or black. And his brother seemed not to own a single garment with more color to it than this nut-brown coat. With his neckcloth neatly but unostentatiously tied, with a single gold watch fob at his waist and not even one ring on his fingers, he felt exactly the way a preacher looks—drab as a sparrow.

There was another reason for the scowl, as well. He had spent a good hour and more this morning over an unconscionably early breakfast being drilled by his brother about life in Oxford, about Mrs. Everbright's garden, about Mr. Everbright's researches, and about their daughter's taste in conversation. But he still felt totally unprepared for this afternoon.

While Robert Trevelyan was becoming increasingly comfortable with his newly assumed peerage, Alec was growing daily more discomfited with playing the role of an Oxford scholar. Regret was an emotion totally foreign to his optimistic nature, but he was definitely beginning to rue the rash wager that had brought him to Vienna in his brother's clothes. He hadn't given this lark of theirs a great deal of thought before springing the idea on Robin back in London. It had simply occurred to him as a way to brighten what had become an ever more boring existence. The Earl of Kitteridge was a creature of impulse—he would readily admit to the flaw— and he had acted impulsively.

True, it amused him to watch his brother, whom he loved dearly, blossoming before his very eyes. Robin was becoming a new person, and Alec was certain he'd never again be content with his stick-in-the-Oxford-mud ways. For that, at least, he was grateful.

But his own success at masquerading as a classical scholar who also happened to be proficient at languages and knew about such useless things as music and mathematics and mythology was trying, very trying indeed. Who'd have thought a fellow had to know so much to be so dull!

And now there was Miss Everbright to add to the equation. She was bright, devilish bright. The thing to do was to stay as far away from her as it was possible to do, for she was bound to catch him out in an error sooner than the cat could lick her ear. But he found he didn't entirely want to stay away from her. And the fact mystified him. Alec didn't enjoy being mystified, especially by an unattractive bluestocking with an odiously pushing mama.

His face grew pensive as he thought of her. He had met her only the night before, but he could easily call her face to mind. It was unfair to call her unattractive, really. True, she had not the glow of a Georgianna Pennington and not a trace of the feminine magic of the Princess Bagration and her kind. And she hadn't a shade of style or elegance. Wore awful clothes and her hair was worse.

But she had a compelling face, especially when conversing on a topic that interested her. She seemed always composed and calm, a trait Alec would have thought would bore him silly but which, in fact, he found strangely compelling. A great deal of countenance was how his mother might describe what Miss Evelina Everbright had.

After the inauspicious beginning of their meal at the Castlereaghs', they had actually got on quite well together. The girl, at least, didn't simper as so many of the schoolroom misses constantly thrown at his head did. He had to tread carefully, of course, for she certainly knew his brother better than anyone else in Vienna did. She could easily give the whole game away.

How amazed he had been then when, over the coffee cream in Chantilly baskets, he heard his own traitorous voice politely requesting the pleasure of taking Miss Everbright for a drive in the Prater the following afternoon.

"Oh, dear," she had murmured, clearly discomposed by the request. "You really not need, sir. And it would only give Mama quite the wrong impression."

"And what impression is that, miss?" asked Alec, sipping his wine and concentrating on the look of intelligence in her quite large, amber eyes.

"Why, that you really might offer for me after all. That this mad dash to Vienna was the right thing to do, just as she thought. And since we are now agreed that you need *not* offer for me, sir, I should think it unfair to lead her to believe that you will."

"But surely a ride in the Prater at the fashionable hour is unexceptionable."

"In the eyes of anyone else, perhaps so," she agreed. "But Mama is, well, rather like a horse with blinders. She tends to see only what is directly in front of her, and then only if she wishes to see it. I love her dearly, of course, but her obsession with marrying me off creditably can be rather..." The words trailed off as she once again concentrated on turning her linen napkin into an accordion fan, the only sign she gave of the acute embarrassment she must be feeling.

"Rather difficult?" he asked and the note in his voice was genuinely kind.

"Yes, sir," she agreed and gave him a thin smile.

"Then she shall be pleased that you are to go driving with me, and certainly she is less difficult when she is pleased, is she not?"

"Considerably, but still . . ."

"It is settled, Miss Everbright. I shall call for you at four." And he smiled at her in a way that Robert Trevelyan had never smiled at her in his life.

Evelina felt herself blushing in an unwonted manner, both at the invitation and at the warmth of that smile. She was thankful that Lady Castlereagh chose that moment to lead the ladies from the room.

So now here he was, thought Alec, frowning once more into the mirror, the tonnish, flirtatious Earl of Kitteridge, dressed in a deadly dull brown suit, still feeling naked without his quizzing-glass, about to take the most untonnish female in Vienna for a drive through the Prater at the most fashionable hour of the day.

He didn't understand it; he didn't understand it at all.

Yet when he plopped his brother's beaver hat with its unfashionably low crown onto his dark locks and left the room, it was with a smile on his face and a jauntiness to his step.

"How lovely it is," sighed Georgianna as she looked down on Vienna. "Like a painting in a frame."

"Yes, it is," agreed Robert Trevelyan.

Georgianna flushed briefly and fidgeted on her horse, for the elegantly clad gentleman beside her had not been looking down on the breathtaking view. He had, instead, been gazing raptly at his companion.

She was not displeased by his scrutiny. Indeed, she had spent quite two hours dressing, fidgeting with her buttons, fussing over her choice of accessories, and scowling uncharacteristically at Rose as that hapless servant arranged her heavy hair. But the end result had warranted the effort. She knew she looked well in her new habit of deep-pile velvet the color of rich burgundy. It was faced with twilled gray silk and cut in a vaguely military style that showed off to perfection her petite figure. A snowy cravat secured with a ruby stickpin and a natty gray toque with burgundy-tipped feathers completed the portrait. The *Föhn*, that enervating, siroccolike wind that blew softly across Vienna for much of the year, riffled the tendrils of dark hair that curled at her temples.

Some two hours after leaving the Schulerstrasse, the handsome pair and their equally handsome horses now rested on the Kahlenberg summit, breathing in the freshness of the air, the green of the Vienna Woods that surrounded them, and the pleasure of each other's company. So far it had been a perfect ride, thought Georgianna. Her companion had been right about the horse; she was a frisky little mare, playful and energetic without being in the least ornery.

They'd galloped with abandon across broad Alpine meadows dotted with late wildflowers. They'd wandered along paths tunneled by overhanging elms, oaks, and chestnut trees gaily dressed in vivid oranges, yellows, and reds, their horses' hooves plowing and swishing through fallen leaves up to their fetlocks. They'd stopped at the Schreiberbach spring to water the horses and couldn't resist cupping their hands to drink the cool, clear water themselves, laughing like children as it dribbled onto their chins. And they'd climbed up, up, up the hill past the terraced vineyards she'd heard called the "Staircase of the Alps," breathing in the scents of musty earth and drying grass and, from somewhere over the hill, the pungent smell of burning autumn leaves.

Now they paused almost 1,600 feet above the city on "House Mountains"; spread before them was a view that seemed designed to turn anyone into a poet.

"I feel like I am at the roof of the world," said Georgianna as she gazed down on the elegant city that from this vantage point looked like a child's miniature panorama. They could see the narrow strip of land dividing the Danube into twin streams bestriding the green and gold of the Prater, the warren of narrow streets twisting around the spires of St. Stephen's Cathedral, and the wedding-cake glory of the Hofburg Palace. The sound of a child's laughter caught the breeze just so and drifted up to reach their ears.

"Yes," agreed Robin, "it's a spot for dreaming and dallying." He gave her a wry, almost enigmatic smile. "I think even my rationalist, unromantic brother would turn into a dreamer in such a setting."

"Is Mr. Trevelyan not a dreamer, then, Lord Kitteridge?" she asked casually. "Lord, no," he replied, then gave a very Alec-like laugh. "Thinks it the height of adventure to wander over the hills of Oxfordshire. At least he did until I convinced him to come to Vienna, though I think he is changing his mind."

"You convinced him?"

"Pulled him along kicking and screaming, but I rather fancy he's glad he came." He followed this statement with a soft chuckle that set Georgie wondering at the joke. "Look there," he went on, interrupting her wondering to point down at the city below. "You can see the Landstrasse." She followed his hand till she saw the great road that led east out of Vienna and disappeared over the horizon. "I've heard it said that Asia begins on the Landstrasse. And look here," he added, gesturing to the precipitous cliffs below them. "Lucky for European Christianity that these cliffs are here. In their sweep westward in the seventeenth century, the Turks fought and lost a desperate battle here. Couldn't scale the cliffs, y'see."

She gave him a quizzical look. "It seems I have been grossly misinformed, my lord. I have it on good authority that you never open a book. Yet here you are expounding on Viennese history—and very interestingly, too, I might add."

"Oh, well, as to that," he said, stammering slightly, "heard my brother speaking of it to Miss Everbright only last evening. Your informant's in the right of it, sad to say. It's Robin who's the bookish one, not me." Careful, old boy, he lectured himself. Bound to give yourself away if you don't watch your step. Think Alec thoughts, he went on silently; but it was hard to do so in Miss Pennington's presence. It was deuced hard to think of anything but how very pretty she was and how very badly he wanted her to like him. The only trouble was . . . which him?

"And did the Turks really get this close?" She interrupted his thoughts.

"So Robin said. Trying to spread their Mohammedanism, don't y'know. If they'd managed the trick, we'd probably be wearing robes and bowing toward Mecca today."

"I don't think I should like that," she mused with a thoughtful frown. "I understand their ladies are never allowed to go anywhere or do anything, and I don't think I should like being compelled to wear a veil whenever I do go out."

"Lord, no! For that, Miss Pennington, would be a truly heinous crime. Can't deprive us gentlemen of such a lovely sight. Wouldn't be at all fair," he said with a grin. There, he thought. Much better. Much more "Alec-ish."

"And you, my lord," she replied, grinning, "look much finer in your riding coat and breeches than you would in flowing Bedouin robes, I feel certain."

He tipped his hat and grinned back. "I thank you for the compliment, miss. Shall we ride on? There's a delightful *heuriger* not far away, I'm told."

"A *heuriger?* Whatever is that?"

"You shall see. At least you shall if my instructions are correct and my sense of direction holds true."

She laughed and turned her horse to follow him. "I trust you to bring me home again, my lord. Lead on." And as they rode down the path she realized she did, in fact, trust him implicitly.

The rest of the afternoon was as delightful as the morning had been. They rode in a leisurely fashion, chatting as they went, with Robin trying hard for the light, inconsequential chatter of his brother and with Georgie being pleasantly surprised by the quality of his mind. Here, up on the hills, the air was so fresh, heavy with the smells of pine and grass and wood smoke, that they both soon felt giddy with it, bosky on air and exercise and something else, something they could not quite define since neither had ever experienced it before but which neither had the least desire to eliminate.

They explored the ruined walls of Leopoldsberg Castle and its nearby church, exclaimed over the large Alpine houses with their steeply pitched slate-tiled roofs, their fanciful shutters, and their large balconies.

As they rode on through the woods they spotted wild rabbits and deer. Once, their horses flushed a pheasant from the brush. The last of the wild blueberries and raspberries still clung to a few bushes, and they picked and ate them, relishing their sweetness, until their mouths were purple and their faces full of laughter.

Finally they came to Kahlenbergerdorf. They happily dismounted before an open-air wine tavern set amid a vineyard at the edge of the village. "Behold, a *heuriger*," said Robin. He doffed his hat with a flourish and bowed low, opening a rustic gate and ushering her into a graveled yard set with oak-plank tables and shaded by towering elms. "I am reliably informed that one has not truly been to Vienna until one has sat in a *heuriger* drinking new wine under the trees. And we seem to be here at the perfect time of year." He pointed to a sprig of pine hanging over the door to the tavern and explained that it meant the very first of the new wine was available.

Robin had a word with a roundly padded waitress dressed in a dirndl and a brightly embroidered blouse. Then he sat next to the young woman he was so quickly growing to love.

Surprising himself with his audacity, he reached out and gently removed her hat and softly brushed a few stray tendrils of hair away from her face. "You are so very lovely," he murmured so softly that Georgie was almost uncertain she'd heard him.

She didn't answer, didn't move. Her face felt warm, not from the sun but from the tenderness of his touch. Her eyes locked with his and she watched his face move slowly into a smile. When the smile was complete she almost gasped, for it was exactly like the smile she had seen her father bestow so often on Suzanne Patterson, a smile filled with tenderness and longing. And love.

"My lord," she breathed. "I . . . I . . ."

The waitress returned and the spell of the moment was broken as she set before them an earthenware pitcher of the tart new wine, a pot of mustard, and a platter heaped with radishes, pickles, slices of cold venison and boar and sausage, creamy cheese, and thick chunks of brown bread spread with *schmaltz*.

"Eat," said Robin in a voice made hearty to hide the emotion racing through him. "You're like a bird the wind might blow away. No one'll believe you've been to Vienna if you don't put some poundage on."

She giggled. "Like the waitress?" she asked as she bit into the chewy bread.

"Well, needn't get carried away, y'know." He reached into a pocket and pulled out a small, slightly crushed packet. Unwrapping it, he revealed a Scotch egg. "Perhaps this will tempt your appetite."

"A Scotch egg! How did you know they're my favorite?"

"I remembered from our picnic on the ship," he said without thinking.

"The ship? But you weren't there, were you? You were in the cabin drinking tea."

Damn me for a total fool, he railed at himself. *When will I think before I speak?* "Well, yes, but, that is, my brother told me when he joined me below," he said feebly.

"Oh," she answered and wondered why the Earl of Kitteridge had felt compelled to ask about her. Still, it had been thoughtful of him to bring the Scotch egg. She bit into it with relish.

The lighter mood was soon reestablished, and they enjoyed

their meal. They exclaimed in wonder over the wine, made faces at the sourness of the pickles, and burned their tongues on the fiery mustard that had horseradish stirred into it.

It was late afternoon by the time their horses clopped along the cobbles of the Schulerstrasse once more. They dismounted and a groom ran up to lead Georgianna's horse away. The pair stood before the door. Neither seemed able to speak for a moment.

"Miss Pennington, I . . ." began Robin.

"Lord Kitteridge, I . . ." began Georgianna at the same moment. They both stopped, tried again, stopped again, and finally burst out laughing. "It has been a perfect day, Lord Kitteridge," said Georgie finally, "and I thank you very sincerely for giving me such pleasure."

"The pleasure, Miss Pennington," said Robin with a deep, dazzling, totally enchanting smile, "was all mine."

He tipped his hat and remounted his horse; she slowly entered the house and closed the door behind her. They had each just passed the most wonderful day they could remember. They each went to bed that night with a smiling face to encounter a night filled with very interesting dreams.

"You drive very well, Mr. Trevelyan," said Evelina Everbright as Alec tooled a high-perch phaeton down the Hauptallee in the Prater. "I've never known you to drive such a sporting vehicle before."

"Well, uh, as to that," said Alec, "it was the only open carriage I could hire, what with the crowds all looking for transportation, don't y'know." She seemed to accept the lie. The truth was that he had gone to no less than a half dozen stables looking for the smart carriage and the pair of lively steppers that pulled it. He knew very well it was a very un-Robertish sort of rig to drive, but he didn't care. He needed one vestige of his true self to lend him confidence.

He never stopped to wonder why he should feel the need of additional confidence in front of a woman for whom he cared nothing. In fact, as he looked at his companion, he wondered why he'd had such a cork-brained notion as to invite her for a drive.

She was rigged out in a ghastly carriage dress of pink sarcenet trimmed with puffs and bows of cherry ribbon and topped with a spencer of red and white stripes that made her skin look positively yellow. Beneath a villager hat edged with pink cabbage roses, her hair had been teased into a pile of curls that had already begun to droop alarmingly. Never before in his life had the Earl of Kitteridge willingly been seen in public with such a quiz. But Robert had, so that was all right.

"Is it difficult to drive such a rig?" asked Evelina. "I should think it would be and am convinced you shan't allow me to take the ribbons as you sometimes do at home."

"At home?" Dash it all, he thought, was Robin really so addle-brained as to let a mere girl handle his cattle? But he couldn't insult her, could he? "Well, of course, Miss Everbright, if you should like to," he said a little doubtfully, praying that she shouldn't want to at all.

"Oh, I should like it of all things, Mr. Trevelyan, and I do most truly thank you for the compliment of trusting me with such beautiful horses. Nicely rounded heads, but not too long in the neck, wouldn't you say?"

"Yes, they are," he agreed, thankful that she at least sounded like she knew something about horseflesh. With a gulp and a prayer, he handed her the ribbons.

He need not have worried, for Evelina Everbright felt more comfortable with horses than she did with most people and knew considerably more about how to handle them. Turning neatly off the Hauptallee into a less traveled lane, she tooled the delicate vehicle smartly along, feathered a gentle curve to perfection, and gave the horses their heads for a few breathless minutes before bringing them to a smart stop.

"Oh, Mr. Trevelyan," she breathed her appreciation. "What sweet goers! I have never driven anything half so fine."

"And I have never seen a woman who drives half so well, Miss Everbright."

Her face had taken on a delicate rose tint, whether from the exercise or the compliment he could not tell, but it lit her face and made her almost pretty. "Thank you, sir, but as it was you who taught me, I should think the honors are yours."

"I did?" he blurted out unthinkingly. "I mean, yes, I did, right, but it's the student makes the teacher, don't y'know."

"As you have heard my father say countless times."

Well, if that don't beat all, he thought. Imagine me knowing a thing like that!

"Thank you for allowing me to drive them, sir," she went on. Her voice had returned to its usual calm, composed manner.

"Any time, Miss Everbright. Any time." He took the rib-

bons from her gloved hands and, giving the horses the office
to start, neatly turned the phaeton around and headed back
down the lane.

What a surprise the girl was, he thought. Who'd have
thought to look at her that she could drive to an inch? As he
headed back toward the more fashionable part of the park,
they conversed quietly, commenting on the beauty of the autumn foliage and the liveliness of Vienna. He liked the sound
of her voice. She didn't twitter or sigh. Her voice was neither
coy nor arch. She didn't flirt with her eyes or her voice. She
merely spoke. He found it very refreshing.

"Would you care for something cool to drink, Miss Everbright?" he heard himself asking before he'd even considered
what he was saying. "Driving can be dusty work."

"Thank you, Mr. Trevelyan," she said quietly. "I should
like that."

"Right," he said, and within moments they drew up in
front of the Green Parrot, one of the dozens of rustic cafés that
dotted the Prater. When he raised his arms to help her down,
he found she was much lighter than he had imagined. His
hands nearly spanned her small waist and it took little effort to
lift her to the ground. That delicate rose tint invaded her
cheeks once more, and he found he was absurdly pleased by
it.

He saw her seated at a table shaded by lime trees and went
inside to bespeak a jug of lemonade and a plate of pastries.
When he returned, she had removed her hat. A pity, since her
tortured curls had all but given up the fight and now straggled
about her face and down her back. But she didn't seem terribly concerned. She merely brushed them back out of her face
and smiled at him in her self-contained way.

"I believe Vienna agrees with you, Mr. Trevelyan," she
remarked as he sat down beside her.

"In what way, Miss Everbright?"

"I cannot say precisely how, but you seem different. More
relaxed. Freer, somehow."

"Do I?" he said, straightening in his chair. He had been
lounging in it in his usual way, one arm thrown across the
back, before he remembered that Robert never lounged. Robert sat.

"Yes," she went on. "I had heard that the Viennese are a
very gay, frivolous sort of people. Perhaps their disease is
catching," she added with a gentle smile. "Do you know, I am

not certain I should mind catching it myself. You will think that very strange coming from me, I daresay, for you know I am not at all frivolous by nature."

"Then you have certainly done the right thing in coming to Vienna. Absolutely impossible to be serious for any stretch of time in Vienna, y'see. Shall I undertake to give you lessons, Miss Everbright?"

"Lessons?"

"In frivolity. Daresay you don't think I shall make a very good teacher, for you know better than most how stiff and prosy I can be. . . ."

"You mustn't say that, sir."

" . . . but I do have an eminently frivolous brother," he went on, ignoring her caveat, "and I have spent a good many years watching him. Daresay I can play the part if need be."

"Mr. Trevelyan," she said with a distinct note of surprise in her calm voice, "I believe you're joking with me."

"Not at all, Miss Everbright," he said and gave her a glinting smile. "And to prove my seriousness, I shall begin at once. Drink up your lemonade like a good girl."

"But what—" she began but stopped with a laugh and swallowed her lemonade as instructed.

He took her empty glass and set it on the table. Taking her hand and pulling her to her feet, he led her across the small yard to a set of swings. "Sit, Miss Everbright," he commanded.

"No, really sir, you needn't . . ."

"Sit, miss," he repeated with mock sternness. "You really must learn to obey the teacher, y'know."

She sat on the swing, carefully arranging her frothing pink skirts about her legs. Alec gave the swing a gentle push, then another, then another somewhat more powerful. In mere seconds she was flying higher and higher, tendrils of brown hair trailing out behind her and pink sarcenet flying up to display a surprisingly delicately turned ankle. Alec took full advantage of the opportunity thus afforded and enjoyed the sight.

"Screech, Miss Everbright," he said after a moment as he gave her another push forward.

"What?" she cried as she swung back to meet him.

"Screech." He pushed. "It's required, y'know."

"I never screech," she shouted as she. swung forward then back again.

"Well, squeal then," he called. "You can at least squeal."

She laughed delightedly as her momentum carried her up and away from him again, a low, clear, full-throated laugh. "I never squeal either," she said as she swung back.

"I'll settle for that laugh," he called and laughed himself in a manner that would have raised many a quizzing-glass back in London accompanied by mutters of "very bad *ton.*" And he enjoyed his own laughter thoroughly.

He swung her for several more minutes before allowing her finally to slow then drift to a giddy, laughing stop, her half boots scuffing against the gravel to act as brakes. She then insisted on pushing him and, much to his surprise, he agreed. When he stopped they were both laughing.

"More lemonade?" he asked with a grin.

"Please." She grinned back, an action unfamiliar to her face but surprisingly comfortable for all that.

"Swinging can be dusty work," they said in unison and burst out laughing again.

They returned to their table and enjoyed the lemonade and the pastries, happily licking their fingers for the last bits of cream.

Alec studied her as she ate, frowning slightly. She caught his change in mood and looked at him expectantly. "Miss Everbright," he said after a moment. "Last evening, you paid me the compliment of being frank with me. May I now be frank with you?"

"Of course, Mr. Trevelyan," she said, wondering at his frown and suddenly very much afraid of what he was going to say. She had been so enjoying herself.

"You oughtn't to wear pink."

"What?" she replied, astonished.

"Oughtn't to wear pink. It don't suit you in the slightest. Makes your skin go all yellow."

She was so taken aback that she needed a moment to marshal her thoughts before speaking. Then she looked down at her gown and smiled. "I know. Isn't it horrid? Mama has the most deplorable taste."

"And you oughtn't to try to curl your hair either."

"How very unhandsome of you to say so, Mr. Trevelyan," she said, but her words were belied by her smile. "Especially since these wretched wisps are solely for your benefit."

"My benefit?"

"Yes. And they required an entire night tied up in rags to achieve. A very uncomfortable night, I might add."

"You oughtn't to have bothered, y'know."

"Well, I wish you will tell that to Mama. She *will* have it that gentlemen prefer young ladies who look like they just stepped out of a candy box."

"Deuce take your mama," he exclaimed, then wished he'd bit his tongue, for that was going a bit far. Robin would never say such a thing. "Mean to say, you shouldn't let your taste be guided by your mother, Miss Everbright."

"I suppose not," she agreed, "for she hasn't the least notion of what suits me. But you know yourself how difficult she can be, especially when she is *quite* determined on any course of action. And it hardly seemed worth the effort of defying her for something as trivial as fashion. Of course, when something of import is at stake, such as allowing me to ride in the hunt or discussing politics with Papa at the dinner table, I can be quite firm with her. But you know what she can be, Mr. Trevelyan. To set her weeping and calling for hartshorn and water over a mere gown does seem foolish beyond permission. Especially since I shall never, you must allow, be a beauty no matter what I wear or how I dress my hair."

"I shan't allow any such thing, Miss Everbright," he replied, eyeing her critically. For the briefest moment, she had the distinct feeling he was longing for a quizzing-glass the better to study her. But that was absurd, of course. She was quite certain Robert Trevelyan had never used a quizzing-glass in his life and probably wouldn't know how. "True, you are not in the common way of being pretty, but . . ." The words trailed off as he studied her closer.

Uncomfortable under such close scrutiny, she busied her hands with her lemonade glass, slowly sipping the last cool drops before setting the glass carefully down again. She was amazed to see that her hand was trembling slightly and she dropped it quickly into her lap. "What ought I to wear, Mr. Trevelyan?" she asked quietly and waited to hear his opinion with an intense stillness she hoped hid her eagerness.

"Gold," he said without equivocation. "Or bronze. Rust. Forest green, even, but never pink. And no bows, no ruffles or ribbons or furbelows. Straight lines and elegant draping. And your hair pulled back off your face."

He too set down his glass. Reaching out with both hands, he pulled the straggling locks of brown hair to the back of her neck, sleeking it back from her forehead and covering her ears. Suddenly he could see that her cheekbones were high and elegantly chiseled. Her neck was not gawky, it was swan-like. And her amber eyes, seeming huge now that her face was so much more open, were lovely. "Like that," he said softly.

Perhaps for the first time in her life, Evelina Everbright actually wished she had a mirror. But she had to make do with the reflection she saw in his eyes, and she liked what she saw. Definitely for the first time in her life, Miss Everbright actually felt pretty.

There was a brief moment of perfect harmony between the two young people before confusion and discomfort once again reigned. Something odd was happening and neither understood it in the least. It seemed the best thing to do was to climb back into the phaeton and return home. So that is what they did.

But for both of them, odd thoughts lingered well into the night.

·••►[*eleven*]◄••·

"No, no, Miss Pennington," said Major von Traunstein with a teasing smile a few days later as he handed Georgie up into an open carriage. "I shall not tell you as yet. It is to be a surprise."

She smiled as she settled herself on the leather seats. "I am not at all certain, Major, that I should be getting into a carriage with a gentleman who refuses to tell me where he is taking me."

The tall officer, resplendent in a green uniform faced in dove gray and covered with silver buttons, smiled back. "I have solemnly promised that you will be safe with me. What is it you English say? Safe as houses? Even without that redoubtable canine of yours to guard you," he added with a grimace, for to say that Talley had not taken a very great liking to Major von Traunstein was an understatement. Perhaps it was all that heel-clicking that set him off. The fellow had been lucky to escape with his skin intact. His boots had been less fortunate.

"Talley does make an admirable chaperone, does he not?" she said with a wicked smile. "But he has gone out with Papa today, so I must just trust you not to kidnap me, sir, and to return me in good time to dress for the Princess Furstenberg's reception."

"My solemn oath!" he declared, hand on heart, and sealed the promise with a vehement click of his heels and a stiff bow. Then he climbed into the carriage beside her and bid his groom release the horses' heads. He flicked the reins, the groom jumped up behind, and they were off at a trot, the major carefully steering them out of the Schulerstrasse and through the zigzag of narrow streets around the cathedral.

Georgie was in a thoughtful mood though she smiled brightly and chattered lightly as the carriage tooled along. She was thoughtful because today's outing was a mere interlude in what had become the primary question of her life. Did she love Lord Kitteridge enough to wish to marry him?

She felt that a moment of decision was approaching even more rapidly than she had planned for it to do. So strong had her reaction to the earl become that it had begun to frighten her. Ever since their enchanted day in the Vienna Woods, she had spent many a night sinking into her feather mattress and staring up into the dimity hangings, thinking of Alec and remembering Olivia's question from *Twelfth Night:* "Even so quickly can one catch the plague?"

True, she did not think of love as a plague and, in fact, she'd left England quite *determined* to catch it. But it had all happened so fast. Too fast. She could not absorb the thought just yet that she might very well have fallen in love. Especially since, such a short time earlier, she had been thinking that the *other* twin, Robert Trevelyan, would make an admirable husband. She would never have guessed such fickleness was part of her nature.

And so she had made herself more available to her other suitors, a phalanx whose numbers increased daily. Surely if she spent more time with other admiring gentlemen, she reasoned, Lord Kitteridge would cease to seem so very special in her eyes.

Thus her acceptance of Major von Traunstein's mysterious invitation today to see "something rather special and truly Austrian."

Their drive was a short one; the major soon pulled the carriage to a stop in front of the Imperial Riding Hall, the baroque masterpiece built by Empress Maria Theresa's architect, Fischer von Erlach. Beaming, he handed her down from the carriage.

"Knowing your love of horses, Miss Pennington, I thought you should like to see where an Austrian nobleman learns to ride. I have had permission from the emperor himself to show you about."

"Famous!" she cried, for she had heard a great deal about the renowned riding school and its equally famous creamy-white Lipizzaner stallions. "I have been so longing to see the horses."

"Come," he said with another bow and offered his arm.

They had a delightful tour, peeking into rooms where the fine art of equitation was taught, visiting the stables which Georgie noted were cleaner than some ballrooms. They watched a number of young boys being patiently but competently instructed in the proper handling of a horse. Finally they were granted the superb honor of making an audience of two as the great white stallions were put through their paces. To an accompaniment of melodic chamber music, they performed caprioles and levades and courbettes of astonishing precision and surpassing beauty. Georgie thought she had never seen anything so graceful yet so powerful. They were astounding animals.

After a thoroughly enjoyable pair of hours, they were on the point of leaving the building, walking down a carved and gilded hallway, when the sound of steel hitting steel and a triumphant shout of "Hah!" sounded through a partially open door.

Always more curious than was good for her, Georgie pushed the door further open and poked her head around it.

What she saw nearly caused her to swoon. She was standing on a balcony looking down into a bare room with about a dozen men spread out along the walls. And in the center of the room, Alec, Lord Kitteridge, saber in hand, was fighting a duel with the Polish Count Wartszewski!

"Oh! You must stop them, Major. You must!" she exclaimed to her companion.

"Stop them? Oh, I couldn't do that," he said, confused.

"But you must! He may be hurt. He may be . . . killed."

"Killed? Who?" He was even more mystified now.

Her eyes were on the combatants. They fixed on Alec as he glided gracefully across the floor, saber flashing. "Alec," she whispered. "Stop them. Please," she begged.

"No, no. Not at all the thing to do, I assure you, miss," said the major. When she moved to lean over the balcony and

shout down at the fighters to stop, he took hold of her elbow
and pulled her back.

Oh, why were gentlemen so bull-headed, so ridiculously
blind and stubborn about their stupid Code of Honor, she
raged to herself. She knew very well that if she ran down the
stairs and into the melee to put a stop to the duel, Alec would
never forgive her. She was tempted to do it anyway, for better
he should hate her than that he should die.

But she knew she could not stop it. At best, she would
postpone it; at worst, she would endanger Alec's life still further. What if he saw her, dropped his guard, and received a
saber through his heart as a result? She would never be able to
forgive herself if he should die because of her. She couldn't
chance such an outcome. She could only watch, hoping her
attention and her prayers could keep him safe.

Parry, thrust, lunge, retreat, the duel moved across the
floor and back again. The sabers flew; she couldn't even see
the points, so quickly did they flash. Their boots thumped on
the polished wood floor. The sharp sound of ringing steel
pierced her ears and her heart which seemed to have taken up
residence in the area of her throat. Her eyes were huge with
terror.

Alec, handsome as the very devil in flowing shirtsleeves
and with his hair falling acrosss his forehead, drove the Polish
count hard. He arched, flicked, parried deftly, and lunged
again. On the sidelines, Robert Trevelyan cheered his brother
on. "Ha-hah!" laughed Alec as the point of his saber slid
across the count's shoulder.

"Good one that," said Major von Traunstein with infuriat-
ing calmness. Had they all gone mad? wondered Georgie. Did
none of them take seriously the notion that one of these men
might soon be grievously wounded? Or . . . dead. She clutched
her hands tightly at the thought.

Had she but known it, the fight was nearly over. Count
Wartszewski was tiring quickly. His sword hand drooped
alarmingly, and every time he let his point drop, Alec managed to score a touch over his guard. Not more than five
minutes after Georgie and the major entered the room—five
minutes that seemed to her more like five hours—the count
was up against the wall with Alec's saber bending against his
chest.

The Pole laid down his sword and raised his hands in surrender, and Georgie started to breathe again. They had not killed each other after all.

And then, to her astonishment, the gentlemen below her all began to laugh, even the defeated count. They crowded around Alec, patting him on the back and shaking his hand. Robin helped his brother into his coat while another gentleman did the same for the Pole. Then the count reached into his pocket, withdrew a purse clinking with coins, and tossed it to Alec, who caught it neatly.

"A deserved reward," said Wartszewski. "You have won your wager fair and truly."

A wager! Georgianna could not believe her ears. A silly, foolish, idiotish wager! And for that she had suffered such an agony of worry. She looked at the discarded sabers. Now that they lay still on the floor she could see the buttons on their tips. "Ohhh!" she exclaimed and very nearly stamped her foot in vexation.

This time she was heard by the gentlemen below. Lord Kitteridge looked up and smiled a friendly greeting. "Hallo, Miss Pennington," he called and ran his fingers through his hair, making himself look even more impossibly handsome. He seemed totally unconcerned at having such an unorthodox audience for what was, after all, a purely masculine pursuit.

Robin, too, dressed for once in his own sober brown coat, looked up and smiled at her, a brighter, more intense smile than his brother's and one that could never be defined by such an insipid word as "friendly." He tipped his hat at her and made a small bow.

But Georgie was in no mood to be smiled and nodded and bowed at. Her fear now past, indignation had rushed in to take its place. How dare they worry her so? She turned to the major. "Please take me home, sir," she said coolly. And the major, wondering what he had done to make her fly up into the boughs, did just that.

An hour later, Georgie was having a serious talk with her mirror. Her vexation had exhausted itself and she now had the leisure to consider her feelings about the afternoon with a clear head.

"Well, my girl," she said as she pulled a brush through her long dark waves. "You certainly had an eye-opener today. When you thought his life was in danger, it was worse than anything. Certainly far worse than the day you saw Lieutenant Farnham off to the front, knowing full well that he might not return. And you were engaged to marry him!" She brushed and brushed, perhaps waiting for the mirror to comment, but it did not.

"Would you have stood quite so paralyzed with fear if it had been Major von Traunstein with that saber in his hand? Or poor young Mr. Smythe-Burns? Or even Papa? Well, yes, certainly if it had been Papa, but hardly the others. You know very well that the thought of danger to *them* might have roused your compassion, even some small degree of worry, but never such absolute terror as you felt today.

"And if you can feel about Lord Kitteridge the same way you would feel seeing Papa in such a situation, what does that tell you?"

She looked a long time at the pixie face in the mirror, studying it, perhaps looking for visible signs that she had truly caught "the plague" of Olivia. But the mirror gave no answer. She was not yet entirely ready to have that particular answer articulated aloud.

Over the next few days, Georgianna spent more and more time with the Earl of Kitteridge, or so she thought, for it was, of course, actually Robin in disguise who squired her about the town. And when she was not with him, she spent a great deal of time thinking about him. Ever since that silly sword fight at the Imperial Riding Hall, she had thought of little else.

That day had solved a problem with which she had been wrestling for some time, and that was the question of which of the Trevelyan twins she preferred. She did not think she would have reacted quite so strongly had Mr. Trevelyan been the one she thought was in danger, though she would admit that she liked him very well.

Suzanne had been wrong, she decided. Lord Kitteridge was the superior brother after all, and the more time she spent in his company, the more certain she became. He was cleverer than Suzanne had implied and much better read. He was kinder, too. True, he was excessively fashionable but what harm was there in that? So was Georgie, and at considerable effort. Each day she felt a little more certain that there was no one with whom she would rather spend her time.

He accompanied her one afternoon to a *salon* held by the Princess Esterhazy where the conversation was primarily literary. The next afternoon saw them at the Kaunitz Palace being entertained by the sharp-tongued gossip of Talleyrand. On both occasions, Lord Kitteridge managed to seem at home. They attended a fête in the Augarten. At a dinner at the Russian embassy, they commented wryly on the lavishness of the meal which included sterlets from the Volga, Périgord truffles, Sicilian oranges, oysters from Brittany, English strawberries, pineapples from Moscow and cherries from St. Petersburg.

Another day they went for a stroll along the ramparts, stopping in a café to sip *kaffee mit schlag* and nibble at pastries. The weather held fine, slightly crisp and sunny, and the days seemed enchanted to Georgie.

She began, slowly but inexorably, to think the Earl of Kitteridge *might* make an admirable husband.

For Robert Trevelyan there were no longer any doubts; he was in love as he had never thought it possible to be. When he waltzed with Georgianna Pennington, he almost ached from the joy of holding her in his arms. She was beautiful, but more than that she was clever and kind and witty. He loved watching how her face mirrored the workings of her mind when she was struck by a new and intriguing idea. He loved the teasing ring of her laughter and the warm smell of her hair.

When he awoke each morning, it was with a smile on his face at the thought that he would soon see her again.

But that smile quickly faded into a hopeless frown as he realized he was falling deeper and deeper into a morass of deceit from which he might never be able to extricate himself. He felt quite certain that Georgianna was not a young lady who would take kindly to the discovery that she had been duped. She was too honest, too straightforward, to suffer such a slap in the face with complacency.

Then, too, how could he possibly think that a girl like Georgianna, a young lady who had any number of princes and counts and majors practically at each other's throats over the privilege of dancing with her, would be content to choose a mere *Mister* Trevelyan as her husband. The arrogance of such an idea appalled him.

He did believe that she was far from indifferent to him; she might even be falling in love with him. But the thought gave him little consolation. What if she was? It was not with *him*, after all, not with Robin, he knew that well enough, and the idea was a bitter one. It was the Earl of Kitteridge she was learning to love. And he was *not* the Earl; Alec was and always would be.

Why, *why* had he allowed this to happen to him? He who had spent so many years carefully constructing a life in which it didn't matter that he was the second son of an earl, a life in which he could be safe from envy of his own brother. And now he had calmly walked away from that safety, slammed the door on it, and plunged straight into what he had spent his life avoiding.

He had dug himself a hole that seemed to stretch halfway to China and he hadn't the faintest idea how to crawl out of it again. He didn't even own a shovel.

He was in agony, but such a ridiculous agony that he nearly had to laugh at himself. He was in an agony of jealousy over Georgianna Pennington, and the man of whom he was jealous was *himself!*

The only consolation on Robin's horizon was the masquerade to be held at the Hofburg Palace this very night. The invitation required that everyone come in fancy dress, an actual costume; a simple domino would not do. Since no one would be able to tell the twins apart by their attire as they usually did, the ball offered both young men a welcome respite from the masquerade they were living daily.

"Don't mind telling you, it'll be a relief," said Alec over dinner in the hotel's dining room that night.

"Well, it was your idea, you know," his brother pointed out drily.

"Yes, and a paper-skulled idea it was, too," said Alec.

"I thought you were enjoying it."

"Enjoying it! Robbie, you know me well as I know myself. D'you really think I enjoy going about looking like a preacher all the time? Or trying to understand frog talk all day? Or having to dine with Mrs. Everbright, for God's sake? I swear I could write a book on geraniums by now."

"Hah! And you thought I was the one who'd be made to look nohow. I think *I* am doing rather well," said Robin.

"You are," said Alec and grinned. "A damn sight too well if you ask me. The strangest people are beginning to tell me that my brother, Lord Kitteridge, has improved amazingly. Did you know Vienna's doing wonders for the flighty earl? Settling him down, y'see."

"Actually, I think they're right. You presumed that this lark would be 'good for me.' Your very words, dear brother. And it has been. But what's sauce for the goose and all that."

They both laughed as they rose from the table. It was time

to metamorphose back into themselves, if only for tonight. They went upstairs to don their masquerade costumes.

Robin was still chuckling as he closed the door to his room. The irony of being grateful to a masquerade for giving him the opportunity to be himself was not lost on him and he could appreciate the joke.

But there was far more hanging in the balance this night for Robert Trevelyan. He hoped to use the opportunity to learn the true state of Georgianna's feelings for him—and for Alec.

···❦❧[twelve]❦❧···

"OH, MISS GEORGIE," sighed Rose as she gazed at her young mistress. "You do look a treat, bless me if you don't."

Georgianna smiled at the young abigail in the mirror. "Thank you, Rose. Mme. Fuseau did do a marvelous job, did she not. It's *exactly* what I hoped for when I described the idea to her. How glad I am we went to Paris."

"I never seen the like, miss, never in all my life. What'd you call it again?" asked Rose.

"A firebird. It comes from a Russian fairy tale about a princess who is turned into a bird." She turned slowly in front of the mirror and tried to peer over her shoulder without dislodging her headdress. "Are my wings straight in the back?"

The maid reached out and flicked a feather into better alignment. "Aye, Miss Georgie, straight as can be."

She was dressing for the masquerade at the Hofburg and not one of the thousands of gentlemen expected to attend was likely to fail to notice Miss Georgianna Pennington. She'd spent hours over the design of the firebird costume, discussing every detail with the Parisian *modiste,* and she was pleased beyond measure with the results of their labors.

The basic gown was of Florentine taffeta in a brilliant cardinal red shot through with gold and embroidered all over in gold, red, and orange flames. After leaving a satisfyingly large expanse of milky bosom bare, it fell straight to the floor in front and was gathered into a short train in back. Over the gown were the firebird's wings, folded smoothly across Georgianna's shoulders and falling down her back to the floor. They were entirely covered with overlapping feathers of red, yellow, and orange, the tip of each feather lightly dusted with gold so that it shimmered in the light whenever she moved. Her dusky hair was piled on top of her head and wrapped with a bandeau of red silk embroidered in gold; feathered wings soared up and behind her at each side. Red gloves and gold kid dancing slippers completed the image.

She looked exactly the way a princess who'd been turned into a bird ought to look, an aristocratic creature with its wings folded safely about it, at rest but able to spread those lovely wings at any moment and take flight. Or go up in flames.

It was particularly important to Georgianna that she look splendid this night. She needed the extra confidence that came from knowing she looked her best, for she had decided to pay especially close attention this night to the Earl of Kitteridge and how she felt with him. Was she in love with him? Oh, she *hoped* she was! How very convenient it would be.

She already knew that she preferred his company to that of almost any gentleman she knew (or had ever known, even—traitorous thought!—her father). She felt impatient whenever she needs must go riding with Major von Traunstein or dance with one of her Italian swains or listen to Mr. Smythe-Burns's insipid verses. And she only felt truly happy again when she was once again talking or laughing with Kitteridge.

And when he gave her that very special smile, the smile he'd bestowed on her that day on the Kahlenberg summit and several times since, she felt a warmth surge through her body and a tingling prickle her skin that was somehow magical.

She felt reasonably confident, whenever she remembered that day and that smile, that he was not indifferent to her. In fact, she felt she might just be able to bring him up to scratch if she wished. The idea gave her gooseflesh.

The odd thing was that he seemed awfully reluctant to take the relationship beyond where it now stood. Despite everything she had been told about the flirtatious earl, he seemed almost shy, afraid perhaps of what she might say if he announced his intentions too clearly.

Tonight, she thought, she would let him know, as subtly but as clearly as she could manage, that she would not be averse to entertaining the idea of accepting an offer from him. Her large eyes blinked as she stared at herself in the mirror. Oh, dear, she thought. This putting of one's fate to the touch was a risky sort of business.

She squared her shoulders, gave her chin a determined tilt, and turned to her smiling abigail.

"Rose, hand me my mask, please."

A large number of heads were certainly contemplating romance on that magical night in Vienna, and a large number of hearts must have sunk with despair on entering the ballroom of the Hofburg. The crush was overwhelming. Even without masks covering every face, it would be a Herculean task for even the most determined Romeo to find his Juliet.

Over three thousand guests had been invited, a number large enough in itself to make things difficult, but the footmen at the door, after collecting the invitations from the arriving guests, had been doing a brisk business in reselling them. Consequently, by the time the Penningtons and Suzanne Patterson arrived, there were already close to five thousand people milling about the halls and galleries and the white and gold ballroom, with more pouring in every moment. They filled the dance floor and the balconies, spilled onto the terraces, and flooded the gardens. No one in Vienna had stayed at home that night, Georgianna felt certain.

Knights and ladies, gypsies, milkmaids, and Barbary pirates bumped into the likes of the Emperor Charlemagne, Queen Catherine de Medici, and Cardinal Richelieu. Papageno and Papagena sipped champagne together in a corner, their bright green parrot heads bobbing as they talked. Julius Caesar flirted with Queen Elizabeth; the Caliph of Baghdad chatted to Lucrezia Borgia. And at least a dozen Bonapartes paraded about, each a broader parody of the defeated emperor than the last.

Heads did indeed turn as Sir Richard Pennington, who made a rather respectable sultan in a striped turban and flowing robe, steered his two ladies through the worst of the crush near the door. Suzanne was an ethereally lovely Marie Antoinette, her hair lightly powdered, her ice-blue gown gracefully hooped and strewn with satin bows, tiny high-heeled slippers with silk rosettes on her feet. As they inched their way through the throng, at least a dozen courtiers from the previous century made her a graceful leg.

"Champagne," said Sir Richard as they at last gained a square of open floor near one of the French doors. "Must have something to drink or we'll all die." Fortunately, a liveried footman chose that moment to appear with a tray of glasses, three of which disappeared at once.

"Have you ever seen the like?" asked Suzanne as she sipped and looked about. Then she began to laugh. "Who on earth do you suppose that is?" she asked, gesturing toward a rather ungainly horse. The rear half seemed not to have the least idea of what the forward half wished to do.

"Don't know about the front," said Sir Richard, "but I'll go bail the rear is Lord Charles Stewart. Always said the fellow was a horse's—"

"Richard!" Suzanne cut him off and they all laughed.

Almost the first person to approach them was a very large King Henry VIII. "Red gown," he said with great joviality. "And feathers! Found you, Miss Pennington, dash me if I haven't."

She had to stare at him a moment before her face lit with recognition. It was the gyrating side whiskers that finally did it. "Captain Bloomfield," she exclaimed, then corrected herself with a laugh. "Forgive me, Your Majesty," she said and sank into a deep curtsy though she remembered to be careful not to crush her wings on the floor.

He offered a great paw of a hand and pulled her to her feet. "Now, now, no need for that. Came to claim my dance, what? Music's starting, you see. Must come, you know, or I shall have your head, what?" And he roared a great laugh.

"Of course, sire," she said with a smile, "and as I have grown rather partial to my head and would like to keep it upon my shoulders yet a while, I shall come dance with you as I promised." She laid her hand on his doublet-covered arm and they went to join the country dance just forming.

Miraculously, with the first strains of music the floor had cleared sufficiently to make room for the dancers. They joined a set with a peacock, an angel, two red Indians, and a pair of Pierrettes.

"Must say, Miss Pennington," said the captain, "you're looking, uh, blooming. That's it, blooming."

"Oh, no, Captain, I mean Your Majesty. Birds cannot bloom, surely. Not even firebirds."

"Well, mean to say, a man can hardly tell a lady she's flaming, what? Or flapping. *That's* what birds do, don't y'know. Flap their wings about. Make a stir. Couldn't very well say that, could I? Wouldn't be polite, what?"

"Of course you could not," she agreed. She must remember there were some gentlemen you simply could not tease. She was glad the movements of the dance took them apart.

When they had met on the packet boat to Calais, Georgianna had studied this man as a potential husband. Then, she knew only that she must find one; she had no idea of what he would be like. How absurd the idea of marriage to such as Captain Bloomfield now seemed. Now that she had quite a clear idea of the sort of gentleman she *did* wish to marry.

And where the devil *was* he, anyway?

The dance went on. Captain Bloomfield went on. He what-what-what?-ed her till she thought she'd scream, and it was with relief that she left him at the end of the dance.

She did not return to where she had left her father and Suzanne. Rather, she began prowling about the room, peering discreetly but hopefully up at the faces of every tall, dark-haired gentleman she encountered.

By the time the Trevelyan brothers arrived at the palace the crowds had swelled even further. It had taken them quite half an hour to make their way through the multitude in front of the palace and then to reach the ballroom. Once inside, they were more or less crushed into a corner, a dashing and colorful cavalier and a sober-looking Hamlet.

They hadn't discussed their costumes in advance, so when Alec had strolled into his brother's room a short while earlier each had been taken totally by surprise at sight of the other. A moment of silent staring, mouths agape, and they'd both gone into whoops. They slapped their thighs and laughed until tears prickled their eyes and they nearly fell over.

"You!" said Robin when he could again speak. "Hamlet! No one'd believe it. The *tonnish* Earl of Kitteridge looking sober as a judge."

"Not sober. Romantic. Lord Byron always wears black, you know," said Alec with an altogether insincere melancholic droop that did make him look startlingly like Lord Byron in tights. "Got to admit Hamlet is a romantic sort of fellow. The ladies adore him."

"Dreary is what he is," said Robin.

"Well, yes," admitted Alec, turning in front of the mirror with a look of satisfaction on his handsome face, "but you know, there's something devilish attractive about a man in tights."

"I do think the skull's got to go, though," said Robin.

"No, no, can't do that. How'll people know who I'm supposed to be otherwise?" He raised the skull he had managed to find only with difficulty and frowned at the empty sockets. "Ugly sort of fellow he must have been. Look at that beetle brow. What's his name supposed to be, then?"

"Yorick," said Robin, striking a pose. "'Alas, poor Yorick. I knew him.' Have to go about quoting the line all night if you insist on carrying the thing."

"Alas, poor Yorick, I. . . . No, bound to forget it. And, of course, I can't dance with the thing in my hand. Bound to scare the ladies, anyway. But I think I'll take the poor chap along for starters. See what develops. Never know, do you?"

"You never do," agreed his brother. And they both laughed.

"But never mind me. Look at you!" said Alec and walked a slow circle around his brother, nodding, chuckling, and finally letting out a long whistle. What he saw was an elegant, almost foppish gentleman in blue satin breeches and doublet, foaming lace in a dozen places, ribbons tied in love knots, and a periwig of heavy black curls falling to his shoulders. A cape of midnight blue satin lined with white was back over one shoulder. And to complete the picture, a small heart-shaped patch resided just to the left of his mouth, below his blue silk mask.

"Suits you down to the ground," said Alec when his perusal was complete. "Have you got a lace handkerchief?"

"No, only a linen one. Why?"

"Got to be lace. So you can flick it about like a true fop, y'know. Here," he said and pulled a surprisingly lacy handkerchief from one of Hamlet's pockets. "Don't imagine Hamlet uses lace, anyway. Danish, y'know." He gave Robin the bit of lace. "Now make me a leg."

His brother did so, and it was very gracefully done, a true courtier's bow.

"*Very* good," said Alec. "You'll do. Yes, indeed, you'll do very well. Shall we?" And Hamlet offered the cavalier his arm and they headed out the door.

Robin had surprised even himself with his choice of costume. If he had ever attended a masquerade in London (which he certainly hadn't), he would probably have gone dressed as a monk—or perhaps as Hamlet, all in black. Now, given the opportunity to be anyone he wanted, he'd gone and chosen one of the most flamboyant periods of English history in which to dress himself. Something mystifying was happening to him in Vienna.

So now here they were at the Hofburg, and despite their decision that each would play his true role this night, they'd each chosen a costume more suited to the other. Maybe this living in one another's skins was getting to be a habit not easily broken.

"Damned crowds," muttered Robin, pulling his cape free from the crush of a fat Wife of Bath behind him. "How the devil do they expect a man to find anyone in this swarm?" He was tall enough to look over the heads of much of the group, but what good did it do him when he hadn't the vaguest notion what sort of costume he was looking for? If only he'd thought to ask Miss Pennington what she would be wearing.

Alec, too, seemed to be searching for a particular reveler among the throng. A frown of concentration marred his handsome face. "Must be among this lot somewhere," he muttered almost to himself.

They grabbed two glasses of champagne from the tray of a passing footman and went on muttering into their wine and scanning the room with their eyes.

Evelina Everbright stood uncertainly in the doorway, fluttering inside but holding rigidly onto her usual calm, self-contained outward demeanor. She was ridiculously nervous. And for the silliest of all possible reasons. She was nervous because she knew she looked more attractive than she had ever looked in her life.

Oh, she was still not a beauty; she never would be, and that was a fact. But her mirror had told her—and she didn't *think* it lied—that she was almost handsome this evening. She had never before cared that she was not pretty and so paid little attention to what she wore or how she dressed her hair. As long as her gown was clean, she was content. And when her mother bought her all those truly awful pink and yellow and pale-blue ruffled confections before coming to Vienna, she saw little point in complaining about them and ending up with a Cheltenham tragedy on her hands. She really did not care enough.

But tonight she cared. She found she cared desperately. For Mr. Trevelyan, despite everything she thought she knew of him, had cared what she wore. He had noticed. And remarked. And suggested. And she had taken his suggestions to heart.

Turning a deaf ear to her mother's prognostications of doom if she did not smother herself in ruffles and pink ribbons, Evelina had designed herself a startlingly simple costume. She was the Greek goddess Artemis, the huntress, lady of wild things, lover of the woods and the wild chase. She wore a straight, elegantly draped gown of bronze hammered satin clasped lightly at her shoulders and leaving her arms bare. Thin gold braid edged the neck, crossed the bosom, and tied at the waist, and a wreath of gilded leaves circled her head. On her feet were golden sandals.

She looked . . . regal. With her hair brushed till it shone then pulled off her face into a Sappho, her neck seemed to go on forever. Her skin had taken on a warm golden hue, and her eyes behind a golden loo mask were the exact shade of her gown and looked huge. Her height now seemed an advantage rather than a liability.

Clutching a small gilt bow and arrows, she swallowed hard and entered the room, the clucking shepherdess that was her mother trailing in her wake.

Georgianna jumped when she heard him. "Birds are made to fly," said a deliciously familiar voice behind her. "But perhaps for now you will be content merely to dance."

She turned with a ready smile to see a pair of gentlemen— a cavalier who would have been at home to a peg in the court of King Charles II, and a Hamlet whose black tights and doublet showed off a remarkably well-developed set of legs. For a moment she didn't know which of them had spoken. She looked at them both, her mind racing. Despite their masks, she knew at once who they were, but not which was which.

She studied them as discreetly as she could. Why did they have to look so very much *alike?* You could never be truly certain which one you were speaking to. Under normal circumstances, of course, she hadn't the least trouble telling them apart, for they always dressed so differently. But what was she to do tonight?

Surely, she thought, the sober Hamlet must be Mr. Trevelyan. It would be very much in character for him, she thought. And the cavalier was precisely right for the dashing, fashionable Lord Kitteridge. How perfectly at home he would have been in Charles's frivolous restoration court.

She concentrated her gaze on him. From his wide brimmed hat with its sweeping ostrich plumes to the red heels on his boots, the gentleman was exquisite.

He made her an elegant leg, sweeping his hat nearly to the floor, and said, "Do firebirds waltz?" He reached for her hand as though he already knew the answer.

"This one does," she answered.

"Done it again, haven't you, dear brother?" said Hamlet. "Why is it you always manage to beat me to the prettiest girl in the room?"

"I am only taking pity on them, dear brother. For who would not prefer dancing with a laughing cavalier to taking the floor with a depressing Dane? *Especially* a Dane with a skull in his hand."

Yes, Georgianna thought. This gay cavalier *had* to be Lord Kitteridge. She was certain of it now.

The brothers laughed identical laughs and the cavalier turned once more to Georgianna. "Miss?" he said and offered his hand again.

Suddenly she had an idea and said, *"Avec plaisir, mon chevalier,"* as she took his hand.

"Mais non, mademoiselle," he replied. *"Le plaisir est de moi. Absolument de moi. Je suis enchanté."*

Oh, dear, she thought, confused again as they took the floor. Lord Kitteridge spoke abysmal French, she knew that well enough, and her cavalier had just flattered her with a perfect accent. Then she must be waltzing with Mr. Trevelyan. But why would he suddenly become so attentive and flattering to her when she'd hardly seen him at all the past few days?

They danced a few minutes without speaking. She ventured a peek up at him, very carefully (for she had to be mindful of her headdress or he might have a firebird feather in his eye) and saw him smiling at her. And it was *precisely* the way Lord Kitteridge had been smiling at her the past few days—that warm smile that made her feel like she was melting.

Oh, dear, she thought again. How can I tell? And the worst

of it was that for one astonishing moment, she didn't care which brother it was. She knew that she should. It must be terribly *wanton* of her not to. But the feeling of his strong arm about her waist, the way his blue eyes glinted with warmth and laughter as he gazed at her, the spicy smell of his eau de cologne, all pushed such thoughts momentarily from her mind. She just gave herself up to the enjoyment of the waltz and basked in that lovely smile as he spun her around the room, her train and her wings lightly sweeping the floor.

"By the bye," he said after a few moments, breaking the magic of the spell, "have you been writing long letters to your Aunt Jane with instructions to save them for that book you plan to write?"

"Book?"

"Yes. What was it? *The World as I See It,* by a Lady. I look forward to reading it, you know."

She thought. Was it. . . . ? Yes, she was *certain* it had been while walking in Calais with Mr. Trevelyan that they had come up with that silly notion of her writing a book. She remembered the afternoon quite clearly, for she had enjoyed his company immensely. So her partner *had* to be Robert.

But Robert didn't look at her in that special way or hold her so closely when they waltzed. Did he?

"Perhaps," he went on with an impish smile, oblivious to the disorder he was causing in her mind, "you ought to call it *All the World's a Salad and All the Horses Merely Vegetables.* You could make Celery and Carrot minor characters with Artichoke as the heroine." And then he laughed, the rich, roguish, twinkling laugh of Lord Kitteridge, the same laugh he'd given her that night at dinner when they'd discussed horses named after vegetables.

Oh, dear, she thought. Oh, dear, oh, dear, oh, dear! She wanted to scream "Who are you?" but of course she couldn't. It just wasn't done at a masquerade. And she wanted to scream "Who do I love?" but of course she couldn't do that either.

Well, my girl, she thought. That's put paid to your grand scheme of bringing Lord Kitteridge up to scratch tonight. You can't very well get a man to propose when you're not even certain he's the man you think you love. Especially not when there's even the slightest chance that you might like his brother just as much as you do him. She felt hopelessly confused.

To give him credit—or absolve him from blame—Robert Trevelyan had not purposely set out to confuse the woman he loved. In fact, he was very nearly as confused as she was. True, he did at least know his own identity, which gave him the advantage of her, but he had been acting the part of his brother so long, he'd almost forgotten how to be himself. And since he had decided he *would* be himself tonight, he was in something of a state.

He couldn't remember what he had said to her as Robert and what as Alec. He didn't know what she expected of one of the brothers and not of the other. But he couldn't stand to say nothing, so he plunged ahead like a bull charging at a red flag, jabbering away like some damned magpie and probably not making any sense at all.

Then he had an idea so brilliant it quite shocked him. A way to explain away whatever he might say. "Devilish thing about being a twin, Miss Pennington," he said with some bravado, a sort of "in for a penny, in for a pound" attitude. "Do you know that sometimes I actually know what's in my brother's mind? Mysterious, I know, but there it is. When my brother says or does a thing, I often just seem to know about it." He was warming to his topic now. "Just sort of pops into my head, and I can follow all the action just as if I was there. Very entertaining, really. Like watching a play."

She thought about this a minute. "I should think rather that it would be highly uncomfortable. Having someone else privy to one's thoughts, I mean. I am frequently made to squirm by merely having to listen to my own. I should be horrified to think that someone else was listening to them as well."

"Oh, well, as to that, I trust him not to use them to his advantage, and I'm certain he trusts me as well."

It was an explanation of sorts, however inadequate, and Georgie began to feel a bit better. This was surely Lord Kitteridge, then, this shining cavalier, and he had simply learned somehow about her conversations with his brother, either by a mysterious sort of transference of thought or simply because Robert had told him.

She let herself relax and enjoy the rest of the waltz, ruminating on the possibility and desirability of becoming the Countess of Kitteridge.

"No," Robin said softly. "Trust Alec with my life."

And her eyes flew to his face again.

* * *

It was nearly an hour before Alec found Evelina Everbright, and when he finally managed the trick, he wasn't at first certain it was she. She was standing across the room, straight as a statue with her head held very high, and she looked entirely different. The color and style of the gown and the new hairdo were vast improvements, even more than he'd thought they would be. She looked almost like the goddess she was portraying.

This tall, composed woman in bronze, if it was in fact Miss Everbright, would be able to hold her own in any company, he thought. And any man who chose to stand beside her need never blush for her appearance.

He had to be certain it was she. He plunged into the crowd, feeling like a fish swimming upstream, weaving, dodging, stepping on a few toes and receiving an elbow or two in his ribs before he had gained the opposite shore. On the way, he wondered about what to say to her.

Her costume, yes, that was it. He could comment on it. But who the devil was she supposed to be? He reached into the depths of recent memory and gave thanks that Miss Pennington preferred violets to roses. That lost wager meant he'd had to actually listen to a lecture from Robin on mythology. Let's see now, he thought. Bow and arrows. Leaves in the hair. Hmmmmm. Aha! Diana, that's who she was supposed to be. Or that other one, the Greek, uh . . . Artemis! That was it. Rather proud of remembering that bit, he was.

He had almost reached her and was considering the politics of simply reaching up and removing her mask to be certain it was Evelina when he heard a voice behind her. It was a voice he'd learned to recognize the way a worm learns to recognize the pecking of a robin.

"I am not saying it is not a lovely gown, Evelina," said Mrs. Everbright to her daughter, "but so, so *plain*. And such a very odd color. Not at all the fashion. You might at least have put some flowers in your hair or worn my coral necklaces when I offered them. Gentlemen do not, I am afraid, pay attention to plain ladies who make no attempt at all to be fashionable."

"Oh, hush, Mama," said her daughter with more than a hint of impatience.

"Well, I only—"

Alec cut her off, all doubts as to the goddess's identity gone. "I have never danced with a goddess," he said as he

bowed over Evelina's hand with a smile. "I do hope that you
will consent to change that lamentable state."

The tiny frown of anxiety that had been creasing her wide
brow disappeared as if by magic at the sound of his voice and
was replaced by a smile that was quite dazzling. And when
the smile worked its way up her face and brought golden
sparks to her wide, amber eyes, Evelina was truly beautiful.

"Well, sir," she said, "as you must know, I am patroness of
the hunt. Perhaps I prefer to be hunted."

"You have been, goddess. For the past hour and more. And
now I have caught you." He turned to her mother and placed
poor Yorick into her bony hands before she could protest.
Then he put his arm around Evelina's slender waist and pulled
her into the waltz. And she went willingly, still smiling that
dazzling smile.

Mrs. Everbright watched in amazement. Evelina, *her* Evelina, had actually been *flirting* with that Hamlet fellow. And
he had flirted back! It was nearly enough to make her drop her
shepherdess's crook in wonder. She certainly *did* drop that
horrid skull he'd handed her, dropped it like an ember right
onto the nearest table. Then she scurried off in search of Lady
Castlereagh to see if she could discover who the fellow was.

Evelina had not the slightest question as to the identity of her
partner. Had she not spent most of the past week in his company? Her surprise had been very great when Mr. Trevelyan
had continued to call even after she had told him so bluntly
that he need not offer for her. After that day in the Prater,
neither of them had again referred to the matter, but the idea
of marriage to him sat in her mind like an owl on a branch,
watchful, unmoving, endlessly patient.

For despite what she might have said to him at the Castlereaghs' dinner, Evelina now very much wanted to marry this
gentleman who held her so comfortably and waltzed her so
expertly around the room.

When she had left Oxfordshire with her family, it was
under protest. She had always enjoyed Robert Trevelyan's
company, but she was not in love with him. And she knew
instinctively that he did not wish to marry her. Now all that
had changed, on her part, at least. She could not know how he
felt.

But he did not *seem* indifferent to her. In fact, he seemed
like quite a different person from the gentleman with whom

she occasionally rode, played chess, or discussed literature in Oxford. Here they had not once discussed literature. Instead they had discussed fashion. They had not played a single chess game. Instead they had ridden on a children's merry-go-round and swung on a set of swings.

Perhaps what everyone said about Vienna was true, she thought. Perhaps there really was fairy dust in the very air and the water was laced with love potions.

They finished their waltz and her darkly handsome Hamlet stayed by her side. They danced a second and, daringly, a third time. Evelina felt like Cinderella, totally enchanted and magically enchanting. Her Danish Prince Charming seemed uninterested in anyone else in the room.

But a metaphorical clock chimed twelve inside this Cinderella's head when a gentleman dressed as a cavalier approached them. "Alec," said the man and she could see that it was the other Trevelyan twin. "You have been monopolizing this lovely goddess long enough. I insist you give up the next dance to me. Go and find your skull or the ghost of your father or something, Hamlet."

Alec laughed. "Oh, very well, Robin. You may have her for the country dance. But I shall return straightaway for the next waltz. That is, if I may, Artemis," he finished, turning to Evelina for permission.

But she couldn't speak. Alec? Robin? Had she been dancing with the wrong brother all evening? But it was impossible. It was ridiculous. It was. . . . She felt the cavalier take her hand, felt herself being led onto the floor, heard the music begin.

And she proceeded to execute the steps of the country dance in as awkward a fashion as she had ever managed in her life, stepping on her partner's toes, bumping into another couple, and turning the wrong way at least twice. Her cavalier seemed to have little to say.

She returned gratefully to her mother at the dance's end only to be given the intelligence that her father, who had been enjoying the evening in one of the card rooms, had suddenly been taken quite ill. They were leaving the palace and she must get her cloak at once.

Artemis stumbled out of the ballroom with her head teeming with unanswered questions.

·◄►{ thirteen }◄►·

"HERE," SAID ALEC to his brother the next afternoon, dropping a heavy purse onto the table. They were sitting in a quiet corner of a café in the Stephansplatz.

"What's that?" asked Robin, not picking up the purse.

"Your century. That was the wager and you've won it. Never thought you could pull it off, but you've done the trick. Make a better me than I ever thought you could. Maybe even a better one than I do myself." With a vacant look, he scanned the room and muttered, "Cork-brained wager, anyway."

Robin frowned; this was not at all the Alec he knew and loved. He reached out and pushed the purse back toward his brother. "Told you so at the start. But we're not finished."

"Yes, we are," said Alec. "I'm conceding defeat."

"Nonsense. You've never conceded defeat in your life, Alec. Besides, I don't want you to concede defeat. Why should you?"

"Because I'm leaving Vienna."

"Leaving Vienna?" replied Robin, so astonished he almost dropped his coffee cup. "But where...why...what sort of hey-go-mad start is this, Alec? You can't leave!"

"Don't see why I shouldn't. You certainly don't need me here, and..."

"The devil I don't," began Robin, but Alec went on as if he hadn't spoken.

". . . and I am needed elsewhere. Mr. Everbright has fallen ill."

That stopped Robin talking. "Ill?" he asked with concern. He was really quite fond of Evelina's absentminded father. "Not seriously ill, I hope?"

"Shouldn't think so," said Alec, "but he seemed deucedly uncomfortable when I saw him this morning, poor chap. Attack of dyspepsia or some such."

"Too much rich food, I imagine. Back in Oxfordshire it's boiled mutton and greens with a treacle tart most nights. But what's that to do with you, Alec?"

"Thing is, the sawbones says he's got to go to some place name of Baden and take a course of the waters. Not far from here, I'm told. Be there a fortnight at least. Only thing to set him back to rights. And, of course, Miss Everbright and her mother will be going along as well. I've offered to accompany them." He finished this all in a rush, looking straight forward and with a decidedly sheepish look on his face.

The thought of Alec gone, Alec deserting him, put Robin in a positive quake. "Well, of all the harebrained starts. Why, by all that's holy, did you go and make such an addle-pated offer?"

"Dash it all, Robbie, couldn't leave them helpless. Two females in a foreign land and all. The old fellow's in mighty queer stirrups, I can tell you, and the mother twittering about like nothing. Not up to making the decisions, he ain't, and nor is she. They need my help. Obliged to do the civil, don't y'see?"

"But why you? You don't even speak German." Robin spoke the first objection that came into his mind.

"No, but Evelina . . . that is, Miss Everbright does." He actually blushed as he said it and fidgeted with his cup and saucer till he sloshed coffee onto the sleeve of his gray coat.

A light went on in his brother's mind. "Evelina, is it?" he said slowly and shook his head at the enormity of the discovery he'd just made. "Well, if that don't beat all." He thought a bit more then nodded knowingly. "If I hadn't seen you dancing with her last night I wouldn't have believed it. Not certain I do now."

Alec, uncomfortable with his brother's perspicacity, huffed about for a minute or two, mopping ineffectually at the coffee stain with a linen napkin. "Simple enough. They need a man to accompany them is all. See all to rights, don't y'see? Stands to reason I should offer to go along. Only gentleman they knew in Vienna who's free to go, after all." He looked up then. "Except for you, of course, and I don't imagine you're anxious to leave Vienna just now."

"Not at all anxious," Robin agreed. The brothers kept few things secret from each other for long, even when they wished they could. "But it won't fadge, Alec. You may think Evelina's a green girl, not up to snuff, but she's no ninnyhammer."

"Course she ain't!" he replied with unwonted vehemence. "Most needle-witted girl I ever knew. Awake on every suit."

"Yes, she is. And that's the whole point. Can't flummery her at all. Don't see how you've managed to pull it off this long. It's a pound to a penny she'll cop to it before you're a mile from the city that you're not me. Then we'll really be in the briars."

"No, she won't, because I plan to tell her."

"You what!?"

"Plan to tell her who I am. Only fair, don't y'know." He dropped the linen napkin—the devil take his brother's coat, anyway!—and looked at Robin a long moment. Robin could have sworn he saw his brother *blush*. "You don't try to flummery the girl you're going to marry, now do you?"

"Marry? You? Evelina?" Robin sputtered. He seemed momentarily incapable of speaking in sentences longer than one word.

"If she'll have me," said Alec softly. He seemed to have grown very interested in the shine of the boot that stretched out before him beside the table. "Which ain't at all certain, I can tell you. I ain't at all the sort of fellow she's used to, y'know."

Robin's instinct was to point out that if Miss Everbright would not accept him, *Mrs.* Everbright most certainly would. What, turn down an earl for her daughter? Why, it was not to be thought of! But Robin loved his brother too dearly to say any such thing. "Of course she'll have you," he reassured. "Any woman would. Why shouldn't she?"

"You know I ain't clever like you, Robbie. And Evelina's as knacky as they come. Knows Greek and Latin and things like that. Probably even plays chess."

"Yes, she does," Robin agreed. "Beats me at it, too."

This made Alec look worried. "She does?"

"Regularly," said his brother. "But what I don't understand is what's made you want to marry the girl. She's not at all in your style."

"Don't I know it," said his brother with a rueful grin. "She's not at all pretty like your Georgianna..." Robin started to protest that, however much he might wish that Miss Pennington was "his" Georgianna, she was no such thing, but Alec went on heedlessly. "...and she don't even know who I'm talking about if I try to tell her the latest *on-dits*." He ran his fingers through his hair in a most un-Alec-like fashion that made him look even more boyishly handsome than usual.

"But..." his brother encouraged.

"But when I'm with her, I feel... I don't know, relaxed, easy. Like I don't have to put on a show for anybody. Tell you what it is, Robbie. When I'm with Miss Everbright, I feel like *myself*. Does that make any sense?"

Robin smiled a huge smile and clapped his twin on the shoulder. "Yes, dear brother. That makes perfect sense. In fact, I'd venture to say that it is the most sensible thing I have ever heard you say. And if that's the way you feel, then you must certainly marry Evelina Everbright."

"I mean to," said Alec and there was determination in his voice.

"Well, this certainly calls for champagne." He turned to a waiter lounging against the wall. "Herr Ober! Champagne, at once." The wine appeared almost instantly and was poured into a pair of fluted glasses. "To my brother and his lovely bride," he said, lifting his glass. "A lifetime of happiness." And they both drank.

"Thought she looked rather well last night," said Alec after he'd put down his glass. "Didn't you?"

It wasn't exactly the way a lovestruck swain is supposed to describe his beloved, but Robin understood it for what it was. "Never seen her look half so well, in fact," he said and poured more champagne. "Downright handsome, she was."

"Yes, she was. Told her she oughtn't to wear pink and I was right. That bronze suited her right down to the ground, though."

At that Robin burst into full-throated laughter. "Trust you to turn even Miss Everbright into a fashion plate." Alec had the grace to join in the laughter.

They drank a few moments in silence, each man deep into his own thoughts. Then Alec looked up. "Think you could teach me to play chess?" he asked.

"Not as well as Evelina does."

"Oh. Didn't think so."

"She rides like the very devil, y'know."

At that Alec brightened considerably. "Oh! That's all right then."

Silence fell again. They drank. They frowned. Finally Robin asked, "When are you leaving?"

"In the morning, soon as I can hire them a suitable carriage."

"The morning," Robin murmured.

"I'll have Chevis pack up a few things tonight. Be a good thing for you, I should think," said Alec. "No need to go on with the masquerade now, y'see. You can relax. Go back to being good old Robbie."

"Yes," agreed Robin. Trouble was, he didn't want to go back to being "good old Robbie." Especially when it seemed clearer by the day that Georgianna didn't care a fig for "good old Robbie." She was too busy falling in love with dashing old Alec. "Oh, God," he groaned and ran his fingers through his hair, but his brother was so wrapped up in his own thoughts that he didn't hear.

And so Alec left Vienna and Robert Trevelyan stayed. And that left Robin impaled on the proverbial horns of a dilemma. Did he allow the Earl of Kitteridge to disappear and turn himself back into Robert Trevelyan, thereby taking the risk of losing the one thing in life he now wanted—Georgianna Pennington? Or did he put it about that Robert had left town—as Mrs. Everbright thought—and go on with the charade, thereby making Georgianna fall more and more in love with . . . his brother?

It seemed a dilemma without a solution, a maze without an exit. And he felt like the Minotaur, confined in the Labyrinth and doomed for all time to roam endlessly along its twisting paths without finding an exit.

He wandered for hours about the city that day, his hands thrust in his pockets and his head bent. He didn't see its graceful houses and smiling people, didn't hear the peal of the church bells or the ring of his own boots on the cobblestones, didn't feel the chilly drizzle that had begun to fall, dripping from his beaver hat and soaking the edges of his brother's greatcoat wrapped warmly about him. His mind was too full of the thought that once again he was not to have the best of life. Not for him the cream. He was a second son, and that meant second best.

It was a familiar, almost comfortable thought. He had, after all, had his whole life to get used to it, to come to terms with it. And he had done so. They why did it hurt so much now?

And he knew the answer. Because Georgianna Pennington was not likely to settle for second best.

He wanted desperately to prolong as long as possible the joy he felt whenever he was with her, the pure delight of seeing her eyes shining with the affection he had begun to recognize there. But Robin was a deeply honorable man. It was bad enough that he had wooed her under false pretenses. He would have trouble living with himself for that. But he would be unable to live with himself at all if he went on with it now, knowing that she was starting to love a man who did not exist.

And so he made his decision. The Earl of Kitteridge would disappear and Robert Trevelyan would take his place—and remain just long enough to make his farewells to Georgianna and all the hopes and dreams she had spurred in him. Then he would leave Vienna and return to the safety—the dull, boring, stifling safety—of Oxford.

His feet dragged him back to his hotel. Numbly, he began stripping off the many-caped coat, the elegant blue jacket and marcella waistcoat, the doeskin breeches and the gleaming new boots, all the outward signs that told the world he was the Earl of Kitteridge. He didn't bother to summon Chevis, for what, after all, did a mere Mr. Trevelyan need with a fancy valet? Then he rummaged through the wardrobe. Alec had packed only a smallish valise, leaving most of Robin's clothes behind.

He pulled on a pair of brown breeches, a pale-yellow waistcoat, and a plain brown jacket. He retied his cravat in a less extravagant style and dropped the sapphire stickpin into Alec's jewel box. He dug out his old boots, scuffed but comfortable, and pulled them on. Then he stood before the mirror.

But strangely enough, he did not see the comfortable Oxford scholar he expected to see there. Somehow, the clothes no longer seemed to fit. Oh, they were the correct size, it was true. But they didn't hang right. They no longer wrapped him in safety.

What had happened to the comfort he'd felt in these sober, dull clothes only a few weeks earlier?

He remembered the image of the Minotaur and the maze with no exit. What was the rest of the story? Then he remembered. Theseus was given a clue that would enable him to escape from the Labyrinth, to find his way out again. And thus armed he went into it fearlessly, almost joyfully. He charged in and he killed the Minotaur. And then he escaped with the lady he loved!

Suddenly Robin knew what he had to do. He would continue to be Alec. But he would *also* be Robin. Alec's decision to leave Vienna with the Everbrights had been so sudden that none of their friends were likely to know of it. And Mrs. Everbright had surely been too busy caring for her husband and packing their things to spread the delicious news that Mr. Trevelyan was to accompany them.

So he, Robin, would become two men. He would teach his Georgie to love the better man—the better man for *her*. He would slay her love for Alec as surely, as mercilessly as Theseus had slain the Minotaur. He would foster her love for Robin, and he would carry her out of the Labyrinth with him.

For the first time that day, Robin smiled.

Georgianna was nearly beside herself when Lord Kitteridge failed to call for four days running. His brother *did* call, every day, and once she agreed to accompany him for a drive in the Prater, but he seemed loath to discuss his brother's activities.

"Oh, he's about somewhere," he replied airily to a casually asked question about Alec's whereabouts. "Never know when or where he'll pop up. That's Alec, flits about like a regular butterfly."

To this, she merely snapped open her parasol and stared out at the trees that were now almost bare.

Another day when he called she just happened to ask if Lord Kitteridge planned to attend a musicale the Castlereaghs were holding the following week.

"Oh, I shouldn't think so," said Robin as he sipped his hostess's excellent English tea. "Not much of a lover of music, Alec. Couldn't tell a sonata from a symphony, I shouldn't think." Then he neatly changed the subject by saying, "By the bye, have you heard about Herr Beethoven's new piece? In honor of Wellington's victory at Vitoria, I understand. It's to be given its premiere next month. Are you fond of his music?" And with that they were off on a thorough discussion of music. They enjoyed their conversation very much, and Lord Kitteridge was forgotten for the remainder of the afternoon.

Another afternoon when it was too cold and drizzly to go driving, they had spent the day together indoors. Robin was fascinated with the heating system in the Penningtons' house which had been turned on now that the days were growing chillier and the evenings positively cold. They made their way down to the cellars so they could examine its workings in greater detail.

When they came back up, he challenged her to a game of chess. The game took over an hour and she enjoyed it thoroughly. She very nearly beat him, for she was an excellent player. But so was he, exactly the sort of player she liked to pit herself against.

"I shall beat you next time," she warned as he folded away the board.

"I think you very well might," he agreed. "You certainly made me work for my victory."

"I often play with Papa," she explained. "Do you play with your brother?"

"Alec? Lord, no! He wouldn't know a rook from a pawn even if he could bring himself to sit still long enough to play which, of course, he can't."

"Oh," she said softly and finished gathering up the chessmen. When he left he kissed her hand in a way that made her wonder.

But the thing that alarmed Georgianna most was a report that came to her ears the very next day. Lord Kitteridge had been seen entering the Palm Palace at midnight; it was home to two of the most beautiful—and most notorious—ladies in Vienna. The Duchesse de Sagan was famous, or infamous, for the number and nobility of her lovers, including Prince Metternich *and* the czar. And Georgianna knew at first hand of the beauty of the Princess Bagration and the freedom with which she displayed that beauty. She remembered the princess's ball; she remembered even more vividly the princess dressed as a harem girl at the Hofburg masquerade: a tiny jeweled bolero barely covering her bosom, billowing harem pants of the thinnest and most transparent silk, and a wide expanse of bare midriff with a huge ruby in her navel. Georgie could not like the idea that a gentleman she'd thought she might wish to marry was paying calls on either "The Naked Angel" or her neighbor.

Then finally she saw Lord Kitteridge again and her doubts and fears melted like the snow on the Alps in summer. It was at a dinner given by Prince Metternich at the Chancellery. She saw him across the room as soon as she'd entered and she couldn't help but smile. He looked handsome as the devil himself in midnight-blue evening dress and ivory pantaloons, his neckcloth in an exquisite Waterfall caught with a diamond pin. The whole was topped with that wonderful grin that made him so irresistible. She felt her poor heart flutter at the sight of him.

Yes, she thought. She *would* bring him up to scratch.

On seeing her, he immediately excused himself from his companions and crossed the room. He lifted her hand and placed a tender kiss on her palm that seemed to burn right through her kid glove. His smile eclipsed the glow of the huge chandelier.

"How I have missed the sight of you, Miss Pennington," he said, holding on to her hand and smiling even more warmly.

"I have not been away, my lord," she pointed out and pulled her hand away, though not urgently.

His grin turned rueful. "Of course not, and I do hope you will forgive me for not calling. You *mustn't* be angry at me. Say you're not."

"I have no right to be angry at you, Lord Kitteridge."

"Do not say so, Miss Pennington," he said softly. He leaned forward and spoke softer yet, almost into her ear. "I hope that soon you will have more right than any other lady to chastise my actions. But, of course, I intend that you shall have no reason to do so."

She felt herself go warm all over. This was as close as he had yet come to a declaration. Surely now he intended to offer for her.

To cover her confusion, she said, "I do not see your brother. Is Mr. Trevelyan not here tonight?"

"No," he said airily. "I believe he had other plans."

"Oh," she said, surprised that she should feel so disappointed by his absence when the man she loved was right here beside her.

Dinner was announced and he led her into the dining room. But he had not been seated next to her. (In fact, he had been careful not to be.) He was, she noticed with extreme displeasure, seated next to the Princess Bagration. Georgianna was left to converse with Mr. Smythe-Burns on one side—he had just penned an ode to her eyes and a pair of sonnets to her hands, one for the right and one for the left—and with Major von Traunstein on the other—who was daily growing more particular in his attentions and whom she was daily growing to particularly dislike.

The gentlemen lingered long over their port while Georgianna fidgeted with her Norwich silk shawl among the ladies in the drawing room. When the men finally rejoined them, she sat up straighter and fluffed her skirts. She had been careful to dispose herself on a sofa with room enough for just two. But Lord Kitteridge walked straight to a settee some distance away where the Princess Bagration was holding court. And there he remained for the rest of the evening!

The last image in Georgianna's mind as she rode home in her carriage was the princess's face. It was looking directly at Georgianna and it was covered with a smile of triumph.

·▸▸❯[*fourteen*]❮◂◂·

THE EVENING OF the Castlereaghs' musicale arrived. And since *every* event, practically every word, that was a part of Vienna in these incredible days had diplomatic or political overtones, the gala affair at the British mission in the Minoritzenplatz was no exception. Ostensibly a social evening, it was in fact intended to be a showcase for British talent and British music.

The guest list was sparkling indeed. The czar had agreed to attend, though his sister, the Grand Duchess of Oldenburg, who had publicly and repeatedly announced that music made her vomit, had declined. No one was likely to regret her absence. Prince Metternich would be there, of course, a fact that severely taxed Lady Castlereagh's seating arrangements. Naturally the Austrian foreign minister must have a position of honor, but he must also be seated as far as possible from the czar, whom he cordially detested.

Monsieur de Talleyrand was expected to attend; he would be happy to perch delicately on a gilt chair in the first row, perfuming the air all around him with the delicate scent of the orange-flower cologne he habitually wore. It was firmly hoped that the enormously fat and enormously unpopular King of Wurttemberg would stay away and that the gentle and ugly

King of Denmark would not. Not one of the lesser lights who could wangle an invitation was likely to miss the evening.

Georgianna had been asked by Lady Castlereagh, a particular friend for many years, to perform. Though no one in Vienna had as yet heard her sing, the Castlereaghs were familiar with her lovely clear soprano voice. She agreed very prettily and asked Mrs. Rimley, the young wife of an equally young embassy official, to accompany her. They spent a pair of agreeable afternoons worrying over their repertoire and practicing together.

On the evening of the concert, Georgianna was nervous. She knew her voice was well trained, and she was comfortable with the music she had chosen to perform—a set of songs by Purcell. But she also knew that Vienna, with its reputation as a city of music, would present her with the most sophisticated and demanding audience she had ever faced. This was, after all, the city of Mozart and Beethoven. Ecstatic and knowledgeable crowds poured into the Opera House nightly. Along the ramparts, maids and hackney drivers, as well as lords, ladies, and burghers, could be heard humming arias from *The Magic Flute* and *Don Giovanni*. Performing for such an audience would strain the confidence of the most skilled professional.

But even this fact would not have reduced Georgianna to the quivering mass she became as she sat in an anteroom with Mrs. Rimley, waiting her turn to perform. No, it was not royalty or diplomats or music lovers she worried about. Were Herr Beethoven himself to be in the audience with his hearing intact, his presence would have affected her less than did the certain knowledge that Robert Trevelyan would be there. It was for him that she wanted to be perfect.

She could not explain it, not even to herself. After all, she was quite decided that it was Lord Kitteridge, not his brother, that she loved. Even the Turkish treatment she'd been suffering at his hands had not entirely dimmed her feelings for him.

But she knew that Mr. Trevelyan was something of a connoisseur. He knew a great deal about music, and the thought that he might be disappointed in her performance was more than she could bear.

She was not alone in her condition. Robin was nearly as nervous as Georgianna was. All his attention was now concentrated on her, all his love, all his longing and caring, and the thought that the evening might prove difficult for her was

one he found painful in the extreme. He had never heard
Georgianna sing; he had no way of knowing the level of her
talent or her training. And he wanted desperately for her to be
wonderful, for everyone in the room to be awed by her as he
was awed by her.

Yet he feared it would be impossible. Like every gentleman
in England, he had been made to sit through an interminable
number of concerts in which the daughters of the *ton* showed
off their musical "accomplishments." He knew only too well
how thinly distributed was the talent. Insipid girls playing
equally insipid harp music, reedy sopranos singing mawkish
ballads, workmanlike but uninspired sonatas plunked out on
the pianoforte by debutantes—that was the norm.

Then, too, Georgie was such a little thing. Surely she was
too tiny, he worried, to have the range and power to fill the
Castlereaghs' enormous ballroom crammed with the elite of
international society. He feared for her. He knew he would
love her no less even if she squawked like a sick crow, but the
others, he was well aware, would not be so charitable. He was
surrounded by the most critical audience Europe could assem-
ble. She was opening herself to biting, brutal criticism, making herself so terribly vulnerable.

He tried to relax in his spindly chair, forced himself to still
his nerves. Lady Castlereagh walked to the front of the room
and the buzzing of the audience quieted. She greeted her
guests and bid them enjoy the music. The concert began.

The first performer was a small gentleman with three gray
hairs combed across the dome of his skull and a bulbous nose
that glowed in the candlelight, and he played the pianoforte in
a perfectly adequate if uninspired performance. Then a young
but highly talented and equally picturesque Miss Withers, a
classical blonde in a gossamer dress of silver and white,
plucked and strummed out a lovely pair of tunes on a golden
harp. Doubtless, several of the more impressionable young
attachés tumbled into love on the spot with the angelic vision
she presented.

Her strumming done, Miss Withers blushed prettily and
bowed demurely in response to the enthusiastic applause. But
Robin was not clapping. He was clutching the paper program
he held in his hands, crushing it until it was well-nigh unread-
able. It did not matter that he'd smudged the ink; he had no
need to consult it to know that Georgianna was next.

As paper programs crackled around him and a few

members of the audience coughed discreetly, Robin held his breath. The door at the side of the small stage area opened, and Mrs. Rimley stepped out. She smiled a brief acknowledgment to the audience and stepped to the piano, sat, and spread her skirts discreetly about her.

A few heartbeats later—and Robin could easily have counted his, so loudly did they thump in his chest—Georgianna entered, smiled at the assembly and at Mrs. Rimley, and took up her spot standing just in the curve of the elegant pianoforte.

Unlike Miss Withers, in her ethereal silver gauze, or most of the other young ladies in the audience who were dressed in soft pastels, Georgianna had chosen to wear brown. But what a brown it was, thought Robin!

Rich as chocolate, warm as her huge brown eyes, it shimmered and glowed in the lamplight. Her gown was cut from silk velvet so soft and fine it seemed to float about her as she moved. Into the luxurious pile of the fabric were woven threads of gold that caught the flicker of the candlelight; they shimmered and danced and reflected a glow back onto her face. The sleeves were slashed and puffed with peach-colored gauze shot with gold, and golden ribbons tied the dress beneath her bosom. A pair of gold filigreed butterflies chased each other through the rich, dark hair piled high on her head.

All in all, Robin thought she looked like a deep brown rose that had been dipped in golden fairy dust. And the brightest of the shimmer seemed to have landed in her big, luminous eyes. They glowed and sparkled and shone as she scanned the audience. And when they landed on his face and held for the briefest moment, he fancied they grew even brighter. She definitely smiled; that he could not have imagined. He smiled back, a smile that combined pride and encouragement, and she nodded its acceptance.

In that moment, Robert Trevelyan thought he would die of cold if that gaze were ever again pulled away from his.

The first notes of the piano sounded, and she did look away then. But her gaze was replaced by a sound so pure and lovely that it held Robin just as firmly as her eyes had done.

"Fairest Isle, all isles excelling," she sang. It was gay, happy music, and her eyes danced over the audience as her voice danced over Purcell's lilting notes from *King Arthur*. "Venus here will choose her dwelling, and forsake her Cyprian grove." The charming air sounded as fresh on her lips as though written especially for the occasion instead of 124 years earlier. "Cupid from his fav'rite nation, Care and envy will remove." A classic English beauty sang of England, playing with the music and with her listeners.

The song was quickly over. She moved into a piece from the *Fairy Queen,* and a new side of her talent was revealed. "Hark! Hark!" she began *a cappella,* the notes long and trilled and fluttered in a virtuoso manner that Catalani herself would have applauded. Lord Castlereagh's audience certainly did as she finished the second number.

For her last piece, Georgianna had chosen *The Blessed Virgin's Expostulation.* And now she was no longer a young girl singing a charming air. She was no longer a singer glorying in what her voice could do. She was a woman pouring out her anguish for her child. She sang with a richness of tone and a depth of emotion wholly unexpected in one so young. She took command of the music and the emotion behind it; the words and the anguish they described seemed to come from the very center of her being. No vocal trickery, no fluttered notes or sparkling eyes were needed to lend a surface patina to the words. This was Mary singing out her soul.

"Gabriel. Gabriel. Gabriel!" the virgin called, and so heartfelt was the plea that the audience might have expected the angel to miraculously appear before them. The music cried and Georgianna cried with it, "of mothers most distressed."

Robin felt himself near to tears. The music rose to its conclusion. "I trust the God, but Oh! I fear the child," she whispered in ending.

She finished with her head bowed and the room was silent for a long moment. No one wanted to break the spell cast by the voice and the words, and the whole room seemed to hold its breath. Then it exploded into applause that echoed off the mirrored walls and reverberated up from the gleaming parquet floor. Even the usually imperturbable Prince Talleyrand rose from his front-row chair and enthusiastically saluted Georgianna with his applause.

She stood with her head bowed, as she had ended the song, then slowly she raised her face, glowing with emotion, toward the audience. Her gaze met that of her father who was beaming his pride almost to the point of bursting. She gave him a warm smile. Next to him Suzanne clapped loudly and smiled broadly and Georgianna smiled back. Yes, she thought, she could finally admit that she loved Suzanne Patterson.

Then her eyes slid across the room to join once more with Robin's. And so very lovely was she that he stopped clapping entirely and merely stared at her. For a long moment, the sound and the crowd around them seemed to disappear, leaving only the two of them in the room, motionless, silent, but with their eyes speaking volumes only they knew how to read.

Then the rolling wave of sound washed over them again, bringing Georgianna back to herself. Smiling brilliantly all around, she made a deep, graceful curtsy, accepting the adulation of the crowd, bowed her appreciation to Mrs. Rimley, and walked off the stage.

Robert Trevelyan sat stunned.

An hour later, the concert was over and the guests repaired to the dining rooms and salons where a cold buffet had been laid out.

When Georgianna appeared, she was immediately surrounded by a throng of admirers as congratulations were hurled on her head. It was quite half an hour before Robin was able to snatch a moment alone with her.

He took the hand so many others had just shaken, and he did not let it go. Bedamned to what anybody thinks, he told himself. This is the woman I love and I don't care if the world knows it. But what could he say to her? he wondered. What could he say that had not been said to her a hundred times already in the past half hour? You sing well? An understatement not to be thought of. I enjoyed your performance? Exactly the sort of banal thing good old Robin would have said, and he was tired to death of being good old Robin. So he just opened his mouth and said what he thought.

"Thank you for the pleasure you have just given me, Miss Pennington. True talent is a rare gift, bestowed on few, used by even fewer. You have honored us by using yours so well and by sharing it with us."

Georgie looked up into his handsome face and basked in his smile. It was his special smile, his magic smile as she had come to call it in her mind. Of course, when she had so christened it, it had been adorning Lord Kitteridge's face rather than his brother's. But she was coming to think it was just as nice on a face above a sober brown coat as it was above a dashing blue one, perhaps even nicer. And she certainly had no complaint with the way he held her hand. It felt warm and tingling, as it had when Lord Kitteridge had held it, but more than that it felt safe. It felt right. She left it there.

"I am glad you enjoyed it, Mr. Trevelyan," she said softly. "I enjoyed singing."

"That was obvious. You could not have sung so soulfully had you not." Then suddenly he grinned. "If I were Shakespeare's Orsino, I would claim that your music was the food of love and say 'Play on.' But the fact is, I am hungry, and I'll wager you are too."

"Starving," she admitted with a laugh. "There is a time for music and a time for food, Mr. Trevelyan, and this is definitely the latter."

"May I, then?" He gestured toward the heavily laden buffet tables.

"Please," she said. "We can join my father and Mrs. Patterson if you do not object."

"I should enjoy their company," he said and walked away, adding silently, But not nearly as much as I will enjoy yours.

The party at the Penningtons' table grew merry. They nibbled on lobster patties and munched on crab cakes, spread slices of cold beef with horseradish or spicy mustard, dug into potato salad flavored with bacon and vinegar, and spooned up fruit ices and almond custard. And they washed it all down with a great deal of champagne.

Both Sir Richard and Suzanne went on at length about Georgie's performance. Both were genuinely proud, and she basked in it. "How good it was to hear you sing again, Georgie," said Suzanne, reaching out to squeeze her hand. "It has been too long. You must give us a private concert one night soon. I long to hear the Handel. You do it so very well."

"Wonderful idea, that," added Sir Richard. "I've hardly heard you at all myself lately, puss, since I've been out when you've done your practicing. You will give us our own concert, won't you?"

"Of course," she said with a laugh, then without conscious thought she added, "but only if Mr. Trevelyan will consent to come, too."

"I should be honored," he replied with a smile.

"And perhaps," added Georgie, still speaking without thinking, "your brother will come as well."

"Oh, yes," said Suzanne. "Kitteridge must come, for he has not heard Georgie sing at all."

"Yes, yes," said Sir Richard. "Bring him along."

"Well, he uh, that is . . ." Robin began and couldn't seem to go on.

"I collect Lord Kitteridge is not overfond of music," said Georgie, bailing him out without even knowing she was doing so.

"That's it," Robin said quickly. "Got a tin ear, Alec does. Couldn't tell a decent soprano from a dying cat. You wouldn't want him there. He'd only fall asleep."

Georgie frowned but Suzanne laughed. "That's true, I had forgotten. Why, Kitteridge is famous for his snores whenever he needs must sit through so much as a single piece on the harp."

"Quite famous," Robin quickly agreed and managed to turn the subject.

They were soon discussing his life in Oxford, and now it was Robin's turn to surprise himself with his own words. "I am thinking of not returning," he said in answer to a question of Sir Richard's.

"But what will you do instead?" asked Georgie.

He gave a rueful grin. "I haven't the least notion," he said honestly. "English gentlemen without estates to care for and with no desire to enter the church or the army have few options open to them."

"That's the truth," said Sir Richard, who had reason to know. A second son himself, he had not inherited his title; he had earned it. "Have you thought of the diplomatic service?" he asked. "A young man of your sense could do much worse."

"Why no, to tell the truth I hadn't," he said, "which is odd. It does seem an obvious choice." He grew quiet a moment as he considered the notion. He had enjoyed Vienna, far more than he'd expected to. And it was not merely the parties and picnics and society he had enjoyed, though he was honest enough to admit he'd had a great deal of pleasure from them. It was not even the presence of Georgianna Pennington that was solely responsible for the enjoyment of his stay, though she was certainly the most important element of it.

No, it had been the politics of the whole show, feeling like he was at the very center of things even if he wasn't an actor on the stage. He avidly read the newspapers every day; he conversed knowledgeably with many of the diplomats. He was concerned and intrigued with the actual work of the Congress.

"I think I should like that," he finally said, softly, as though he were unsure he had the right. "I think I should like that very much."

"Well then," said Sir Richard. "Come see me tomorrow. Three o'clock if that's convenient. We'll discuss it. See what can be done."

"Why, thank you, sir. That is very good of you. Very good indeed," said Robin, truly pleased and flattered.

"Not at all, for I'm not an altruistic sort of fellow when it comes to whom I want to work with. Fact is, we need more good young men of just your sort," said Sir Richard. "We'll discuss it tomorrow."

Robin did not know it yet, but his future had just been secured.

The conversation drifted into other channels and soon it was time to go home. Robin, who was fond of walking and had not brought his carriage along, declined the Penningtons' offer of a lift and strolled back to his hotel whistling a tune. Then he began humming. By the time he turned into the Schulerstrasse, he was singing softly, "Fairest isle all isles excelling"—except that he substituted "maid" for "isle."

···❧[*fifteen*]❧···

TIRED, GRATIFIED, PLEASED, and slightly confused, Georgianna tumbled into bed and fell immediately to sleep. Venus skipped through her dreams, forsaking her Cyprian grove. She was soon joined by Cupid who was busily removing every care and envy from his fav'rite nation. And behind them came Purcell himself, shooing them here and there and admonishing them not to dare to sing off key.

They faded and the music with them, to be replaced by a vision of Robert Trevelyan sitting opposite Talleyrand and Metternich and crazy old King George. He was pulling off one brilliant diplomatic coup after another while they all watched in envy. When he finished, he scolded them all like a headmaster with a room full of unruly pupils: "Now go home and don't bother me any more," he said. "I want to listen to my wife sing."

And she sang, beautifully, soulfully, and just for him, and he smiled at her in that magic way he had. As she continued to sing, Lord Kitteridge came into the room, listened, and did *not* fall asleep and begin snoring. Instead, he smiled, too, and his smile held just as much magic as his brother's.

Her voice faltered as her gaze flitted back and forth between the two of them, but she kept singing, singing, singing as though the music would give her an answer. But soon her song was interrupted. Someone was cracking hard nuts next to her ear, the sound sharp and piercing. When the shells opened, she thought the nutmeats must have gone rotten. An acrid, pungent smell poured from them, making her cough.

The coughing continued and jolted her partially awake. She thought she heard the walnuts crack again, but that was ridiculous. She came more fully awake, remembered where she was, and realized she must have heard the chestnut branch cracking against her window. But the smell of the rotten nuts did not go away, and she could not seem to stop coughing. Something was not right.

She forced her mind to clear and opened her eyes. They smarted and teared at once, but not before she saw that her bedchamber was filled with smoke.

Smoke! She jumped from her bed and looked wildly around. Next to the far wall, smoke wafted lazily up through the pierced steel grating covering the vent of the heating system of which Count von Hohenstalt was so proud. The cracking sound came again, but this time she knew it didn't come from the big chestnut outside her window. It echoed up through the grate, and it was the crackling of an angry fire raging somewhere below.

She ran to the grate and touched it lightly, then pulled her hand back with a jerk. The grate was burning hot. Even the bare wooden floor around it, usually so chilly even with the heating system turned up, felt warm on the soles of her unshod feet. There was a fire below, and it was not a small fire that would quickly be doused. She had to get out; they all had to get out, at once!

She ran to the door of her bedchamber, flung it open, and practically threw herself into the hall. Here the smoke was much thicker. She could see no flames, but an eerie orange glow danced across the walls at the end of the hall, just at the top of the stairs. For a moment, it occurred to her that the glow was exactly the color of orange marmalade.

It was not a steady light that shone there; rather it danced and flickered and shifted its color from the marmalade to lemon yellow to bloody red.

Georgianna ran toward that strange, lurid light and looked down on a blazing inferno. The fire must have been burning for some time before the smoke woke her, because the flames had already eaten their way up two flights of stairs. The hall immediately below her was a furnace. Flames licked at the bannister and chewed at the carpeting, eager to claw their way up yet another floor to where she watched, horrified.

She stood immobilized by the sight. She saw her mother's face in the flames, heard again her mother's cries as they had been on that horrible night four years ago in Spain. "Get out, Georgie," her mother had cried then. "Get out!" She heard the words as clearly now as if her mother had returned from death to shout them at her again.

"All right, Mama," she said with ridiculous calm. Then she turned and began running back down the hall toward her father's room. Just as she opened her mouth to scream "Papa!" the door to his bedchamber was thrown open.

"Georgie!" boomed his voice followed at once by his substantial form. He was clad in his nightshirt; a brocaded dressing gown, its sash dangling untied, had been hastily wrapped about him. His nightcap was askew. "Georgie!" he screamed again, a strong note of panic edging his voice. He thundered down the hall toward her room, barreling through the thick smoke and almost colliding with her in his haste.

Seeing his beloved daughter safe and whole, he scooped her into his arms and held her close for an instant. "No," he shouted into the smoke. "Not Georgie too. I won't let you take Georgie too!" Then he started to pull her toward the stairs.

"No, Papa," she cried. "We cannot go that way. The fire is blocking the stair."

"The back stairs," he exclaimed, and they turned and ran to the other end of the hall.

When Sir Richard opened the narrow door to the servants' stairs, tongues of flame shot through the opening. He jumped back and stumbled, his thick black eyebrows singed right off his face but otherwise unhurt. Georgie kicked out at the door and swung it shut again, blocking off the angry flames for the moment.

She looked back over her shoulder. The flames had reached the top of the main staircase now and were eating their way down the hall toward them, feasting on the thick Persian carpet, seemingly insatiable. They had almost reached the door to Georgianna's chamber already. Her father, still stunned, sat on the floor where he had fallen. He seemed unable to move or even to think. He simply stared up into her eyes as though she were already dead from the flames and he had killed her. "I'm sorry, Bella," he murmured to his dead wife. "I'm sorry."

"Come, Papa," Georgie said as calmly as she could. She put her hand under his elbow and pulled him to his feet. "We must go."

Pulling her father after her, she ran into his bedchamber and slammed the heavy oak door shut behind them. By this time both of them were coughing violently from the acrid black smoke that grew thicker with each heartbeat. It billowed through the heating vent and crept under the closed door. Looking around frantically and trying to think clearly, Georgie grabbed a small but heavy Persian carpet and threw it across the vent. The smoke pouring in through it was immediately reduced to a trickle. Then she reached for the pitcher of water sitting on a washstand and dumped it onto the Persian carpet, hoping to keep it from igniting.

Watching her movements and understanding her motives, Sir Richard snapped into action. He immediately pulled the damask coverlet from the bed and began stuffing it under the door, wedging it firmly so it blocked out the curling tendrils of smoke. "The windows," he cried to his daughter. "Open the windows."

Georgie, berating herself for not thinking to do it first thing, ran to the French doors that opened onto a tiny balcony overlooking the Schulerstrasse. In her impatience and her anger at herself, her fingers fumbled with the latch. She could not get the French doors open. She began pulling uselessly on the handle, near to panic.

A voice sounded in her mind. "Slow down to hurry up," her governess used to say. She stopped yanking uselessly at the door, counted to three as her governess had always made her do, then looked closely at the latch. Just like the one in her own bedchamber which she had opened easily a hundred times, it had a simple latch that had to be turned instead of lifted. She turned it easily, and the French doors swung open.

With a cool rush like a taste of heaven, the fresh night air surged into the smoky room. Georgianna stepped onto the balcony and gulped enormous draughts of the stuff into her burning lungs, choking and coughing violently as she did so.

Her father was right behind her. With one hand clutching at her shoulder, as if to reassure himself that she was whole and safe, he bent over the iron railing of the balcony, retching horribly from the smoke he had inhaled.

They were safe, for the moment, but they both knew it was

a precarious safety. Even as Georgie looked back into the room, she could see tiny tendrils of smoke edging their mean and obstinate way past the coverlet wedged under the door. Steam hissed up from the wet carpet over the pierced steel grating that must by now be red hot. Soon, flames would batten down the solid oak door that sealed them safely off from the conflagration.

They had to get out, but how? Through the tears that poured from her stinging eyes, she looked down onto the street so far below. Her eyes met a busy scene.

Talley ran back and forth below the balcony, barking up at her and wagging his tail as if he were asking her to come and join a game. Johannes, the footman, and Keller, the butler, were looking up at them too, beside their own faithful Tom Coachman. They were all three waving their arms and seemed to be yelling something, but she could not hear them. The roar of the flames had become so loud she could hear nothing. Immediately below her, untamed streaks of scarlet flame danced through the windows of the music room, like the ribbons of a little girl's hair dancing in the wind. Below that, the front parlor spit flames like poison.

Her father was still doubled over, retching and coughing. "Come, Papa," she said as gently as she could and still be heard over the growing roar of the fire. "We must go now." So collected was her voice, despite the searing pain in her throat, that she might have been suggesting they leave some boring hostess's drawing room after a standard fifteen-minute duty call. "Can you stand, Papa?"

He answered by rising to his full height, though he clutched at the balcony railing a moment to steady himself. "I am fine, Georgie," he managed to say. "What must we do?"

It was as though they had been plunged back four years to that horrible time after Georgie's mother had died. He had looked to her for support and direction then, too. "Well, I think we really must go," she said, though she had no idea how they were to manage it.

She looked down again at the barking, running dog, the servants with their agonized faces, and the dozen or so others who had gathered in the street to witness the horrible spectacle. Between her and them stretched what seemed an enormous gulf of nothingness, a void unbroken by anything that could help in a descent. It was too far to jump, she knew. The fall would probably kill them; at the least it would break a dozen or more bones apiece.

Then her eye landed on the chestnut tree outside her own room. How often she had railed in her mind against the lazy gardener who had left it so many years unpruned so that it woke her in the night with its constant lashing against her window. Now she blessed him, for it might be their salvation. They could easily reach its broad branches from her own balcony.

But that balcony was so far away—the distance looked as long as a cricket field, though it was probably closer to fourteen feet—and the only thing that spanned the distance was a very narrow ledge of brick. She studied it for a moment, mentally measuring its width and comparing it to the size of her foot—and her father's larger one.

Dimly, through the fire's howl, she heard the clanging of bells as the fire brigade hurried toward the house. It might have been reassuring to know that help was on the way, but Georgianna was smart enough to know that there was little they would be able to do. The house was gone and unless she acted, and at once, she and her father were gone with it. Just as her mother had been swallowed by the flames of a hired house in Spain. No, she thought. I will not give up. Mama would not like it.

She looked at the ledge again. Well, if it was the only thing that would keep the two of them alive, then it must be made to do, she told herself sternly, though she shivered violently at the thought of stepping from her comparatively safe perch on the balcony out onto such a precarious crossing.

"Come, Papa," she said again in that same collected way. "We are going for a walk." But to her horror, when she turned to smile encouragingly at him, he was no longer beside her. She turned back to the bedchamber and saw with alarm that he had gone back into the room. The carpet over the grating was now burning hotly, flames dancing above it at least a foot high. Smoke poured in all around the door; it would disintegrate in flames any second.

"Papa!" she screamed. She could just make out his image through the thick black smoke. He was rummaging through the top drawer of his dresser, throwing things over his shoulder in his search for something. "Papa!" she cried again. "Come out!"

Then he found whatever it was he was looking for, dropped

it into the pocket of his dressing gown, and rejoined his daughter on the balcony. Running one hand over his hair as though to reassure himself that it was properly combed and knotting the fringed sash of his dressing gown firmly about him, he said in a very calm voice, "I am ready now, Georgie."

She laughed, actually laughed, to see him so clearly don his dignity once more. Then she said, or rather shouted, over the din, "Come then. It is not so very far, and we shall soon be on the ground."

She lifted her nightgown, heedless of the growing number of gentlemen watching interestedly below her. This was certainly no time for missishness or maidenly airs, and she couldn't very well climb over a balcony railing without hitching up her gown no matter that all the world would be treated to the sight of her bare legs. She swung one leg over the railing, then the other, and perched a moment on the wrought iron, suddenly terrified of that nothingness just below her.

"It's quite safe, old girl," shouted her father. "No one more nimble footed than my Georgie, you know. Off you go."

Still she hesitated. Then a vicious crash sounded behind her, and she knew the solid oak door guarding the room from the conflagration had surrendered to a stronger power. Almost at once, clouds of smoke billowed out through the French doors.

"Now, Georgie!" said her father. "No more time to wait, I'm afraid. I'm right behind you."

With a gulp and a prayer, Georgie stepped out onto the narrow ledge.

It was at that very moment that Robert Trevelyan bolted down the street, his breath rasping in his throat and his heart pounding with terror. He had been awakened by Chevis who, for possibly the first time in his life, was almost incomprehensible with excitement and anxiety. It had taken the valet a few moments to explain to Mr. Trevelyan what he had seen.

A very poor sleeper, a fact he deplored with every fiber of his being, Chevis had been awakened a few minutes earlier by the wild clanging of the bells as the fire brigade pounded past the house. Grumbling, he had looked out his window only to see a scene of chaos. People running, dogs barking, the windows of neighboring houses flying up as heads craned out to see what was going forward. He smelled the smoke and then he saw the brilliant red glow of the fire. He knew instinctively and at once that it was coming from the Penningtons' house, some hundred yards down the street. He ran to tell his master.

Within five minutes Robert Trevelyan was out of bed and out the door, his nightshirt sloppily stuffed into a pair of hastily donned evening breeches and his carpet slippers jammed onto stockingless feet. He arrived on the scene just in time to see his beloved, so appallingly far above his head, begin to inch her careful way along a ledge that was narrower than the length of her tiny foot.

Robin had heard and read the phrase "His heart stopped in his breast." It seemed to be a staple in the more dramatic popular novels of the day. He had always thought it more than a trifle overblown. But now he felt his own heart, if not actually stop, then certainly lurch violently within him. He held his breath, fearing that if he moved, if he so much as blinked, taking his eyes for even the smallest fraction of a second from that diminutive white form on the ledge, he would never see her again. It was as though he believed he could safely pin her to the wall with his gaze, and he dare not look away.

In the pale autumn moonlight filtering through the almost bare trees, Georgianna looked like a ghost, a beautiful wraith floating between the two balconies. "Don't look down, Georgie," Robert called out to his love even though logic told him she could not hear him. "Don't look down."

"Don't look down, Georgie," Sir Richard called to his daughter who was flat against the cold brick, her palms spread at her sides. "Just look at where you are going. Keep your eyes on that railing."

She had stopped for a moment, her fear writ large in her eyes. But the sound of her father's voice seemed to steady her and renew her determination. "I am fine, Papa," she said with an unusual calmness. "I shan't be a moment more. Mind you come right after me."

To her love, watching so helplessly below, her progress seemed agonizingly slow, as though she were moving through treacle. The nightmare went on and on. The growing crowd watched as if mesmerized. Encouragements rang up toward her through the din in a half dozen different languages, but she heard none of them. She heard only her own heartbeat, her father's encouraging voice, and the roar of the fire.

Like an inchworm, and just as slowly, she crept along, nearer and nearer to the other balcony. Then suddenly her foot, feeling its way along the coping, hit a loose stone. A chunk of the ledge crumbled away, sending showers of stone down onto the heads of the gasping crowd, and for one horrifying second she lost her footing. Far below, Robin shot forward as though to catch her, even though the rational part of his mind knew it would be useless even to try.

An involuntary gasp, almost a yelp, escaped from Georgianna, and she waited to be overtaken by the sensation of falling through space. But instinct would not let her fall. Her hand flew up and wrapped itself firmly about a drain spout, a horribly leering gargoyle just over her head. She steadied herself once more.

A gush of relief rose from the crowd. After a frozen moment to catch her breath and stop the swimming sensation in her head, she began her slow progress again. Finally she could reach out her hand for the balcony railing. A step more, an inch more. She stretched her hand further.

And then she was across! Robin felt his breath surge out of him as if whooshing from a burst bubble as he saw her grasp the iron railing of the balcony. She pulled herself all the way toward it and swung her legs lightly over, rewarding her love and the now considerable audience that had joined him with a glimpse of two beautiful ankles, a shapely pair of knees, and a flash of one creamy thigh before she stood safely on the balcony and shook her nightgown down around her again.

Now that his daughter was safely across, Sir Richard began his own crossing. He moved even more slowly than Georgie had done and with greater difficulty since he carried so much more weight and his own foot was so much larger on the tiny ledge than hers had been. Georgie smiled at him reassuringly and murmured words that only he could hear above the din, words of strength and calm, words that told him that he *must* make it across, for how would Georgie be able to go on living if he did not?

Inch by inch, foot by foot, he shifted his powerful body even closer until he was nearly there. Georgie, still speaking in a calm, reasonable voice, said "The railing is somewhat hot to the touch, Papa. Do not let it startle you." Another foot and she added, "Here, give me your hand, Papa."

He tried. He reached out for her, stretching. His fingers brushed hers. And then he slipped. A large chunk of coping showered into the street and he fell. Georgianna screamed, "Papa!"

As he felt his footing disappear below him, Sir Richard threw his body toward his daughter and managed to catch hold

of a piece of iron railing. His hands slid to the base of the
balcony, but they held there. Legs dangling, veins standing
out on the backs of his hands, he hung far above the street,
eyes huge and face red, coughing out the smoke, but he did
not let go.

Georgie saw him catch himself and positively *willed* herself to speak to him calmly. "That was very well done, Papa.
Now you must simply pull yourself up a little." And she
smiled at him.

He did not smile back, not just yet, but the sight of his
daughter so near seemed to give him courage. Marshaling all
the strength of his powerful arms, he pulled his body up,
placed one leg on the remaining bit of ledge. Then, hand over
hand, he climbed up the railing until he held the top edge.
Another minute—a minute that seemed like an hour to Robin
watching below and a lifetime to Georgianna just a few inches
away—and he was up. Georgie held his shoulders while he
swung his legs over the rail, then he stood beside her, panting,
coughing, bending over in an attempt to regain his breath.

A cheer went up from the crowd below, and Talley, running back and forth below the balcony, barked playfully.

With the safety of the iron balcony beneath both their feet,
something seemed to break in Georgie. She began to shiver
violently. Sir Richard, finally regaining his natural sense of
command at the sight of her, quickly removed his dressing
gown and put it around her. He held her close a moment until
the shivering lessened. "Here, put it on properly," he said, and
like an obedient child she donned the robe and let him tie it
about her. Then he chucked her under the chin. "Now, my
little hoyden," he said. "I hope your tree-climbing skills are
not grown rusty."

Both his words and his manner seemed to steady her. "Not
at all, Papa," she said with a smile that was only a little
forced. "I will wager mine are better than yours."

"Hah!" laughed Sir Richard, "I've climbed more trees than
you have years, my girl, *and* come down them safe again.
Never a broken bone yet." And with that he reached for a
branch of the chestnut tree. "Here, I'll go first to test the
branches." The few bronze leaves remaining on the tree fluttered dryly as he pulled on the branch. It bent with his weight.
He hung on to it a moment, testing his weight on it before
swinging his legs up.

The branch gave a loud creak of protest and Sir Richard

froze while Georgianna's hand flew to her mouth, but the bough did not break. In another moment, he was standing on it, reaching for smaller branches over his head to help keep his balance, and moving steadily along the branch toward the point where it joined the main trunk.

"There!" he said to his daughter in triumph. She looked so very white in the moonlight, and so very small, thought Robin. "Think you can do it as neatly?" added Sir Richard in his most bracing tone.

"Of course," she replied, but her voice quavered.

She moved to the far edge of the balcony and reached out for the branch. But just then the French doors behind her exploded. The noise was deafening, even above the cacophony of the fire. Glass rained everywhere—onto the balcony, into the sky, onto the heads of those standing below. The crowd screamed and scattered, but Robert Trevelyan did not move.

Neither did Georgianna. She stood as if stunned. Robin couldn't tell if she had been badly cut by the flying glass. He wanted to scream out his helplessness.

"Georgie!" came a scream above him. Sir Richard's anguished cry seemed to bring Georgie out of her trance. With a start, she realized that flames were shooting from the broken window. The draperies billowed like towers of flame; one savage tongue had licked at the trailing hem of her father's dressing gown still wrapped about her.

Moving as though in a dream, Georgianna slowly removed the flaming dressing gown. While her fingers fumbled with the sash, its long silken fringe touched the fire and burst into flames. Finally the knot came loose. Her arms slid from the sleeves. Slowly, so slowly, she kicked away the burning pile of fabric. It slid through the railings and down to the ground, trailing a shower of sparks as it fell and landing but inches from where Robin stood. A bystander stamped out the flames. Robin never took his eyes off Georgianna.

He was in agony. As he had watched the flames crawl up the robe, he had felt his own flesh burn. He had counted innumerable hours while she slowly removed it, feeling the flames searing his own body. And he sagged with relief when she kicked it away and he could see that the thin cotton of her nightgown had not caught fire as well.

Then the world speeded up to normal again and even accelerated well past that speed. In a trice, Georgie had scrambled up onto the broad chestnut bough. She scampered along it like a particularly agile monkey and, following her father's lead, climbed to the ground.

Her father scooped her into his arms and carried her across the street, safely away from the flames, where they both collapsed onto a stoop among the cheers and prayers and "Praise Gods" of the crowd. Talley ran after them, barking furiously, his flag of a tail wagging as hard as it could go, and licked Georgie all over her soot-smeared face.

Father and daughter collapsed into a combination of laughter, crying, and coughing. Someone handed Georgie a ladle of cool water. It tasted sweeter than the finest wine, sweeter than honey, sweeter than heaven, and she drank it so quickly she almost choked. Someone else wrapped an old coat around her shoulders.

And then he was there, the man Georgie loved. Brushing past her ebullient father and her frolicking dog, uncaring of the dozens of interested spectators, he scooped her into his arms and held her till she feared her ribs would crack.

"My love, my love," he murmured over and over into her smoke-scented hair. As he held her, rocking her like a baby, stroking her head, his voice croaked.

Georgie realized he was sobbing with relief even as she had been doing. "It's all right," she said into his chest, bare beneath the open collar of his nightshirt. "I'm all right," she said and sagged contentedly against him, breathing in the warm, spicy scent of him and relishing the slight roughness of the tiny hairs curling across his chest and tickling her cheek. She could feel the reassuring thump, thump of his heart beneath her ear. How she loved him, she told herself.

The same thought seemed to have occurred to him at the same moment because he took advantage of her closeness to raise her face to his and kiss her with a thoroughness that left her breathless. Heedless of the impropriety of his act, heedless too of her father sitting not five feet away and of the dog tugging at her hem, he kissed her as though he wanted to drown in her.

And she kissed him back just as thoroughly. All the fear, the dread that had gripped her on the balcony, the certainty that she was about to die, floated out of her. All her terrors for her beloved father drifted away on the smoky air as she gave herself up to the delicious feeling his kiss aroused in her. The warmth she felt surging through her had nothing to do with the flames still raging so near. This fire burned inside her, and she had no wish to see this one quenched.

She was dimly aware of the bustle all about her—the fire fighters trying their best to stem the raging inferno and keep it from spreading to the other houses on the street, the volunteers bringing water from the pump at the end of the road, bucket after bucket of it passing from hand to hand, and all sorts of people milling about, watching, pointing, and exclaiming. But mostly she was aware of how very good it felt to be kissing him and how little interested she was just then in thinking about anything else.

But then he stopped kissing her to gaze lovingly into her eyes. And with the removal of his soft probing lips from her own, she was able to think again. And the first thought that sprang, unwanted and ugly, into her mind was horrible. Not even the intense heat from the fire or the bright glow of the flames could fully account for the brilliant crimson that stained her cheeks as Georgianna came to a terrible realization.

She did not know whom she had just kissed!

·····❯❯❯[*sixteen*]❮❮❮·····

GEORGIANNA HAD NEVER been more confused in her life. The last half hour had simply been too much for her. Her mind was in a shambles, her composure in shreds, and her heart rent in two. Her lungs and throat were burning from the smoke she had gulped, and her knees were still weak from the terror of it all. And now this.

And the worst of it was that the gentle arms of one of the Trevelyan twins were still comfortably around her, and she didn't want him, whoever he was, to let her go. Not ever.

He didn't seem as if he were going to do so any time soon. As she caught her breath on a tiny sob, he gently lifted her chin. In the dancing, flashing reddish glow from the fire, she could see that his face held a look of tenderness and deep concern.

"It's all right, my love," he said soft as a sigh. He brushed away a tear that spilled from her huge, stinging eyes and wiped a smudge from her cheek. "You are safe now."

"I know I am," she said in a small voice. It must be Mr. Trevelyan, she thought, dear Robin, for he was being so tender, so sweet. Only Robin looked at her with such concern.

But could she be quite certain? She *had* to know. Cringing with embarrassment, she took a deep, searing breath to steady her nerves and asked, "But which one are you?"

Stunned by the question, Robin stared at her a moment with a blank face. Then, unaccountably, he grinned, a wide, happy, boyish, devilish grin. He never knew afterward what made him do it, why he didn't simply tell her there and then who he was and be done with it. But he did not. Instead, he cocked his head, allowing one dark, uncombed lock to fall over his brow, chuckled softly, and said, "Why, I am the one who loves you to distraction, of course."

No, she thought, he is Lord Kitteridge. For only he, dear, boyish, irrepressible Alec, smiled at her that especially engaging way and teased her so with his eyes. It had to be Alec. "Really, my l—" she began, but she was brought up short by a high-pitched scream piercing through the fire's roar to rain down upon them.

She jerked her head around and looked back up at the still raging fire. The front of the house was engulfed in flames. They poured from every window except those at the very top of the house. And from one of those top windows, two very small, very frightened white moons of faces could be seen.

"My God! It's Rose!" cried Georgianna.

Leaning through one of the tiny dormers was Georgianna's maid. Behind her, looking over her shoulder and screaming hysterically, was Hannah, the chambermaid.

There was no chestnut tree for them to climb down, no ledge to inch their way along. If they jumped from that height, they would certainly be killed. Nonetheless, Hannah was scrambling madly for the window, trying to squeeze past Rose and throw herself through the little opening. Rose fought with her, trying valiantly to pull her back from certain death. And below, Georgianna watched in an agony of fear for their safety and a deep guilt that she had not thought of them sooner.

Everyone around her seemed frozen to the spot. No one seemed to know what to do. But how could they just stand there and watch two young women die?

Behind her, Georgianna heard the voice of her love. "Blankets!" he shouted in tones of firm command. "Bring some blankets! Good strong ones. And large!"

A pair of boys ran into the nearest house as though they were foot soldiers who'd just heard a command from a general.

He then cupped his hands around his mouth and shouted up to the frightened maids. "Rose, pull her back in and keep her

there. Can you hear me? Keep her there! And keep calm. Both
of you. We'll have you safe down in no time."

Rose, well trained if terrified, nodded her ashen face and
called back, "Y-y-yes, sir. Very good, sir."

The boys ran back from the house, towing a very large,
solid looking *hausfrau* in a ruffled nightdress and an enormous
mobcap. With a protective sir, she clutched a pair of sturdy,
serviceable blankets to her substantial bosom and wore a look
of caution on her wide face. She was not about to offer up two
of her best winter blankets—the best Alpine wool, they were,
too—until she knew to whom they were going and why.

Robin bent over and spoke in her ear. Her eyes flew up to
the window in alarm, she nodded and thrust the blankets into
his hands. Then she rushed back into her house, doubtless to
prepare whatever it was she thought fire victims would find
most restorative.

"Five men!" called Robin toward the bystanders and began
rolling out one of the blankets on the ground. "I need five
strong men here." Sir Richard tried to rise, but found he could
not stand just yet. Tom Coachman came running, but no one
else approached. *"Funf mannen. Hier!"* Robin then shouted.
In a flash, a crowd of strong young men rallied round, ready
to help.

With Robin shouting instructions, they grabbed a blanket,
three men to a side, rolled the edges to get a better grip, and
moved to stand below the window at which the maids still
struggled, Hannah still trying to jump out and Rose still valiantly restraining her. The position of the men with the blanket
was precarious, for the flames from the lower windows licked
out at them furiously and the heat was worse than any furnace.

"Closer," Robin admonished them in German. "We'll miss
them if we stand too far back." He turned his head to a man in
the bucket brigade. "Water! Douse us all thoroughly. And the
blanket too." And soon buckets of freezing water were poured
onto the young men, sticking their shirts to their broad backs
and streaming into their shoes and slippers. From those nearest the flames, steam began rising almost at once.

When they were at last positioned directly below the
dormer window and holding the blanket stretched taut between them, Robin shouted up to the terrified maids to jump.
"We shall catch you, I promise," he added.

But now Hannah, so eager to dash herself to death against
the pavement a few minutes earlier rather than burn to death in

her room, froze with fear. She balked like a stubborn mule and refused to jump. She cried and yelled for her mother and called on the heavens for mercy and begged Rose not to make her jump.

Rose, out of all patience with the girl and eager to get safely to the ground herself, shook Hannah by the shoulders and told her in no uncertain terms to stop being a goose. Her words did no good at all; Hannah *was* a goose and a goose she would always remain.

Though Hannah was a good two stone heavier than she, Rose decided she would have to take matters into her own hands which meant taking Hannah into her own hands. She slapped her hard across the cheek to stop her screaming for a moment, then, while the younger girl was still in a state of shock, Rose picked her up like a sack of meal. Then with a hearty "Off you go, my girl," she gave a heave and pitched poor Hannah through the window.

Screaming all the way down, the chambermaid landed square in the middle of the blanket, bounced up again a few feet as though she were being tossed for fun at a county fair, and finally came to rest. The men let the blanket gently down, someone offered the maid a hand, and the *hausfrau* from across the way led her off, one doughy arm wrapped about the young girl's trembling shoulders and all the while clucking at her in German.

The blanket was readied again, and Rose stared down at it. She was clearly frightened. "It's all right, Rose," cried Robin. "We shall catch you."

"Come down, Rose," Georgianna shouted up to her. "Please come down. I need you so."

And that, as Georgie had known it would be, was that. Her mistress was calling. Rose hiked up her nightdress, thrust her legs through the small opening, shouted, "Tally ho!" (which seemed appropriate even though she was a little unclear as to its exact meaning), and sailed down into the blanket, her nightdress billowing about her and her braided hair trailing behind. With a soft thump, she hit the woolen surface.

She soon followed Hannah into the substantial embrace and the even more substantial kitchen of Frau Landtsmann.

The men retreated from the fire and headed for the water buckets to drink greedily and wash away the smoke from their throats. Robin drank too, then congratulated his crew and turned to his love.

But she was now safely wrapped in the embrace of her father as well as a sturdy blanket with her maid clucking at one side and Frau Landtsmann at the other. The *hausfrau* was urging the homeless Penningtons into her house and they went. At the door, Georgianna turned around. Her eyes flew over the faces of the crowd until they came to rest on Robin. She gave a tremulous smile, he nodded, and she turned and disappeared into the house.

Georgie slept little for the rest of that night. In truth, she didn't even try for much of it. Instead, she sat with her father in Frau Landtsmann's tidy parlor, talking through the events of the evening, compulsively reliving the horror, the terror. They had been petted and fed, wrapped in warm robes, and given barley soup and pumpernickel bread and thick, sweet coffee. Realizing how close they had each come to losing the other, they held on tightly to each other long past the hour when they should have been sleeping to recoup their strength. The fact that Georgie's mother had died in a fire lent special poignancy to their embrace.

"How fortunate that no one was seriously hurt," said Sir Richard. "Good thing I'd given them all the evening off."

It was indeed fortunate that Sir Richard was a lenient master to his servants. When he granted them a free evening, all but Rose and Hannah had joined together for an outing to the opera, sitting in the gods near the ceiling of the top balcony. They'd returned home excited and humming and had been sitting about the big kitchen table sharing a hearty pot of coffee and Cook's cream buns when three things happened in as many seconds.

First Shippington, Sir Richard's valet, raised his head and said, "Does anyone else smell smoke?" Next a thundering crash sounded from the front hall. And lastly, the cellar door exploded in flames.

The men immediately threw open the green baize door that divided the servants' quarters from the front of the house and rushed out into the hall to warn the family. But the entire space was already engulfed in wicked flames, blocking any access to the stairway. They tried the back stairs only to find they were even worse. They couldn't get up the stairs. There was nothing they could do but run out the area entrance into the street, hoping to save themselves. The fire was spreading as though the breath of the gods was blowing it like a bellows.

Once outside, several had searched fruitlessly for a ladder. it would have done no good; the floor on which the Penningtons slept was too far above the ground for any ladder to reach. In any case, only moments after their arrival on the street, they saw Georgie and Sir Richard step onto the balcony.

The servants could only stand and watch the odyssey of their master and mistress as they inched their way along the ledge.

Fortunately, the stables were in a mews, far enough removed from the house that they were never in danger. Tom Coachman, the grooms, and the carriage horses were all unhurt. It was, indeed, a miracle and a blessing that every member of the Pennington household, even Talley, was safe.

Gathered safely in Frau Landtsmann's parlor, they talked all at once for an hour and more, congratulating themselves, reliving the adventure, explaining what happened. But finally they drifted off as their extemporaneous hostess found bedding and space for eight unexpected guests. Georgie and Sir Richard were left alone in the parlor.

"Why did you go back, Papa?" asked Georgie after a silence, still holding tightly to his hand. "I turned around and you were gone. I thought I'd lost you."

In answer, he reached for the charred dressing gown someone had retrieved from the pavement below Georgie's balcony and which now reposed in a sodden lump on the floor. He reached into the pocket and handed something to Georgie.

"Oh, Papa," she breathed as she took the small oval from his hand. It was a miniature of her mother framed in pearls. He had loved his dead wife so much that he had risked his life to retrieve his only memory of her. Georgie felt tears sting her eyes, hotter than the burning of the smoke.

But he surprised her again. "For you," he said. "I couldn't stand for you not to have it, Georgie." He managed a small smile. "Looks like it's all you've got, too. That and a shockingly dirty nightdress."

"Oh, no, Papa," she said as she put her arms around him. "I've got a great deal more than that. I've got you."

Father and daughter held each other close a long time before they finally agreed to go up to the simple but comfortable bedchambers Frau Landtsmann had readied for them.

* * *

First thing next morning, Sir Richard sent a note to the embassy explaining their situation. It was replied to not half an hour later and in person by Lord Castlereagh himself with his lady in tow. The foreign secretary and his dowdy but very kind wife arrived at Frau Landtsmann's little house with clothing, salves and bandages, port-wine jelly, sympathy, and a carriage to carry them all back to the embassy.

"Of course you must come to us," said Lady Castlereagh before either of her potential guests could object. "Where else should you go? If the British embassy cannot provide help in a situation like this, what earthly good are we? *So* fortunate we took the Liechtenstein Palace after all, is it not, Cas?" she said to her husband then turned back to Georgianna to cluck some more. "It's enormous, you know. I haven't even begun to count all the rooms." She reached into a copious carpetbag and dug out a gown several sizes too large and handed it to Georgie. "Here, my dear. I know it is ghastly and will hang like a tent on you. I'd make at least two of you, more likely three. But it will at least cover you decently until we can get you home."

Georgie felt enormously comforted by the older woman's mothering.

In no time at all they were ensconced in the big house in Minoritzenplatz. A doctor arrived to see to any and all stray cuts, scratches, and bruises, and to prescribe a cordial for raw and burnt throats and special drops for stinging eyes. A tailor and a dressmaker were sent for to immediately begin the process of making the Penningtons decent. They and their entire household had lost every stitch but what they wore and would all have to be completely re-outfitted. And a large number of footmen were sent running with an even larger number of notes informing friends and acquaintances of the change in their address and their circumstances.

Georgie was in a muddle as to what to do about the Trevelyan/Kitteridge matter. She, who so prided herself on knowing her own mind and acting on that knowledge, knew only that she was in love, completely, absolutely, and irrevocably in love—with two very similar but very different gentlemen. And she now knew with absolute certainty that one of them was in love with her. He had kissed her and held her and called her his love.

But which one?

To be safe, she decided to send two identical notes to the

König von Ungarn, one to each twin, thanking him for his assistance of the previous night and informing him of their current whereabouts. This was done and Georgie retired to an airy, ornate bedchamber where she promptly fell into a deep sleep and slept for nearly four-and-twenty hours.

When she awoke at last it was to make several discoveries. Two daytime gowns had been quickly stitched for her so she need not face the world in her shift; her room was positively overflowing with flowers and notes from her many acquaintances and admirers; and she was starving. She tugged on the bell pull and Rose appeared almost at once, dressed in a starched if slightly baggy dress belonging to Lady Castlereagh's own dresser.

"Oh, Miss Georgie, you do look better," Rose chirped as she came in laboring under a huge tray covered with plates of eggs, sliced ham, kippers, muffins, and hothouse strawberries. A bowl of porridge was provided in case she should not yet feel up to eating anything more demanding, and a silver pot steamed the rich smell of fresh-brewed coffee into the room.

"I feel better," said Georgianna as she sat up in bed and prepared to pounce on the tray. "And what of you, Rose? Are you well? Should you not be resting?"

"And leave someone else to look after you, Miss Georgie? I should think not. I'm right as a trivet, I am. Only a pair of bruises in a spot no one won't never see them. Not even that Shippington if he knows what's good for him." She set the tray down and arranged it properly. "Did you ever in your life see so many flowers? And in October, too. Wouldn't you like to see the cards, Miss Georgie?"

Georgie washed down a strawberry with a gulp of coffee and nodded her head. Rose was already bustling about pulling the cards from each of the floral tributes. "This one here's from that major fellow, Troutstein?" she said of an enormous spray of mums and dahlias that looked like it belonged on a duke's grave.

"Von Traunstein," Georgie corrected with a giggle.

"Them white roses is from Lord Creighton and the daisies from Captain Bloomfield. The asters come from..." She squinted to read the card: "...the Honorable Jonathan Smythe-Burns III."

"Mmmmm," Georgie acknowledged with a mouthful of eggs.

Rose then picked up a lovely and huge arrangement of roses, red, orange, and yellow ones beautifully displayed in a golden basket. "Lord Kitteridge," she read the card. "They're from the earl, miss."

Georgianna choked on a bit of ham, coughed, and reached eagerly for the card. "Let me see," she demanded. Rose handed her the card. She studied the engraved name and turned it over. "Flaming roses, flaming hearts, but *not* a flaming Georgianna, please." It was signed "Kitteridge."

While she was studying the card and pondering the message, Rose carried over a delicate and beautiful arrangement of violets nestled in a silver bowl. Before she could hand Georgianna the card, her impatient mistress was plucking at the flowers for it. "Robert Trevelyan," she said softly and smiled completely. She turned the card over. "If you had died, I would have died, too," read the simple, straightforward, and exquisite message. And he had signed it "Robin," a name she had never used for him except in her mind.

She fell back against the goosedown pillows with a smile on her mouth and a frown on her brow.

Robin had decided it was time to end the charade. After the night of the fire, he knew he had to put his fate to the touch. He could no longer go on not knowing how Georgianna felt about him. About *him.* He hoped she would accept his love and return it. He thought she might, especially after the way she had kissed him. But he had to know.

He had sent a note round to the embassy asking if Georgie was receiving yet. Until the very moment of the note's arrival, she had not been, but she immediately sent back an affirmative reply, noting that she would be at home at four o'clock.

He spent his morning deciding what to wear, what to say, how to convince her that she really loved him and not Alec.

Georgianna spent the morning sitting quietly with Lady Castlereagh, stitching new petticoats and chemises to wear under the new gowns she must have. Thank goodness they had found a *modiste* who could make her up a couple of dresses on very short notice. She was prettily attired in one of them now, a lilac round gown tied with a violet sash and with a violet ribbon pulling her dark curls back from her face.

The fire that had destroyed Count von Hohenstalt's beautiful house had taken a full twenty-four hours to put out and it seemed that nothing at all would be salvageable. They were merely thankful that the blaze had been kept from spreading to the neighboring houses in the narrow street and that no one had been injured. All Vienna talked of it. Even the peccadillos of the Duchesse de Sagan and Prince Metternich were temporarily forgotten.

So now Georgianna stitched and Lady Castlereagh talked, an accomplishment at which that lady excelled. But she was so kind and full of good will that Georgie didn't mind her chattering. In fact, she was thankful for it, for it gave her an opportunity to think.

She had played the scene in front of the burning house over and over in her mind. A dozen times in her memories the man she loved kissed her; a dozen times she reacted with passion and love. She saw his smile and heard his laugh. She watched him again as he moved so forcefully and confidently to save the lives of Rose and Hannah. She heard him commanding the others in perfect German.

Now that she had the leisure to think it through very carefully, noting every minute detail of the scene, she had come to the conclusion, and with a certainty that startled her, that she had been kissed by Mr. Robert Trevelyan.

And rather than being disappointed by the discovery, she found she was overcome by joy. When she'd received his note asking if he might call on her, her heart had soared. Yes, it was all happening, everything she had come to Vienna to find. Soon, her father would be free to marry Suzanne, knowing that his daughter was happily settled. And when Georgianna finally left the nest she was going to soar higher than she'd ever thought possible.

The thought of her father's marriage to Suzanne no longer bothered Georgie at all. In fact, she was eager for it, knowing, now, what love could feel like. He deserved it so much. And he would not be abandoning his daughter. She knew that she was loved by him. She always would be. No one would ever replace the special part of her father's heart that was reserved just for her. And she would be welcomed in her father's home —her father and *Suzanne's* home—at any time because they loved her. But when the visit was through, she would return to her *own* home and her own love. Today would tell the truth of all this, of that she felt certain.

She stitched and sighed and dreamed with a contented smile on her face. Before long the post was brought which gave Lady Castlereagh a new source of topics on which to talk. She would read a letter, describe the sender in minute detail, add several interesting bits about the correspondent's antecedents or progeny and the prospects of each, then move on to the next letter. Georgianna found the wave of sound quite relaxing.

Until Lady Castlereagh opened her last letter and began to chuckle. "Really," she said, "I always knew Constantina Everbright was a ninnyhammer, but now I really think she must be all about in her head."

"Mrs. Everbright? I'd heard they had gone to Baden for Mr. Everbright's health. I hope he is improving."

"Oh, yes, seems the waters are doing wonders for him. She, however, belongs in Bedlam rather than Baden, I believe. Listen to this part, my dear. I never heard such twaddle." She read from the letter:

> *I simply don't know* what *we should have done had not Mr. Trevelyan offered to accompany us to Baden. He has been so very* kind *and* considerate, *so good in his care of us. He has been* particularly *nice in his attentions to Evelina. My dear girl is positively* blooming. *I know I need not hide from you, dear friend, that I am in* Daily Expectation *of being able to make a very* Interesting Announcement. *I could not hope for better for my* dear, *my* very dear, *Evelina.*

She put the letter down with a chuckle. "Whatever can the silly widgeon be thinking of? She has always been one to see what she wished to see, but truly! I do believe her wishful thinking has led her straight over the edge, for of course Mr. Trevelyan is not in Baden with them. He is right here in Vienna and has been all along. Why, he shall be calling here this very afternoon. Did you not tell me so, Georgianna?"

But Georgianna did not answer. Her mind was too busy spinning with thoughts and she did not at all like the pattern they were weaving.

···⊷⊷❴ *seventeen* ❵⊷⊷···

THE CLOCK IN Robin's hotel room struck the three quarters. The hour of truth was nearly at hand. He must set out at once if he was to be at the embassy at four. He was ready. Well, actually that was not true. Not at all. In fact, he was quaking in his very elegant Suvaroff boots. He even looked down at them and was amazed that the tassels were not dancing about.

But he was as ready as he was ever likely to be, so he may as well get the business over with. He tried to reassure himself. It's only natural you should be a bit nervous, he counseled himself. After all, you have never before proposed marriage, even under ideal conditions, and that description could hardly be said to apply just now. But other men have done it and survived and so will you. Now go!

He set out from his hotel with a determined step. He'd decided to walk to the Minoritzenplatz. It would give him time to marshal his arguments, and his nerve. He could do it, he knew he could, and that in itself was a wonder, for two months earlier, Robert Trevelyan of Oxford would have turned tail and run.

But this time in Vienna had provided Robin with a powerful and much needed lesson. For most of his life, he had been trying to deny a part of who he was, the most vital part. Since he couldn't be Alec, the eldest, the heir, the earl, he had tried to deny every aspect of his character that was like Alec's, to disguise himself as a simple, scholarly, sober (and, yes, dull) man, to hide in the shadows where no one would compare him with his more glittering brother.

Now he knew, he knew to the bottom of his being and with a confidence that grew with every step and that would make it possible to face Georgianna now, he could combine the best of the Robin he'd tried to be for all those years with the best of the Alec traits he knew he possessed but had tried so hard to bury. And that, he felt certain, would make him exactly the right husband for Georgianna.

By the time he lifted the knocker on the embassy door, he was no longer quaking. He was smiling. For the first time in his life, Robin felt whole.

Georgianna was raging. She was a very bright girl and after hearing Mrs. Everbright's "nonsensical" letter it had not taken her the whole morning to piece together the truth of the matter. A few careful questions had elicited from Lady Castlereagh the exact date on which the Everbrights had left Vienna for Baden. She recounted her own movements during that period and, more importantly, those of her twin suitors.

Why had she not seen it before? she wondered, railing at her own stupidity. Why had she never wondered why she suddenly no longer saw the Trevelyan twins together after the night of the masquerade? The sudden cessation of their togetherness coincided exactly with the morning that the Everbrights had left for Baden, supposedly with Mr. Trevelyan riding beside their carriage all the way.

Call it intellect or intuition, Georgianna knew with absolute certainty that for the past week she had seen only one of the Trevelyan brothers. She could not be entirely certain which one it was. Indeed, she was no longer certain she knew anything at all about either one of them. If the past week was a charade, who was to say the entire time they'd been in Vienna had not been one as well?

It didn't matter. Not a whit. She didn't *wish* to know. She didn't wish to have anything more to do with either of them. She was livid. How dare they use her so? How dare he (whoever *he* was) make her fall in love with him as some sort of a joke? How *dare* he!

She remembered seeing Alec (or so she thought) flirting

shamelessly with the Princess Bagration. Well, she was welcome to him! And Evelina Everbright wanted Robert Trevelyan? She could have him with Georgianna's very good wishes! She wished she were Pontius Pilate standing before a screaming crowd so she could very publicly wash her hands of both of them.

And now one of them was coming to call. She could hardly wait to tell him what she thought of him, and where the devil *was* he? The clock was chiming four even as she raged.

The last note of the chimes faded away only to be replaced by the banging of the knocker.

"That will be Mr. Trevelyan," said Lady Castlereagh, rising to await her guest. "Such a nice young gentleman. Cas has been talking about finding a place for him here on the staff. A valuable addition he will make, certainly."

The butler threw open the double doors to the drawing room. "Mr. Trevelyan, ma'am," he intoned.

"Humph," Georgie grunted but no one heard her.

"My dear Mr. Trevelyan," said Lady Castlereagh, sailing toward him with outstretched hands. "So good of you to call and give us all another opportunity to thank you for your prompt action of the other night."

"I'm glad I had the opportunity to be of some assistance, ma'am. There was a serious fire in a factory near Oxford last year while I was at hand. I was able to observe how a blanket could be useful."

"Do come and sit down. I was about to order tea. Would you ring for it please, Georgie?"

Georgianna, who had not even stood when he entered, did so now and walked to the bell pull. She gave it such a yank it nearly came down on her head. Then she returned to her sofa and sat. She had said not a word.

He was looking at her, a wondering look. Well, let him wonder, she thought. He will know soon enough why I am glaring at him. And just look at him, her mind rolled on. He *says* he is Robert Trevelyan, and yet he is dressed like neither of them usually dresses. A very fine dark-blue coat typical of the earl over a waistcoat and pantaloons of dove gray typical of Mr. Trevelyan. A neckcloth beautifully tied but not ostentatious. Shirtpoints starched but not pointing to his ears and immobilizing his head. One fob at his waist rather than Alec's usual two or three; one signet ring on his finger; a small black pearl in his cravat. He looked wonderful, she had to admit.

I don't care, she told herself. I shouldn't care if he looked like the blessed King David himself or Adonis on the very day he mesmerized Aphrodite with his beauty.

"I hope you are quite recovered from your ordeal, Miss Pennington," said Robin. It sounded odiously flat in his ears, not at all the sort of thing he wished to say to her.

"Quite," she replied and said nothing more.

"And your father?" he tried again.

"Is quite well."

"Good," he said, started to say something else, stopped, started again, and finally added another "Good."

The kind fat face of Lady Castlereagh was beginning to look just a trifle distressed. "Georgianna . . ." she began, but luckily the tea tray was rolled in at that moment. "Oh, good. Tea shall make us all quite comfortable. Will you pour, Georgie?"

She did. She put one lump of sugar in his cup, though she knew very well that Alec liked three lumps at least and Robin preferred his tea unsweetened. He took it without complaint.

As it was growing clearer by the moment that Georgianna had no intention of speaking to their guest, Lady Castlereagh, wife of a diplomat that she was, rose to the occasion, filling the air with chatter and questions and observations about other fires she had witnessed, about mutual friends, about the weather, about the almost certainty of Mr. Trevelyan joining the embassy staff. But it was heavy going even for her.

The foreign secretary's wife, for all her dowdy clothes and her placid demeanor, was not stupid. She knew a row brewing when she saw one. She also knew the best way for a young lady and a young gentleman to deal with such a matter and that was alone and propriety be hanged. So after a few more moments' chatter, she looked at the plate of cakes and biscuits. "Oh, dear, Cook has forgotten the macaroons. You simply must try his macaroons, Mr. Trevelyan. They are quite a specialty with him. I shall just go off to the kitchen and see that some are sent up, shall I?"

"You need not trouble yourself on Mr. Trevelyan's account, Lady Castlereagh," said Georgie coldly. "He does not care for macaroons."

"On the contrary," he said at once. "They are my favorite treat. I should dearly love to try your cook's recipe, ma'am."

"Good," said the lady with relief. "I'll just run and see

about them. Shan't be a moment." And she hustled herself through the door.

They both watched her go. Then Robin turned and looked a long time at Georgianna before speaking. "Are you going to tell me now why you have been looking daggers at me ever since I walked into the room?"

"I should be happy to tell you, *Mr. Trevelyan, if* that is indeed your name?"

Somehow, he was not even surprised. "Ah, I see," he said on a sigh. "Know about that, do you?"

"I am relieved, at least, to see that you have no intention of wasting my time by denying what I know to be true."

"Well, I might if I thought you'd believe me," he admitted with a rather sheepish grin.

"I most certainly would *not* believe you. I would not believe *anything* you chose to tell me, not even if you said the sun will rise tomorrow and the Viennese like whipped cream."

"There is one thing you can believe," he said and looked at her with honesty writ large in his face. "You can believe that I love you, Georgie."

The words did not affect her. Well, only a little. She *willed* herself not to be affected by anything he might have to say to her, for it was almost certain to be untrue. "Love me?" she said, her voice heavy with sarcasm. "You can say that to me? And expect me to believe you? I don't even know for certain who you are."

He stood and bowed. "The Honorable Mr. Robert Trevelyan at your service, miss."

"Honorable! I sincerely doubt you know the meaning of the word, sir." She huffed and glared and fidgeted on the sofa and poured herself more tea to have something to do with her hands then left it to turn cold on the tray. Finally she asked, "Are you really Mr. Trevelyan?"

"Robin," he corrected. "I think it's past time you began calling me Robin. And yes, I really am and have been all along."

"What is that supposed to mean?"

"I think it is time I told you the whole of it, don't you?"

His tone was so gentle she began to feel guilty for her own rage, but rage was what she still felt, so she huffed a bit more. "What leads you to think I am interested in hearing it?

"I'd go bail you are *very* interested, but it doesn't matter whether you are or not, for you are going to hear it just the same."

"How dare you . . ." she began, for her temper was at its zenith.

But he stopped her by moving to sit beside her on the sofa and taking both her hands in a grip that allowed no escape. And then he told her the story, all of it, right from that very first day in Jackson's Boxing Saloon when he had made the decision to come to Vienna with Alec. He left nothing out and did not spare himself in the telling of it.

She was admittedly intrigued by the story, occasionally asking a question, letting out with a gasp, or making him repeat something. Once, when he recounted the sudden appearance of the Everbrights on the scene, she was late stifling a giggle.

"It was a dashed stupid thing to do, worse than a school-boy's prank," he said when he was done. "I know that better than anyone and you can never berate me for it more than I have berated myself for my behavior. But now that it's over," he said, squeezing her hands and looking deep into her eyes, "how very glad I am that I did it," he finished simply, "for look what it has brought me."

Intrigued though she was, she was still suffering under a strong sense of ill usage and was not yet ready to let go of it when she had been at such pains to build it up. "You have played your part well, Mr. Trevelyan," she said coldly. "So well, in fact, that you have well and truly taken on your brother's characteristics. You are now fully as arrogant, as conceited, as much of a coxcomb as he is!"

"Now that *is* unfair, Georgie," he said with a smile. "Alec is not a coxcomb."

"Lying, pretending, sneaking about. How I hate it all! And all the time you were both *laughing* at me." She was perilously close to tears now, but she refused to give way to them. She would rather die first. She sniffed. Hard.

"Oh, Georgie, Georgie," he said softly, reaching out to stroke her hair. "I have never laughed at you, and I never will." He lifted her chin to look into her eyes and she saw it, that smile, and she felt all the old magic it had conjured up in her for so long.

"And if you think you can get round me by turning on the famous Kitteridge charm," she said in a rapidly weakening temper, "you are in for a very large disappointment."

"Oh, no, not the Kitteridge charm, my love. The *Trevelyan* charm. I am finished with trying to be my brother. But more importantly, I am finished with trying *not* to be my brother. Can you not understand, Georgie? I have been living a lie for most of my life, trying to be someone I'm not so that I would always be safe. It is time to stop." He took hold of her shoulders and, even though they stiffened beneath his hands, he turned her, gently but firmly, to face him. "From now on I am going to be only me. And that me, the Honorable Robert Trevelyan, loves you, Georgianna Pennington, more than I thought it possible to love anyone or anything in his world."

Try as she might to hang on to the fine temper she'd developed—and quite righteously, too, she felt—she was having trouble managing it. It kept being nudged aside by another feeling, one equally strong, equally compelling, and considerably more enjoyable.

This other feeling seemed to begin in her shoulders, just where his hands burned through the thin muslin of her gown. From there it radiated down into her body, through her limbs, into her soul. It burned inside her till her anger melted away. She could no more hang on to her wrath than she could grab hold of a block of ice that had been left too long in the sun. It simply didn't exist any longer.

"But why . . ." she began, but she was not allowed to finish her question. Robin, sensing that she was weakening, stopped her talking in the best way known to man. He kissed her.

And to Georgie the kiss was utterly familiar. There was no doubt in her mind that this was the man who had kissed her on the street in those moments after her escape from the fire. But it was more than that that made the kiss feel so . . . right. Kissing Robert Trevelyan, letting her arms tighten about his neck, feeling him pull her closer and closer, Georgianna felt like she had come home.

Finally he released her and she had to gasp for breath. She was frightened, so very frightened at the strength of her response to him, at how much she loved this man. She tried once more to distance herself from it.

"It's not fair," she said in a small voice. "I don't love you. I love your brother. You've seen to that."

"Well, I'm afraid you can't marry him," said Robin calmly.

"Why not?" she said mulishly, completely ignoring the fact that Lord Kitteridge had not asked her.

"Because he is going to marry Miss Everbright."

That shocked her eyes wide open. "Miss Everbright! Miss Evelina Everbright?"

"The very same. I've had a note from him not an hour since. He popped the question this morning over a glass of the spring water at Baden and was accepted before the bubbles had time to tickle his nose. This afternoon, he intends to break the sad news to Mrs. Everbright that her daughter is not to marry the upstanding Oxford scholar she has so long prayed for as a son-in-law and will instead have to settle for an earl."

A surprised giggle escaped her. And then they were both laughing until they cried.

And then they were kissing again. And she hadn't the least desire to either laugh or cry. Especially when she realized, fully realized in a moment of startling clarity, that all her confusion over which twin she loved had been for naught. She loved a man, not a name, and this was the man. He always had been. When he was Alec, she had loved Alec; when he was Robin, she loved Robin. It was as simple as that. She wanted to go on kissing him, her Robin, her funny, clever, handsome Robin, forever.

At length, at very great length, he pulled reluctantly away from her. Neither of them seemed to find it odd that Lady Castlereagh had not returned. In fact she had done so, taken one look at the lovers seated on her sofa, smiled happily, and disappeared again, muttering, "That's all right, then."

"Am I forgiven?" Robin asked.

"Yes. No. Oh, I don't know. Kiss me again and we shall see."

"Ask me properly," he teased, but his face was serious.

"What do you mean? Isn't it unmaidenly enough that I have asked you at all? Truly proper young ladies do not, you know." She peeked up from the comfortable place where her dark head rested on his elegant jacket. "Kiss me. Please," she said in a small, almost plaintive voice.

"Robin."

"What?"

"Kiss me please, Robin. Don't you see, my love. I need to know that it is me, really and truly me, that you want to kiss, me that you love."

She smiled a slow, warm, winning smile, a smile full of sweetness and love, and she lightly touched a finger to his cheek, his chin, his lips. "Kiss me please, Robin," she said.

"With the greatest pleasure in the world, my love," he replied softly.

And so he did.

*If you enjoyed this book, take advantage
of this special offer. Subscribe now and . . .*

GET A *FREE*
HISTORICAL ROMANCE

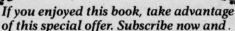

—— **NO OBLIGATION**(a $3.95 value) ——

Each month the editors of True Value will select the four best historical romance novels from America's leading publishers. Preview them in your home Free for 10 days. And we'll send you a FREE book as our introductory gift. No obligation. If for any reason you decide not to keep them, just return them and owe nothing. But if you like them you'll pay *just* $3.50 each and save at least $.45 each off the cover price. (Your savings are a minimum of $1.80 a month.) There is no shipping and handling or other hidden charges. There are no minimum number of books to buy and you may cancel at any time.

send in the coupon below